Tea & other Ayama Na Tales

For Evie and Henry—
With much affection and
many memories - Ellie

Tea & other Ayama Na Tales

Enjoy your travels in
Ayama Na —

Eleanor Bluestein

Winner of the G.S. Sharat Chandra Prize for Short Fiction
Selected by Marly Swick

BkMk Press
University of Missouri-Kansas City

Cover design: Ashley Shearer
Author photo: Sherri Goldman
Book interior design: Susan L. Schurman
Managing editor: Ben Furnish

BkMk Press wishes to thank Gina Padberg, Cara Lefebvre,
Elizabeth Gromling, Shane Stricker, and Paul Tosh.
Special thanks to Nathan Becka.
The G. S. Sharat Chandra Prize wishes to thank Leslie Koffler,
Evan McNamara, Linda Rodriguez, and Jane Wood.

"The Cut the Crap Machine" first appeared in *GSU Review*.
"AIBO or Love at First Sight" was featured in *ForeWord Magazine*'s online Book Club.

Library of Congress Cataloguing-in-Publication Data

Bluestein, Eleanor
  Tea and other Ayama Na tales : stories / by Eleanor Bluestein.
    p. cm.
    Summary: "Ten short stories, set in a fictitious, but realistic,
Asian country called Ayama Na. The stories resonate with tensions
of family life, governmental corruption and instability, and tradition versus westernization"--Provided by publisher.
    ISBN 978-1-886157-64-4 (pbk. : alk. paper)
1. Family life--fiction. 2. Asia--Fiction. 3. Culture conflict--Asia-
-Fiction. I. Title.
  PS3602.L857T43 2008
  813'.6--dc22

                                    2008041001

This book is set in Adobe Caslon Pro, Big Caslon, and Edwardian Script.
Printed by Walsworth Publishing Company, Marceline, Missouri.

For Harry

Tea & other Ayama Na Tales

Acknowledgements

My thanks to the San Diego Writers Studio,
to Edna Myers,
to Nathan Becka,
to Ben Furnish and his crew at BkMk,
and to Marly Swick, of course.

Foreword

In this original, sparkling, culturally savvy and highly entertaining collection of linked stories set in a mythical but utterly believable small country in southeast Asia, Bluestein displays a brilliant sense of craft as well as cultural ventriloquism, writing equally convincingly from the point of view of both Westerners and Easterners—a tour guide, a feminist beauty queen, an impoverished farmer working on an assembly line that manufactures robot dogs, an American artist run amok in Ayama Na, two playwrights with different philosophies of life collaborating on a doomed production—these are just some of the unforgettable characters in this striking collection. In the tradition of Robert Olen Butler and Bob Shacochis, this is a writer who illuminates our cultural differences while exploring the intricacies of the human condition.

—Marly Swick
Final Judge
G. S. Sharat Chandra Prize for Short Fiction

Pineapple Wars

A dull throb pounded in Koriatt's head as he drove home from work. At every clogged intersection, he leaned on the horn, venting his frustrations at the day's catastrophes—two of four repair bays out of commission, his ace mechanic home with a malaria flare, and that maniac of a customer, Loopat Slimree, flashing a mouthful of ugly gold teeth and threatening to kill him. How could the worst lemon on the lot, a Lexus with electrical shorts in the dashboard display, end up in the hands of a hit man for Ayama Na's sleaziest drug cartel? And why didn't that *purae* Hundai in front of him force its way into the traffic circle?

Koriatt wanted to get home to the cold *Yama Hi* his wife would have put on on the coffee table for him. Suri worked eight to two at the dealership (billing and accounts receivable) and knew firsthand the aggravations he had to tolerate. Before he walked in every night, she set out that beer, plugged in the fan, and herded their sons into the kitchen so he could unwind and watch the news before the onslaught of family life.

Koriatt threw his tie on a chair, popped the cap off the *Yama Hi*, and flung himself into the sofa cushions. Comforting sounds filtered through the closed kitchen door—the sizzling wok, the earnest voice of his eldest son, thirteen-year-old Lam, reciting the individual letters of the week's spelling words as his brother quizzed him, one word at a time.

The TV screen blinked and flickered until a ragged stack of rubble emerged, footage from an accident at the Sleephat Center, a shopping mall under construction on Weeskiescoopackiak Street where, earlier in the day, a wall had shattered and crushed a brick mason and two luckless pedestrians. The pundits speculated that the prime minister, widely known to be on the take, had accepted massive campaign contributions from the Slotupranskayat Construction Company, the perpetrators of this fiasco, already indicted twice for pasting walls together with watered down cement.

"The connivers! The thieves!" Koriatt muttered, railing against the government and at the same time aware of the satisfaction he derived from political scandals. Koriatt had dreams of running for parliament, becoming the savior of his vice-ridden country, and the corruption on the TV fueled his vision of himself as Pin Dalie's Serpico. The more cops on the take, the more postal employees with their hands in the till, the more members of parliament lining their pockets with *ghree* while the country's infrastructure crumbled, the finer Koriatt would look when he cleaned up the mess. And who would clean it up if not a young honest businessman like himself?

Didn't he run his dealership with scrupulous integrity? Did he ever overcharge a customer or underpay an employee? Hadn't *Ayama Na Today* cited him as one of the country's ten most exemplary employers for his commitment to health care benefits? Including a dental plan!

Sure, he and Suri had business loans to repay and two sons to educate. Of course he'd be as happy as the next guy to live in a mansion on Raspinkopiriat Street (where that good-for-nothing who owned the Honda dealership lived) instead of in this cramped rental, but to fleece customers and exploit workers in a country that had been through so much amounted to a crime against the next six generations. What kind of example would that set for his boys?

Ack chee mi yobat! That corrupt prime minister with his skinny mustache and his disappearing chin had the gall to stand there with a smile on his face and deny the allegations. "You greedy hypocrite," Koriatt yelled. "You scoundrel. You enrich yourself while the citizens who elected you can't buy medicine or educate their kids." In the groove now, Koriatt ranted and raved, his fantasies at full throttle, his head clear, his muscles relaxed, the day's tribulations compartmentalized away. Then the phone rang.

"Not home yet," he said to himself. That's what Suri, dark-eyed and pretty, would say to whomever dared to intrude on his hallowed twenty minutes. His sweet wife wouldn't disturb him if King Mindao called in person requesting delivery of a brand new hybrid fuel-efficient Prius to the palace doorstep.

But what was this? The unthinkable was happening. Suri was approaching him, slotted stir-fry spoon in one hand, phone extended in the other, her wide, freckled face pinched at the need to do this to him. "Sorry but you better take this, my love."

He accepted the phone, heart filled with dread, and the voice he heard was the sharp scratchy country vernacular he'd feared and expected—old man Nee-Poo, the eighty-one-year-old pineapple farmer who owned the hectares that abutted his father's. This time, Koriatt thought, Mr. Nee-Poo would tell him his father was dead, but Nee-Poo hadn't called to report a death. He'd called to describe to Koriatt the latest evidence of his father's dementia and scold Koriatt for neglect.

"Naked! You hear me. From one end of the road to the other with his *yoyo* swinging," Nee-Poo said. "How many times I have to call you? What you waiting for? You want me to phone you one day and tell you your Papi is dead? Time you take him to live with you."

"Thank you, Mr. Nee-Poo," Koriatt said, and sought to fend off the rest of the old man's lecture with a pathetic, "I'll take care of it."

"If you don't, Mr. Big Shot Toyota Dealer, there will be curses on your children's heads. Your mother, may she return to live in a mansion with thirty-three servants, wouldn't know the boy she raised from a toad in a shit puddle."

"Thank you Mr. Nee-Poo, I'll remember that," Koriatt said. Above his right eye, his headache renewed itself with throbbing vigor. What day was it—ah, this was Thursday, the day before his son Lam's spelling test. He couldn't leave the lot on Friday or Saturday, the week's two biggest sales days. Impossible. He'd have to spend Sunday, his one day off, his day to take his children to the soccer park, driving a hundred miles out to the country on roads so impassible it would kill the whole day to get there and back. And for what? What would the trip accomplish?

He'd muted the TV when Suri gave him the phone and he left it that way. He'd do what he vowed not to do again for a minimum of six months. He'd call her—his only sibling—the selfish younger sister with whom he hadn't exchanged a single word since their blowup over this father of theirs three months ago.

"Nice of you to see if I'm alive, *slivo nuki*," she said, tagging him with the abusive epithet that had incensed him during that last conversation, its rough translation, *big geek with blackheads*. "To what do I owe this sudden concern for my welfare?"

"I ask how you are and this is what I get? Did you want me to tell you bad news in the first ten seconds of this call when we haven't spoken in three months?"

"Three months and two weeks," she said, giving herself away.

His silence had disturbed her. Older brothers protect their younger sisters even when their younger sisters are difficult, that was the accusation her acid tone hurled at him. What a shrew she was, so opposite to his wife who never raised her voice. But he softened toward her; she'd missed him. "It's been a long time, Moonri, hasn't it?"

"So let me guess why you're calling. Our father walked naked through the middle of the village."

What? He could strangle her! Obviously old man Nee-Poo had called her first and she'd told Nee-Poo to call him, a chain of events that proved how self-centered she was, this sister of his, unmarried, no children, and yet unwilling to assume the traditional responsibilities of an Ayama Nan daughter and move in with their father to ease his last miserable years. "Nee-Poo called you, didn't he?"

"He calls me twice a month and tells me our mother wouldn't know me from a goose gizzard with huge ugly pin feathers. I figured it was your turn to be on the receiving end of his curses."

She laughed, and he remembered her as a little girl. Nine when she was born and at first merely relieved no longer to bear the stigma of only child, he'd quickly fallen under the spell of her smooth baby skin, that spiky black hair, the funny giggle—a remnant of which he imagined he still heard in her peevish cackle. Until three months ago, Koriatt had seen Moonri at least once a week, meeting her for lunch or inviting her home to dinner so his sons would know his sister.   A mistake, because now his sons missed their tall skinny aunt who brought them gifts of forbidden chocolates and whose drawings of anatomically correct animals made them laugh. It was for his boys' sakes that he tried yet again to reason with her. "You're an artist, Moonri. You can paint anywhere. You don't need to live in Pin Dalie."

"I paint cityscapes, *slivo nuki*. How come you can't remember that?"

Same response she gave last time, same nasty slur. Cityscapes, ha; she painted blobs and squiggles, could be anything on those unintelligible canvasses of hers. "To me what you paint looks like agricultural fields, visions of the countryside. I suspect your work owes at least as much to our father's pineapple fields as to the city." Hadn't he used that argument last time? This conversation evoked in him a crushing *pathchukai lem*—*déjà vu*—that feeling he'd heard this before, juxtapositions depressingly familiar: his logic, her irrationality; his calm attempts to persuade, her pig-headed and disrespectful resistance.

"You have no idea what inspires me," Moonri said.

"Then take photographs of the city to the country with you. Artists work from pictures all the time."

"How would you know how artists work?"

"I…"

"You what? You paid for my art education, that's what you started to say wasn't it?"

"No, it wasn't," he said.

"Liar. I'm waiting. Let's hear it. Go on, say it. Say what you're thinking. I paid for your art classes. I paid for your canvasses. I bought you a three-year supply of oil paint. Go on. Say it."

Koriatt had been thinking exactly that: a dozen tubes of titanium white, ten of chromium yellow, forty prestretched canvases, dozens of brushes—the entire inventory scrolled in his head. "Don't be ridiculous. When do I ever mention your debt to me? Have I ever asked you to repay it?"

"You don't have to. I hear it in your voice. Next you'll say you'll forgive the debt if I take care of our father."

"I would, Moonri, in a minute."

"See? I knew it. You are so transparent."

He guessed that soon she'd remind him that she'd nursed their mother through pancreatic cancer and he owed her for that. She'd milk those ten last days of their mother's illness for the rest of his life. "Let's not do this to each other," he said. "Meet me out at the pineapple farm Sunday. It'll be good to see you. We'll figure something out—maybe hire some help."

"Oh right. That'll work."

Six months ago they'd hired a local widow, a competent woman their father had promptly ejected, arguing she brought shame on his house. In his world, children, not strangers, cared for their parents. "Things could be different now," Koriatt said, thinking that perhaps their father, in his diminished awareness, would no longer know who was or wasn't in his house, or that Moonri, face to face with her father's plight, might relent.

The roads had deteriorated since Koriatt last made this trip. If he ran the country, in his first year in office, he would build two-lane paved highways instead of squandering IMF loans on handouts to cronies who dumped useless dirt into the country's potholes. For the first fifty kilometers, his if-I-controlled-the-world scenarios protected him, but at the halfway point, the old country traditions invaded his thoughts. It was not strictly true that the responsibility for the care of aged parents fell to the eldest daughter, nor did the custom stop at the boundary between urban and rural. Everyday, it seemed, one of Koriatt's employees or customers, both male and female, described the havoc created when a venerated mother or father moved in. Pisek's mother had loose bowels; Ransopa's father criticized his wife and spoiled the children; Pwalalet's mother-in-law insisted on mashed herring paste with breakfast, lunch, and dinner, ruining everyone's appetite; and Pramsin—a customer who bought a new Camry every other year—hadn't had sex since the arrival of his father-in-law. Pisek, Ransopa, Pwalalet, and Pramsin were fulfilling obligations of honor and devotion at great inconvenience to themselves, but Koriatt couldn't decide if wrecking a peaceful family life was admirable or a retreat from the twenty-first century, and he really didn't want to think this complex question through to a conclusion. Even if he wanted to transfer his father to his apartment in the city, he couldn't. Suri's mother had abandoned her family, and left Suri, at age fourteen, to run the household, deal with her distraught father, and submit to the whims of the in-law intruder her mother had fled, a bossy old woman who always had to be right. As a condition of their marriage, Koriatt had promised Suri that her history would never repeat itself. There'd be no invasion of in-laws. He'd given his word all those years ago, before it mattered, before his mother had died, before his father took ill, before his *famuta* of a sister revealed herself as selfish and conscienceless. Before old man Nee-Poo had a cell phone to harass him with.

⊞ ⊞ ⊞

His father lay on the bed, breathing through his mouth, his snores sporadic and uneven as if any one of them could be his last. As soon as Koriatt entered the two-room thatched house raised up on stilts, he had to cover his mouth and nostrils with a cupped hand to ward off the stench. Above his hand he saw wormy larvae squirming in a busted sack of rice in the near corner and on the counter a rotten pineapple, its cut surface black with ants. He dared another look at his father on the bed, his abdomen concave, his ribs visible through his T-shirt, a ten-day stubble on his cheeks and chin. He'd wet himself, and the house reeked of urine-soaked sweat pants (pants Koriatt had brought him on his last visit), rancid pineapple, and animal excrement. The old dog, Foof, skinny as Koriatt's father's arm, lay sleeping on the floor at the side of his father's flimsy cot, too weak and arthritic to drag himself out to the yard.

Koriatt had last visited the weekend after his father's seventy-sixth birthday, four months ago. He'd come alone, leaving Suri and the boys in the city. His father's situation had been deteriorating for a year and he wanted to protect his sons, not from their grandfather's illness or mental deterioration, but from the fact that their grandfather was in trouble and their father wasn't doing enough to help.

Koriatt couldn't keep looking at his father, alone and abandoned, lying in his own filth, so it was Foof that broke his heart—the fur matted, the eyes encrusted, the old dog half starved to death. Koriatt felt suddenly frantic, unable to bear the sorrows pressing at his head. How had it come to this?

He hurried from the house back to the yard, eyes lowered, hand clutching his forehead, envisioning old man Nee-Poo's accusing eyes staring at him from across the space of two yards, imagining Nee-Poo running toward him, calling him the miserable names he deserved. Koriatt slid into his Corolla, rolled up the windows, locked the doors and sat there, head slumped on the wheel while the car turned into a solar oven and sweat soaked through his shirt and pants. His hands slid off the slick steering wheel and flopped around on the slippery leather seat as he waited, vaguely aware of the danger of the car's rising interior temperature but determined that no matter how hot the car got, he wouldn't open the door until Moonri arrived. He wouldn't face old man Nee-Poo alone. Among every other sentient being on earth, only Moonri could understand what he felt. No one else knew how hard their father had worked in the pineapple fields, how, even during the drought, he'd pulled the crop through and still mustered the energy and time to play with them when he came home at night. She knew, as Koriatt did, how proud their father had been of his perfect family: a son to help care for the fields, a daughter to help care for him and his wife when they could no longer tend to themselves.

Twenty-eight now, Moonri had been eight when the cod vendor at the village market put the puppy in her arms. Koriatt did the subtraction and multiplied by seven. In human years, Foof was 140. That dog had no right to still be alive.

The motorcycle that roared in his feverish dreams pulled up behind his car and sputtered to a halt, confirming what he should have guessed—that Moonri wouldn't come to meet him alone. But he hadn't guessed. He'd been caught off guard, and he stumbled from the Corolla with an intense and lonely rage. Always, she had some "brilliant young artist" hanging around, mooching her huge supply of oil paint. Today's artist resembled all the rest, tall with long, straggly hair and an anarchist's smile. They were all anarchists, these artist types, too enlightened to work nine to five. She untangled her smooth, brown arms from her boyfriend's waist and jumped off the bike.

"My brother, the *slivo nuki*," Moonri said to the biker, ignoring Koriatt's bright red face and drenched pants and shirt.

Amused by the irreverence and disrespect in her introduction of an older brother, the biker laughed as he peeled leather off the tips of his fingers, but he did notice Koriatt's state. "Man, what happened to you?" he said. "You look wasted."

"Hot car. And the name's Koriatt."

"Oxeed." The biker extended his hand.

Oxeed's nails were stained with oil paint, probably paid for by me, Koriatt thought, feeling his anger spike. He turned to confront his thoughtless sister for her failure to respect the privacy of their family in this delicate and painful moment of necessity and decision, but Moonri had started walking toward the house.

"Don't go in there," Koriatt yelled, surprised by his sudden desire to protect her the way he'd protected her when they'd lived here as children, an older brother insisting his little sister wear shoes, even inside the house, as a precaution against parasites; his young hands stretching the edges of her mosquito net every night; and when the river flooded, his agile feet running after her if she ventured too close to the bank, knowing even then how many dark things could take a life. "Don't go in there."

"Why? Is he dead?" she called over her shoulder from the step in front of the door, flippant, for all her supposed artist's sensibility, unable to imagine the horrors inside.

"You don't want to see him like he is right now. I mean it Moonri, turn around."

"I took care of mother when cancer rotted her body, or did you forget she died in my arms? I think I can handle a little dementia." She disappeared through the door and in the time it would take to breathe in and out twice, she'd run back to the yard. "How could you?" she screamed at Koriatt. "How could you?"

For an unguarded instant, Koriatt believed she'd asked the appropriate question. Every effect has a cause, and he had caused this, hadn't he? If he hadn't won the regional spelling contest that carried with it a crown scholarship to a high school in Pin Dalie, he'd have worked along-side his father cultivating pineapples for the rest of his life. Moonri would have married the man their father had chosen for her, and their father would have grown old surrounded by family, just as his father, and all the fathers before him, had.

By what stretch of the imagination did he think Moonri, whom he'd provided with the same advantages he'd won for himself, whom he'd turned into a modern woman with twenty-first century ideas in her head, could move back here when he never could?

Moonri sobbed in her boyfriend's arms.

"What's happening in there?" Oxeed gestured with his shoulder toward the house.

"Our father is snoring and the house is a mess," Koriatt said, upgrading the situation, for his own sake, from unbearable to merely awful, half believing his answer, trying to convince himself he hadn't seen what he'd seen, trying to believe his sister was overreacting.

"So look who's showed up. The ungrateful children." Old man Nee-Poo had appeared out of nowhere, balancing in his shaky hands a tray on which a steamer of rice and a bowl of tea tottered. "Who you think feeds him?" Nee-Poo said. "Who you think keeps him from starving to death? Everyday, lunch and dinner, lunch and dinner, lunch and dinner. I cook for myself, I cook for him."

Oxeed pried himself from Moonri's grasp and took the rattling tray from the old man's hands.

Koriatt felt his face grow hot and redden with guilt, hotter and redder than he'd felt in the inferno of his car. Plunging his hands into his pockets, he emptied them of *ghree* and forced the money into Nee-Poo's hand.

"Keep your money, Mr. Toyota Salesman." Nee-Poo let the *ghree* flutter to the dirt. "I knew you before you were born, Koriatt Raeesoritt. You were a good boy. What happened to you? Why don't you do what's right?"

"I'm trying, Mr. Nee-Poo, I'm trying. We're going to see if Mrs. Leeskospanoota is still available." He felt himself duck his head, as if to avoid a blow, for Mrs. Leeskospanoota wasn't what Mr. Nee-Poo had in mind, Koriatt knew that.

Moonri turned on her brother. "Are you crazy? Did you forget that a year ago your father beat her with a stick?"

"You saw *your* father in there," Koriatt said, reminding her that the father in there was hers too. "Do you think he could beat up anyone now? He won't even know the old woman is there."

"I'll know," a voice called from inside the house. And then his father appeared at the door, so frail and vacant-eyed, it seemed impossible he'd spoken.

⊞ ⊞ ⊞

Koriatt couldn't focus on his driving even though, if he wanted his Corolla to survive the treacherous return journey to Pin Dalie, he had to pay attention. The car kept slipping into potholes, bottoming out, damaging the shocks. When the front right tire fizzled to a flat he cursed his father for being alive. And if his father had to be alive, did he have to be the same stubborn man he'd been all his life? Koriatt guessed that even if his father ceased to know his own name, even if he could do nothing but lie on his bed and slobber day and night, if Mrs. Leeskospanoota showed up, he'd beat her with a stick.

And if Koriatt felt anger at his father, he positively hated old man Nee-Poo. Were it not for Nee-Poo's having come round with his vitamins and his antibiotics when his father had pneumonia last year, his father would have expired in his bed, sparing himself and his children this unbearable end. Who was Nee-Poo to intervene in the natural course of events? And now, when his father attempted to starve himself to death, Nee-Poo shoveled food into his mouth. How dare he force feed a man who, for all of his life, walked the rows of his pineapple plants ruthlessly culling the ones that bore weak fruit or no longer produced, sacrificing yield for hearty stock. There was a lesson in that, a lesson old man Nee-Poo never understood.

Nee-Poo's hectares, with the equivalent soil, sun, and rainfall (or its lack), produced pineapples half the size of his father's and a quarter as sweet. His father would look at their dry, porous flesh and brownish-yellow hue and joke that Nee-Poo fertilized them with baboon drool. How Nee-Poo must enjoy seeing his agricultural rival in a state of degradation; how irresistible it must be to him to prolong his neighbor's humiliation. Whose pineapples were sweeter now, Nee-Poo was undoubtedly saying to himself.

Well, Koriatt wouldn't let Nee-Poo get the better of his father. Koriatt would take matters into his own hands, do what his father would beg him to do if he were in his right mind. Finally, Koriatt saw what he needed to do.

For the rest of the drive, Koriatt assessed his decision, gauging if it pinched anywhere, but as the kilometers piled up, the decision seemed right. Nothing hurt, nothing rubbed the wrong way—in fact, the longer he considered his plan, the better it felt.

Why should he and his sister remain estranged? Why deny his boys their aunt's company? Why accumulate more memories of their father as a broken and pitiful wreck? He preferred to remember him in the fields, strong and clever, harvesting the big, juicy, sweet pineapple crop, chuckling at the specter of Nee-Poo's inferior fruit.

※ ※ ※

As soon as she'd updated the spread sheets and posted the bills, Suri locked the backups in the file cabinet and shut down the computer. He watched her drive off the lot in her month-old Camry, this competent and lovely wife of his. Every fall, he and Suri traded their cars for the newer model, a luxury they allowed themselves (although in no other way did they live big) because the cars they drove advertised the business, promoting sales so they could pay their employees a living wage and provide generous health benefits.

It was Monday (the day Lam would bring home a new set of spelling words) and Koriatt's decision still felt right. Throughout the morning, he'd monitored himself for signs of inner turmoil, promising himself that if his hands shook, if he had a sudden tremor or an insight that signaled a mistake, he'd abandon his intended course of action. But instead of a headache, the morning brought one triumph after another. He worked the lot himself and sold two cars, a used Spyder and a new Land Cruiser, the most profitable vehicle on the lot. Moreover, after months of searching, he found an experienced mechanic who could start the next day and would help clear the backlog. All of this struck him as proof of the rightness of his plan. It seemed he could do no wrong now that he had taken charge of his fate.

Returning to the office after his wife departed, Koriatt locked the door and dialed Loopat Slimree's cell phone. The big-shot drug dealer had no land line, only untraceable mobile numbers.

"You worried, Raeesoritt? You want to know if that crappy piece of shit you sold me is behaving itself or if I'm going to detach your head from your neck? At least the tires haven't fallen off, so what do you want? Make it quick, I'm in the middle of a personal grooming session."

Picturing Slimree with a whore rubbing oil on his back, Koriatt told him he needed his help for a personal matter. Slimree gave him the address of the restaurant where he "conducted business." Koriatt met him there and, by the time he left, he and Slimree had a verbal contract.

The next day, after his wife left, Koriatt locked the door to his office again. He felt an obligation to speak the literal truth to his father's neighbor, and choosing his words carefully, he asked old man Nee-Poo to tell his father that after this weekend, his troubles would cease. No longer would he live alone in the old leaky house.

"Tell him," Koriatt said, "that I'll come get him Sunday afternoon."

"You taking him to live with you?" Nee-Poo said.

"That's the plan." Koriatt pictured an urn full of ashes in his living room.

"About time," Nee-Poo said. "You lost ground in this life, but you help yourself now. Yesterday you on road to come back a stink bug. Today you have chance return as a lizard. Big step up. I'll give Papi your message."

"You do that, Mr. Nee-Poo."

※ ※ ※

"I did you a favor. I threw in the dog," Loopat Slimree said when Koriatt met him at the restaurant the following Monday.

"Yeah. I saw the dog." Foof had been lying alongside his father, dog and man at the same stage of rigor mortis, mouths uncloseable, toes stiff and curled upward. There were no signs of violence. It was a clean hit, just as Koriatt had requested, giving the appearance his father had died in his sleep.

Nee-Poo had been sitting on his father's step on Sunday afternoon when Koriatt arrived. The old man had come to feed and shave his neighbor, get him ready for his move to the city, and say his goodbyes.

When Koriatt saw the dog, he feared the simultaneous deaths might have aroused Nee-Poo's suspicions. But Koriatt had nothing to fear. For Mr. Nee-Poo, these events added up to proof of a different kind. "Your Papi not meant to leave his pineapple farm," Nee-Poo said. "And Foof not meant to leave your Papi's side."

"Place stunk like a shitbox," Slimree said, looking at Koriatt through narrowed eyes.

"My father wouldn't allow anyone to take care of him. He was a proud man who..." Koriatt stopped. He didn't owe Slimree an explanation. Slimree was a cold-blooded killer who gunned down the healthy in the prime of their lives. Who was this murderer to stand in judgment of him?

The agreement had been that Slimree would charge by the hour, including driving time to and from the country. Koriatt wanted this thug out of his sight. "What do I owe you for services rendered, Mr. Slimree?"

"Services rendered, hmmm?" Slimree mulled the phrase. "You got a way with words, you know that, Raeesoritt?" Slimree looked Koriatt up and down and Koriatt saw that Slimree viewed him in an entirely new light. No longer was he just a puny self-righteous little businessman, he was someone worse than that—he was a dishonorable son.

"Just tell me the total." The briefcase at Koriatt's side contained thousands of *ghree*.

"No charge for my friends," Slimree said.

Koriatt didn't like that. Loopat Slimree wasn't a friend.

"In fact, *I'm* going to pay *you* for allowing me to *render services*." Slimree grinned, his mouth flashing gold.

Was Slimree mocking him?

"I'm guessing, Raeesoritt, that a good-looking, honest businessman such as yourself with an attractive wife and two clean-cut sons could run for parliament and win. I'm thinking you might be a damn good investment. Me and my associates, we've decided to fund your campaign for office in the next election."

"I don't think I..."

"Right, you don't have to think. From here on, me and my associates, we'll think for you," Slimree said, as he escorted Koriatt from the restaurant. "All you and your pretty wife need to do is pose for pictures and smile and wave." Slimree grabbed Koriatt's arm and waved it back and forth a few times. "Like this," he said. "Now I'm about to get into this vehicle you unloaded on me, Mr. Candidate, and as I drive away, when I look in the rearview mirror, I want to see you practicing your smile and your wave. Get it?"

Koriatt stood on the sidewalk, silent and shocked as Slimree turned the key in the ignition.

"What'd I say I want to see?" Slimree yelled out the window.

Koriatt smiled and waved, and when he couldn't see Slimree anymore, he continued to smile and wave until his grin felt cemented in place. Then he stood there for another minute, contemplating his future as a member of parliament, generating a mental list of the important civic improvements he would put into place so the citizens of his poor beleagured country could have a better life.

Hamburger School

If the oil heated to the proper temperature, the fries would be acceptable, but if the generator quit or the timer went on the fritz, the fries would end up burnt on the outside and raw on the inside or pale and soggy with an oily spurt in every bite. This time, the batch Mahala lifted out looked good, most of the fries crispy, flecked with brown, nice and stiff.

Mahala gave the basket a shake, poured the contents into the bin and sprinkled on the premeasured dose of salt. To fill the orders, her co-worker Raylee, also her lab partner in chemistry at the Pin Dalie Sector Twelve High School, scooped the fries into cartons. The thing about Raylee that everyone noticed sooner or later was how seriously she took her job—way too seriously, in Mahala's opinion. Some days, with some batches, like this one for instance, Raylee pulled limp fries out of the scoop on their way into the cartons even though the preponderance were more than acceptable and if a few imperfect ones slipped through no one would notice. For Raylee's own good, Mahala had to tell her to knock it off.

"Sorry," Raylee said.

Raylee might as well have added, "I can't help myself," because in truth she couldn't, a predicament Mahala understood. Like Raylee, Mahala was sixteen, the age of maximum idealism, and had compulsions toward perfection herself. She, too, would have liked every french fry this McDonald's served to be perfectly cooked. For that matter, Mahala would have liked every slice of cheese on every cheeseburger—single or double—to be flawlessly melted, every chicken burger—a specialty item on the Pin Dalie menu—to be juicy and tender, all parents in Ayama Na to earn enough money to feed their kids, all amputees to regrow their limbs, all wars to cease, every tourist to spend a fistful of dollars, and the oil for the fries to heat to the proper temperature every time despite the vagaries of the timer and the generator.

But unlike Raylee, Mahala knew a few things about perfection. She knew that if you spent your life chasing it instead of accepting its limits, you'd lose the ability to function and your failures would shrivel your spirit. Besides, you should put your energy to more doable tasks, such as saving money to get into medical school, architecture school, or city planning so you could be a credit to your family and a benefit to your country, which was struggling so hard to rebuild itself.

Mahala understood things like this because her father's first family, a wife and three children, had died during the country's descent into mayhem, and her father treated her, the only child of his second family, the way a grandfather would, meaning he asked what she thought, listened to her opinions with respect, and followed up with questions designed to lead her more deeply into what she professed. As a consequence, she could think for herself. Raylee, at the other extreme—because god knows what went on in her family—seemed to have no personal guidelines and therefore operated from naïve behaviors such as this unhealthy quest for perfection and a pathetic and desperate need to please everyone in sight, which led her, for example, to switch days off with anyone who asked, to swap shift jobs even if she ended up cleaning tables and restrooms ten times more than anyone else, and to give her make-up away to every female co-worker who envied her eyeliner or cheek blush. Raylee couldn't figure out how to give herself a break—at least that's how Mahala sized up the situation.

Even before the Big Accusation, that hideous moment at the monthly shift meeting that spelled Raylee's doom, Raylee appeared on the verge of a nervous breakdown. She'd failed algebra last semester and had chronic stomachaches, plus the troubles at work. It was against the rules for the employee filling orders to handle the food, and if the shift manager noticed her pulling fries from the carton, he'd get nasty and cite her with another incident report, which is why Mahala tried to stop her. But Mahala might as well have asked rice not to be white.

Still, if luck had been with Raylee for once, the customer destined to receive the handled fries would have been that kid with the yellow-tipped, punk-jellied hair, a gold ring through his eyebrow, and the silver cell phone at his ear who wouldn't have cared if he found a human finger in the carton. But the customer who did get the fries was a germ-phobic, middle-aged tourist whose eyes opened wide at the thought of eating food touched by

Ayama Nan hands. "I saw that girl touch my fries," she said. "I want a different carton."

During the on-site training sessions for new employees, the shift manager, Rae Ko-Vo, had stressed that the most critical rule was *The customer is always right*. This American concept, he said, was the single most important thing he'd learned at Hamburger School, and he repeated it a million times a week. So the cashier, also a student at Mahala's high school, told the customer, "No problem—new fries coming right up." But meanwhile, Raylee had filled the take-out bags with the rest of this batch, so the lady had to wait for the next basket to emerge from the oil, and while she waited, she took a bottle of sanitizing liquid from her purse and squirted enough in her hands to sanitize an elephant.

And meanwhile, her McWhateverBurger had cooled off and she asked for a replacement for that as well. This was too much, so the sandwich assemblers treated her to the Evil Customer treatment, meaning one of them slipped a big roach from the cup of smashed roaches, hoarded for this purpose, between the tomato slice and the bun, pasting it in place with an extra dose of catsup, a caper they got away with because, according to the morning shift (not high school kids, but mostly older guys who'd survived forced labor in the mines), bugs tasted like condiments, an assertion verified by Mahala's father, an artisanal baker who supplied crusty baguettes and specialty rolls to the fancy tourist hotels in Pin Dalie, but who'd found it necessary to eat a few bugs in his time.

On general principles, of which Mahala had many, she didn't approve of roach retribution, so at times like this she spaced out over the hot vat of oil and watched the bubbles float to the surface, a ritual that produced a kind of exit from her immediate surroundings and also had the paradoxical effect of accelerating time. Before she knew it, without any sense of waiting, the timer buzzed. When Mahala explained to her father the tricks time played at work, the way impatience slowed time down, the way not thinking about it speeded it up, he assured her that the passage of time in one's mind wasn't time playing tricks, but the mind's own reality. The mind, he said, understood time in a way the clock didn't—which gives you an example of the quality of things Mahala's father said and also explains how she ended up, at that juncture in life, able to think for herself. Anyway, when the buzzer sounded, startling Mahala back to reality, Rae Ko-Vo, the shift manager, had already squared off in front of Raylee to reprimand her for touching the fries.

"How many times have I warned you," he shouted. "I ought to fire you." He ordered her from behind the counter and told her to clean the restrooms even though she'd done the spit-and-polish shift yesterday and today's spit-and-polisher had cleaned the restrooms not ten minutes earlier.

"What are you looking at?" Rae Ko-Vo glared at Mahala.

Mahala glared back, staring him down the way you should stare down bullies, especially bullies who make threats they don't carry out. Long ago, Raylee had exceeded the six documented incident reports required to fire an employee unless the employee committed an unpardonable infraction, such as stealing from the cash register or menacing another employee with a knife or hot oil. So if he'd been inclined to fire her, he would have fired her fifteen times already. But he would never fire her, because with her big brown soulful eyes, perfect skin, statuesque height, beautiful figure (even in the stupid McDonald's T-shirt), and wedge-cut jet black hair, Raylee looked like a movie star or an ice-skating champion, and who would fire that? Least of all Rae Ko-Vo because after Raylee went into the women's restroom with the mop and the bucket, he dragged the Closed for Cleaning sign in front of the door and followed her in.

※ ※ ※

"You don't have to let him touch you," Mahala had told Raylee a thousand times, occasionally augmenting her argument by adding that the time that *slivo nuki* tried to get familiar with her, she threatened to file a grievance with his supervisor, and although in the exchange that followed, Rae Ko-Vo had said stuff like "It'll be my word against yours" and "You dress like a slut," he never bothered her again.

"You don't make mistakes the way I do," Raylee had said. "Besides, I need this job. You're an only child but I have seven younger sisters and brothers and I have to help out."

Raylee could have added that Mahala would never understand because Mahala's father had his own business and Mahala's mother wasn't worn down to the nub of a broom from one thing and another, but she didn't. Even if Raylee wasn't just plain too nice to make comments like that, Mahala knew that Raylee couldn't think fast enough on her feet to say the things that by all rights she should say when other people tried to tell her how to run her life. She could barely answer a question or look anyone in the eye, let alone assert herself.

For example, one time when school closed early on account of a generator breakdown, Raylee went home with Mahala to kill an hour before their McD's shift, and in the small flat, one flight above the bakery, Raylee met Mahala's friendly and vivacious mother who looked almost like a teenager herself and read detective stories and drove the bakery's delivery truck and also met Mahala's father who asked her if she liked working at McDonald's. And then, because that's the way Mahala's father was, he asked if she considered the franchise well run and Raylee blushed and lowered her head and couldn't answer because, probably, in her whole life, her parents never asked her opinion of anything.

"I understand you need the job, Raylee," Mahala said, "but Rae Ko-Vo would never fire you. Customers come in here just to look at you. Don't go into that restroom with him anymore."

Raylee patted Mahala on the back. "It's no big deal, Hallie. Honestly," she said.

When Mahala asked her father how Raylee could think being forced to go into the restroom with Rae Ko-Vo was no big deal, he answered, "Do you suppose that may not be the worst thing that's ever happened to her?"

"What could be worse?" Mahala said, stumped. But in bed that night, she decided her father might have a point because most of the time, when Rae Ko-Vo slid the Closed for Cleaning sign in front of the restroom and followed Raylee in, Raylee's father was sitting right there in the restaurant.

He came in nearly every night after he got off work as a guard at one of the tourist sites, but probably not right after because, judging from his breath, he'd stopped at a bar somewhere along the strip. He sat at an out of the way booth, where he drank coffee and rubbed his big nose and his puffy, half-lidded eyes with his huge hand, and when he came to the counter to order the coffee—two or three cups a night—if you happened to be the cashier you went to, you could hear how he slurred his words, plus see the black hole where two teeth were missing. It was a month before Mahala knew his identity, which turned into a huge embarrassment, because everyone, herself included, called him Zig-Zag after the shape of the scar on the side of his oversized head, a gash where hair didn't grow, and everyone also made derogatory remarks about him behind his back, comments Raylee certainly must have heard.

A lot of the time, this Zig-Zag had his eyes on Raylee in a lurid, unpleasant way. It wasn't unusual for people to look at Raylee, considering how beautiful she was, but how Zig-Zag ogled her made the hair on Mahala's arms stand up like the hair on a Venus fly trap, and that happened before she even knew who he was. It struck Mahala that Zig-Zag might be stalking Raylee since he rarely showed up on her days off. When she asked Raylee if she'd noticed the same, or if she felt frightened of him, Raylee swabbed the counter under the catsup dispenser so hard every drop of color drained from her face. "We can turn him in to the franchise supervisor. We can call the police," Mahala said.

At that, Raylee's arm flung out, knocking the straw dispenser off the counter. Then her knees buckled and she sank to the floor. Mahala knelt to the floor to help retrieve the straws from everywhere, and while down there, Raylee whispered to her, "As soon as we get up, follow me," which of course Mahala did. After they closed the door behind themselves in the walk-in cold storage locker, as spooky a place as a stand-up coffin even with that bare light bulb dangling from the ceiling, Raylee swore Mahala to secrecy and told her Zig-Zag was her father. The revelation caused Mahala such a deep sense of shame at the disrespectful stuff she and the other employees had said about him in front of his daughter, that although it was so cold in the locker boxes of frozen hamburgers breathed clouds of ice, Mahala felt like her head was on fire.

"Who do you think Raylee fears most right now?" Mahala's father asked when she recounted this latest development to him, breaking her vow of secrecy because she trusted her father and could tell him anything.

"The shift manager and that drunken ugly father of hers," Mahala said without hesitating, confident she'd named the two biggest tyrants in Raylee's life.

Mahala's father shook his head, so Mahala thought a moment, and then named herself, shocked at how true and right the answer felt. Because if she went to the police or the store supervisor, if she confronted Raylee's father, all normal impulses for an idealistic sixteen-year-old who wants to put the world right, she could plunge Raylee's life into total chaos. She could make Raylee's life a worse hell than it already was.

So things continued in this disgusting way, with Mahala reassuring Raylee every day that her secret was safe and with Raylee walking around with a tear in her eye, or at least that's how Raylee's eyes looked to Mahala until months later when Mahala looked back and realized the eyes with the tears hadn't been Raylee's, they'd been hers. Nothing changed until the shift meeting after work on the day the lady with the sanitized hands got Raylee in trouble for trying to serve her a perfect carton of french fries.

Once a month, the shift manager, Rae Ko-Vo, held a meeting, attendance mandatory, including if you had the night off you had to come back when the restaurant closed and if you worked a half-shift supper hour, you had to return four hours later, which, as anyone who'd ever sat through one of these meetings knew, wasted your time and might have led to a staff uprising except the company paid you for an hour, even if you got out in ten minutes.

Without exception, until that night, every meeting began the same way. Rae Ko-Vo handed out one or two insincere compliments, another technique he'd picked up at Hamburger School, then he read complaints from the customer complaint box, then he listed out loud the number of incident reports everybody'd accumulated in the previous thirty days, then he announced management opportunities in such places as India and Sri Lanka, and then the meeting would end. But this meeting started differently. For one thing, Rae Ko-Vo's supervisor came; for another, Rae Ko-Vo said he was going to turn the meeting over to the supervisor immediately and they should prepare themselves for the disturbing thing he had to say.

The shift employees, about twenty all together, slouched at various tables, but when they saw the supervisor walk toward Rae Ko-Vo, a few sat up straighter, and one guy, a really tall, really skinny kid who happened to be in Mahala's English class, took off his McDonald's cap, blue with red arches on the front, and put it on his lap. So after the employees rearranged their bodies and after the supervisor planted himself at Rae Ko-Vo's left, Rae Ko-Vo introduced him and he took charge of the meeting. He had a low voice, a timbre so much richer and smoother than Rae Ko-Vo's nasal squawk, this alone, in Mahala's opinion, could account for the supervisor's position as a supervisor and Rae Ko-Vo's as a shift manager.

"Let's get right to the point," the supervisor said in his serious voice. "Someone in this room is stealing money from the cash registers." He paused to let the Big Accusation sink in. Then he said, "I'd like the thief to stand up so we can do this the easy way." His eyes moved from person to person, looking for guilt on a face. Then he said, "So, not only is the guilty party a crook, he or she's a coward too."

He'd reviewed receipts and deposits, he said, and the thievery dated back to one month after King Mindao and Queen Hova cut the ribbon to open the restaurant, Ayama Na's first McDonald's franchise, a circumstance that put the entire country at risk as a venue for future American enterprise. "If the thief doesn't confess in the next twenty-four hours, I'll fire everyone in this room and hire employees I can trust." He waved fifty completed job applications in the air. "We're not talking *fulae mav cahoulic* here, we're talking 70,000 *ghree*," he said, using a local idiom to contrast "small potatoes" with 350 dollars, give or take, depending on the exchange rate. Then he said stuff like: Only one person has to lose his or her job; We can work out a schedule of reparations and avoid the police if the guilty party comes forward. If not, someone will do jail time, he could promise that. Understood? Meeting adjourned.

To be accurate, prior to "Meeting adjourned," he stared at them and said nothing for a good thirty seconds. Some people gave each other the fish eye, some shuffled their feet, coughed or shifted in their seats. Mahala's classmate with the cap, which incidentally employees weren't required to wear but this guy always did, twirled it around on one finger, probably figuring to eliminate himself as a suspect by acting natural. Raylee, as usual at these meetings, stared at her knees. Mahala felt sick to her stomach because she believed she knew the identity of the thief, and because like the supervisor said, 70,000 *ghree* wasn't *fulae mav cahoulic*. It was serious money you could work many years to pay back.

※ ※ ※

"So you think it's Raylee?" her father said when she got home. He and her mother were in the bakery, setting up the loaves and rolls to rise for the midnight baking. "Why would she do such a thing?"

"She wouldn't, unless she was forced to."

"You think Raylee and her father were co-conspirators?" Whenever she could, Mahala's mother spoke like the people in the detective books she read.

Mahala nodded.

"What makes you think so?" Her father's expert hands formed a baguette and placed it in a line of baguettes on a rectangular baking tray.

"Seventy thousand *ghree* isn't *fulae mav cahoulic*," Mahala said. "Even in five months, you couldn't short-change customers that much or filch it from the registers. You'd need an outside person to hand significant cash to when you made change, like after a person paid for his coffee."

"Is that evidence or a guess?" her father said. "Is Raylee the only cashier her father ever buys his coffee from?"

Mahala's mother, who was stoking the fire under the bread oven, turned and said, "Don't be naïve, Lito. Zig-Zag would create red-herring suspects. He'd buy coffee from everyone. I'm with Mahala. Raylee and her father had motive and opportunity."

"What's the motive?" He slid the tray, lined with baguettes that would rise in the next few hours, into a grooved slot in the tall rolling tray carriage. From a lower groove, he pulled an empty tray to fill.

"Seven siblings," her mother replied. Mahala nodded as her young mother reminded her father that children need food, clothes, and a roof over their heads.

Mahala's father stopped working. He rubbed his hands, which with their floury wrinkles and knobby knuckles had plenty of character, on his big white apron and put them on Mahala's shoulders, leaving white fingerprints on her navy blue T-shirt. "Would you call the shift manager a moral man?" he said.

Mahala didn't know what he was getting at, but his questions always helped her understand things better, so she answered that she certainly wouldn't, and as evidence, she reminded him of how Rae Ko-Vo followed Raylee into the women's restroom. "And as long as we're talking about immoral people, how about Raylee's father," she said. "He should have killed that *slivo nuki* the first time he saw him pull the Closed for Cleaning sign outside the restroom and go in there with his daughter. Isn't that what you'd do if it were me in that restroom?"

And right then, Mahala understood the whole awful situation. Raylee's greedy despicable father had sold Raylee to the shift manager. Rae Ko-Vo, himself, stole from the registers and gave Zig-Zag wads of cash. Rae Ko-Vo worked the cash registers more than anyone else because of course he never took a turn cleaning tables and counters or bathrooms or standing at the greasy fryers or the hot smoking grill. He made change for Zig-Zag when he came to McDonald's at night, and Zig-Zag drank coffee and made sure his daughter held up her end of his bargain.

"Wow," Mahala's mother said.

※ ※ ※

Mahala lay awake in bed, Raylee on her mind. She recalled all the times she'd seen Raylee's father at cash registers Rae Ko-Vo manned, and all the times

Raylee looked guilty and sad, and that time out back of McDonald's with a few other co-workers on a break, when the conversation turned to how everyone spent the money they earned, and Raylee said three of four paychecks went to help the family buy food and pay the rent, but every fourth week, her father—the father Mahala knew but nobody else knew they knew—took her to the big beauty supply store on Prinsalasakaphorina Street and made her spend the whole check on cosmetics because he wanted her to look good. "Nice," someone had said.

One thing Mahala would bet her life on: As soon as Raylee could give her father the slip, she'd confess to the crime. She'd assume the burden herself; she'd save everyone's job; the shift manager would escape punishment; Zig-Zag would go home to the family; and Raylee would go to jail or spend the next decade of her life working for free at McDonald's to repay the stolen cash plus lots of interest.

If Mahala intervened, tried for example to tell the supervisor the truth and blow the whistle on Rae Ko-Vo, even if the supervisor believed her, he'd say he didn't because these *slivo nukies* stuck together. And if by some miracle, he didn't pretend not to believe her, if he called the police and Rae Ko-Vo and Zig-Zag ended up in jail, Raylee's worn out mother and her seven sisters and brothers would have to fend for themselves.

Mahala could think of only one thing to do to help her friend. She would put all the money she'd earned, every *ghree* of which, because she had a lucky life, she'd been able to save for her higher education, into a paper bag and deliver it to the supervisor. She'd tell him the guilty party gave it to her to return, "no questions asked." If she had to, she'd even confess to the crime herself.

On general principles, Mahala felt good about her decision. If Raylee found out, Mahala would tell her it was a loan that she could pay back later in life. Meanwhile, with the theft discovered, Rae Ko-Vo wouldn't dare funnel more money into Raylee's father's hands, which would free Raylee from that awful situation in the restroom. Mahala got out of bed and went downstairs to the bakery where her father, asbestos gloves on his hands, slid trays of warm bread from the oven. When she told him her plan, he said exactly what she expected. "You earned that money, Mahala. You can decide how to spend it." So while her father watched, Mahala unlocked the safe and transferred the leather pouch to the zippered compartment of her backpack. Then she returned to bed.

Since the supervisor didn't arrive at his office before ten in the morning, Mahala could go to her computer science class, so when her mother swung by in the middle of the route to reload the delivery truck and pick up Mahala for school as she did every morning, Mahala jumped in.

In the light of day, Mahala held firm to the belief that she'd chosen the correct plan, although she downgraded the odds of its helping Raylee out of her plight. Raylee's father could easily sell his daughter to someone else. But Mahala could live with a decision that didn't yield perfect results because she'd long since accepted the reality that you couldn't achieve perfection in any area of life. If her actions wouldn't make things better for Raylee, at least they wouldn't make things worse.

But as soon as Mahala got to school, a sprawling structure with wood plank walls and a front lawn that was mostly bare dusty dirt, everyone was milling around outside exchanging the new gossip. Mahala quickly learned that no matter what she did, things could get neither better nor worse for Raylee, that day or ever, because early in the morning, in that sleazy Sector Nine, the police had pulled the body of a beautiful teenage girl from the Pin Dalie River.

※ ※ ※

They killed her, Mahala sobbed to her father. She'd run from the school straight to the bakery in such a dark state of mind she'd forgotten to tell Professor Savanateekoi she'd be absent from his computer science class. Things got even darker when she passed McDonald's and saw the day-shift employees scurrying around filling breakfast orders as if nothing out of the ordinary had happened in Pin Dalie that morning.

Mahala ran to the bakery instead of to the police station because she didn't know if the evidence pointed at one killer or two, but while sobbing in her father's arms, she decided it was a technicality whether Rae Ko-Vo or Zig-Zag had thrown Raylee's body in the river, and she'd tell the police all the disgusting things she knew about both of these terrible men. But before she got out the door, her father started asking his questions.

"Why would Rae Ko-Vo kill Raylee," he said. "Even if Raylee were to have accused him, he could have denied everything and wouldn't it be his word against hers? Didn't you say these management types stick together?"

Mahala had to admit that while Rae Ko-Vo had opportunity, he lacked motive. "Then it had to be Zig-Zag," she said, picturing the scar on his head, evidence of his violent lifestyle and probably of his chronic drunkenness as well. "Raylee's mother must have found out he'd sold their daughter for sex and threatened to turn him in. He had to get rid of Raylee because she could corroborate what her mother said."

Her conclusion felt logical to her until her father asked if she thought a man like Zig-Zag couldn't figure a way to silence his wife without sacrificing a daughter whose beauty was a source of income for him. And although nothing in Mahala's experience of family life taught her the answer to the question, there are some things everyone knows just from being alive.

So if Rae Ko-Vo didn't kill Raylee and if Raylee's own father didn't kill her, who did? She asked this aloud, but before the words left her mouth, she knew. And sure enough, that afternoon, Raylee's letter came in the mail to Mahala's house, addressed to Mahala herself. In the letter, Raylee apologized for taking her own life and for stealing the 70,000 *ghree* from the register and asked Mahala to give her confession to the supervisor.

Mahala showed her father the letter and then, without asking his advice, she ripped the letter into shreds and threw the shreds in the flames under the bread oven. She wouldn't let Raylee confess to a crime she didn't commit; at least she could do that much for her. And as for destroying evidence, Mahala felt proud of herself. Maybe it was that pride that carried her through those first few days after Raylee's body washed up on the riverbank, or maybe it was the excitement and melodrama that accompanies a sudden death, because in the weeks that followed, weeks in which, since Mahala had quit her stinking rotten job and had time on her hands, all she could do after school was lie on her bed, drained of energy, feeling horrible.

Mahala's mother attempted to cheer her up, attempts her father put a halt to because he knew from experience that it took time to get from one side of grief to the other, and as usual, her father was right. After a month, Mahala stopped spending every afternoon in her bed. She had her hair cut into a bob, she filled out an application to architecture school, and she found that she could think about Raylee without her mind going blank. Instead, when she thought of Raylee's beautiful face and her sweet personality, Mahala wept, inconsolable for hours at a time, a big step up from feeling nothing at all. The crying phase gradually diminished and then disappeared altogether, turning into a kind of scar inside her that her father said he could see in her eyes.

One day, while looking in her eyes, her father asked if she remembered what she'd learned about time, how she'd told him the tricks it played, how it could slow itself down or speed itself up. Certainly she remembered, she said, and to demonstrate to her father that his words had staying power, she recalled aloud that the way time passed in your mind wasn't time playing tricks. It was the mind understanding time the way the clock didn't.

"If you think about that," her father said, "you'll realize that under certain circumstances every day can be longer than twenty-four hours, much longer in fact. An outsider might think someone who died at sixteen died too young, but the person who died might have felt they'd lived a very long life, even longer than mine. One day, Mahala, you'll understand this."

And, of course, Mahala already did. But that is not the same as saying she was comforted to know that when Raylee died, she already felt terribly old.

AIBO or Love at First Sight

Dali-Roo's troubles began in the last year of the drought that spanned the millennium and sucked the green from the countryside. By March of that year, the tributaries of the Faro River that provided water to Pin Dalie's agricultural suburbs flowed like drops of weak spit. Unable to coax another grain of rice from his parched fields, Dali-Roo exchanged his farmer's life for the factory. His old gray ox stood on the parched, cracked earth, swishing flies from its dry itchy back, and watched Dali-Roo hoist himself onto a motorbike to join the surge of motorcycles heading from the rice paddies to the industrial outskirts of Ayama Na's capital.

As he rode off every day, Dali-Roo would promise himself not to steal from the factory again, but every evening, filled with disgust for himself, he'd pull the cardboard box from the shelf in the shed behind the house and add another item that didn't belong to him. A computer chip, a memory stick, a connector input line.

Dali-Roo's good-natured wife, Bancha, convinced that her husband had fallen under a spell, left their young son with her mother, who lived with them in the house Dali-Roo built, and walked seven miles beneath a scorching sun to the village with the wooden church tower—a leftover of the country's missionary craze—to consult with Oiric Lun, a disciple of Fundabas Vee, the country's leading aboriginal faith healer. During a fifteen minute audience, the bearded disciple prescribed a broth of boiled ficus bark, brown longan pods, and dried lemon peel. Bancha cooked this bitter brew for Dali-Roo every night, and every morning before he roared off to the Sony factory he held his nose and drank, for he too believed he was not himself.

Yoi, Dali-Roo's belittling mother-in-law, cursed the day her late husband had contracted Bancha's marriage match. "I warned your father," she grumbled to Bancha. 'Dhow-Li,' I said, 'a defective gleam shines in that boy's eyes.' But would Dhow-Li listen to me?"

"You and your defective gleam," Bancha said, her loyalty to Dali-Roo as steadfast as the day she married him. "You saw that gleam in my brother-in-law's eye too." Bancha was speaking of her sister Soko's fat spouse, now the preeminent hog butcher in Pin Dalie, able to extract edible parts from the slaughtered hog no other hog butcher could. "My sister is rich. She can buy whatever she desires. Good thing my father ignored you."

"Money? Is that what you imagine I wanted for my daughters? Soko stinks of pig from lying with that butcher. And you? You stink of corruption from lying with that thief you are married to."

Dali-Roo feared he'd end up in a cell, creating un-pardonable hardships for his sweet wife, including his mother-in-law's thousand reminders that she'd told her so. A clumsier thief never lived. The metal parts in his pocket rattled against the coins; the memory stick clanged against the sides of the lunch pail; bits of some shiny chrome thing he'd tied to his shin caught the sunlight at the hem of his pants. It wasn't a question of whether he'd get caught, it was only a question of when. Already, his friend Yanko, whose fields had suffered the same fate as his and who worked alongside him in the assembly line without losing his head, had spotted him popping a pair of hinged black lips into his pocket. "Are you crazy?" Yanko said. "The line supervisor watches us like a magician's assistant."

But the unwitting thief couldn't keep his hands to himself, powerless even though he understood he was gambling his family's future, even though he believed that a thief in this life returns as a worm in the next. His fate had been sealed the very first day at the factory when he sat with Yanko and ten other field-coarsened men at a long gleaming table in an orientation room. At the head of the table, a skinny woman in a blue silk suit stood with her hands in front of her chest, fingers formed in the pitched roof of respect, bowing slightly toward each man as she asked him to identify himself. Vinree, Kim-ree, Dar-Vee, Simncc, Okap, Ripdup, Siplee, Slip-sup—all these were men Dali-Roo knew. He'd seen them for years on alternate Saturdays at the tri-village market, trading (in better times) bags of rice for serpent fish and carp trucked in from Lake Sporee. He'd seen these men's wives at the market too, exchanging chicken eggs for tubes of lipstick or buying an eyebrow pencil with the *ghree* they earned stitching T-shirts. Yoi and Bancha did piece work as well, accumulating fifty or a hundred *ghree* by market day.

The factory would pay Dali-Roo and the others more *ghree* than that for eight hours work—500 *ghree* a day, a sum that caused a sensation among the farmers and their wives. "Five hundred a day to start," the recruiter had said, "and 750 if you become a shift supervisor." The recruiter joked about how rich they would be, slugged their shoulders, patted their backs, and handed out maps to the Sony factory.

Dali-Roo had expected to see that grinning, slap-happy guy with the maps that first day at the factory, not a skinny Japanese woman with lopsided hair and city shoes, in front of whom he felt the humiliation of his failed crops. Ashamed to look at her, he focused intensely on the object she slid out of the shiny hard-sided case in front of her.

"This is AIBO," she said, stroking the gleaming metallic animal she placed on the table. "AIBO is Sony's robot pet, a perfect adult companion." It was the size of a small dog or cat, sleek, modern, and hi-tech.

"A *purae* toy!" his friend Yanko whispered, spitting out the Ayama Nan expletive with which he punctuated his sentences. "Is this what these *purae* people do all day while we break our backs growing rice and vegetables for them to eat? What is that dumb thing? I thought we'd be making computers, at least!"

Dali-Roo had thought computers too, but he didn't share Yanko's disappointment. He watched wide-eyed as Ms. Moto, her tiny breasts little points under her suit jacket, gave the robot orders. "AIBO," she said, "show these gentlemen how pleased you are to meet them." The metal animal rotated its pointed unidirectional ears and wagged its curled tail. "Voice activation," she explained. "I tell it what to do and it does what I say."

"Get the ball, AIBO," she said, and AIBO plunged forward, moving its articulated legs in jerking awkward motions. It missed the ball repeatedly and tried and tried again, plugging away so persistently that when it finally succeeded in batting the ball with its nose, the men broke into applause, all but the disaffected, cynical Yanko who whispered "*purae* waste of time" under his breath. Dali-Roo felt angry at his friend and at the same time felt intensely sorry for AIBO, intensely sorry and intensely protective. And an intense surge of something else.

Something he couldn't name because he'd never heard of love at first sight. His marriage to Bancha, in the way of country marriages, had been arranged by his father when he was twenty-one and she eighteen, and although she wasn't from his village, he'd seen her with her parents at the community rice mill, or with her sister scrubbing clothes against boulders on the banks of the Faro. Now and then she'd even shown up at the tri-village primary school he'd attended sporadically himself. He'd been pleased by the match, for although she wasn't a spectacular beauty, she had a soft velvet voice and long-fingered hands, marks of a calming tenderness, but he had not understood that he loved her until two years after they'd wed, when she contracted a high fever and he found himself at her side, pleading with the gods to let her live.

In the early days of Dali-Roo's thievery, when Bancha watched him take the box from the shed and add a cable to it or an electronic sensor, she'd listen to him recite the list of additional components he still needed to steal from the factory—legs, paws, vibration sensors, infrared distance monitors, another one-degree of freedom ear, a miniature microphone, light emitting diodes, orange rechargers, the raw materials for the generator he would also have to build since the rural electrification projects had not yet reached their village—and she would try to reason with him. "If this AIBO holds such an attraction for you, why not just buy yourself one?"

Dali-Roo had shown her AIBO's picture, and the object of his desire looked stupid to her, a dumb ugly toy, not soft and cuddly like the stuffed animals their son Lopo played with, not intriguing like the colorful talking alphabet box with the forty-four characters of the Ayama Nan alphabet Dali-Roo had bought their son with his factory wages. But if Dali-Roo wanted one of these AIBO things, who was she to object? He stood on the assembly line every day from morning to eve and he earned many *ghree*. He'd bought her three bracelets and two necklaces she didn't need; he'd come home last week with so much meat it had changed the smell of his skin; he'd bought her mother a new straw sun hat to replace the old hat that melted comfortably along the contours of her head. If he saved the money he spent on things they didn't need, in a few weeks or a month, he could buy himself this thing.

"Ha!" he said. "Do you know what AIBO costs? Do you understand how valuable it is?"

"Tell me," she said and thought to herself: Rice is valuable. A sewing machine is valuable; a skein of thread, a watering can, a spade, a sharp knife. What could this thing do that mattered to anyone?

"Five hundred thousand *ghree*! If I save every *ghree* I earn after putting food on our table, by the time I save enough, my hair will be silver, my corneas scarred, my spine compressed, my fingers knotted, my skin shriveled, my foot in the grave."

Five hundred thousand *ghree*. Bancha did the calculation in her head—approximately 1,500 USA dollars—and scoffed. Surely, in his delusional state, because this

AIBO was so precious to him, he misheard the price. The actual figure must be 5,000 *ghree*, she thought, not 500,000, a figure Yanko could verify. She could sell the useless jewelry Dali-Roo bought her and buy the robot for him herself, stop his stealing before it deprived her son of a father.

That evening, after she tucked Lopo under his mosquito net, she told Yoi and Dali-Roo she was taking soaked rags to the neighboring house where a feverish wife shivered with malaria, but she left the rags at the neighbor's door and swerved behind it to cross the fields that led to Yanko's house. The fields, now a thatch of dry prickly watermelon vines, the remains of Yanko's last hopeless crop, scratched her ankles and crackled beneath her feet as she walked. The only other sounds she heard were the owl's hoot and the weak chirps of parched crickets dying of thirst.

Yanko greeted her with a big open-mouthed smile that showed his stained purple teeth and slippery red gums, evidence of his incessant chewing of addictive red beetle nuts. Although Yanko's wife had died seven years earlier, and a man alone with his grief and a habit with stimulants could run afoul of the precepts, Bancha hadn't hesitated to come to his house. As her husband's trusted friend, he'd never failed to treat her with respect, although, now that she was here, she realized she'd never been alone with him as night fell, and the manure from his water buffalo scented the air, and the acrid smoke of his waning cooking fire prickled the nostrils.

"What does it cost, this AIBO that has such power over him?" she asked in her breathy voice.

"Five hundred thousand *ghree*. And that is without the *purae* carrying case they make you pay extra for."

Bancha felt herself grow faint. She dropped to her knees on the woven floor mat stained with the reddish purple of beetle gum spit and threw her hands out before her to brace herself. She couldn't save her husband; he would be taken from her. She poured out her worries to her husband's friend.

"Distract him," Yanko said. "Have another child. The added responsibility will bring him to his senses."

"Impossible," she wailed. For two years, Bancha had begged Dali-Roo to make love to her without the protection he acquired for free every month at the tri-village market's International Family Planning booth. The youngest of three brothers, Dali-Roo had inherited ten of his fathers thirty hectares. He wanted Lopo to inherit all ten of his, the bare minimum that could meet even a small family's needs. Bancha, on the other hand, yearned for a daughter. She'd promised Dali-Roo she'd walk to the village with the wooden cross for a potion to insure a daughter and not a son. "That's no guarantee," Dali-Roo had told her. "Do you want to risk a son who will fight with Lopo over our land the way my older brothers' sons did? Do you want bad blood among your offspring and two sons who can't feed their own kids?"

Bancha sat cross-legged on Yanko's straw mat, her high forehead and taut banded hair gleaming in the light of Yanko's oil lamp, her eyes moist and haunted, and explained her husband's position. Yanko leaned against the edge of a table pocked with the lack of a woman's care, nodding as he listened. "You are married to a wise man with an intelligent vision for your son's future," he said. "Lands divided and divided through the generations create impoverished families, even in years when the climate cooperates."

"How can you call him wise when he risks shaming his son by going to jail?" She spoke without sarcasm, seeking illumination. "Explain to me the attraction of this toy." Bancha was warm, alive, and clever. How could it be that while she offered Dali-Roo real intelligence, he preferred artificial; while she offered him human skin to press himself against, he lusted after metal body parts? Every night she tried to make love to him in an effort to show him the joy of what he already possessed, but he usually rejected her and went out to the shed to stare at his box of stolen robot parts. She begged Yanko to explain her husband to her.

Cheeks pulsing a wad of red beetle gum, Yanko concentrated on Bancha's question as though he'd never before thought to ask himself exactly what it was about AIBO that so captivated his friend. He himself couldn't have cared less about the idiot thing that rolled off the assembly line. When he yearned in the middle of the night, he yearned for his dead wife and their unborn children. Perhaps the answer was as simple as that: Dali-Roo had a wife and a child, making it necessary for his yearning to lie elsewhere. But Yanko wouldn't risk suggesting this to Bancha for it might hurt her. He told her instead what might also be true—that AIBO's technological sophistication must seem a miracle to Dali-Roo.

"And the miracle of a real human wife and son he takes for granted?"

Yanko almost reached out to her as she rose from the mat. But he stopped his tongue from speaking the words in his heart and he kept his hands to himself.

It was pitch black. The moon had dipped below the northern mountain, and Yanko insisted on accompanying Bancha to the edge of her house. She refused, but not twice, for she feared straying and tripping an explosive. As the two walked, Yanko maintained a respectful distance from Bancha. At the moment of parting, as she thanked him, she reached out and put her long fingers against the side of his neck.

Overcome, he leaned to her ear and lowered his voice. "If your husband goes to jail, I will provide for you."

"You are kind," she whispered, ashamed of herself for arousing a lonely man's ardor, "but you will not be called upon for such help. My sister married well."

■ ■ ■

As the parts accumulated in the cardboard box in the shed, furrows of worry appeared in Bancha's forehead and sleep often eluded her. Yoi stopped carping about Dali-Roo's transgressions and nagged Bancha to rid herself of him. Mother and daughter would sit side by side, working at their sewing machines set up in the yard while Lopo played nearby, and Yoi would start in.

"Remember Le-amo, the eldest daughter in the Rip-Stune family?"

Bancha shook her head.

"You remember the family," Yoi insisted. "They had that deaf and dumb cow that gave rancid milk."

"I don't remember," Bancha said.

"Yes you do." Yoi became shrill. "They grew dry season chilies."

"Okay," Bancha said to calm her mother. "I can picture them.'"

"Le-amo married Pran, the second son of the Hhoon family from across the Faro. Remember that?" Bancha nodded, for it was useless not to. "When Le-amo was eight months pregnant," Yoi said, "Pran was found in bed with the wife of Lee-Soom, the chair maker."

"And Le-amo divorced him."

"See, you knew the whole story."

"I didn't know the story, but how else would this end? Yesterday it was Soon-Ray divorcing Omkip for lying with his wife's sister. The day before it was Cheesta divorcing Koro after she caught him with one hand on Lappo's breast and the other in her *yaya*. To hear you tell it, there is not a man in the entire Kingdom of Ayama Na with his *yoyo* in his own wife's *yaya*."

"Insolent daughter. Listen to me. If you wait to divorce your faithless husband until he's in jail, the countryside will brand you a disloyal wife and no man will go near your *yaya* ever again. And you only twenty-four. Get rid of him now."

"Have you forgotten who puts the food in your stomach!"

"Food? I would rather starve to death than see you spend the rest of your life with a thief and a shopper." She spat out the last word with contempt. "That hat he bought me doesn't even hold rice. Those bracelets on your arms turn green in the wash water. The toys he buys for Lopo will ruin him for hard work. Buy, buy, buy. Want, want, want. You see where it leads. Your husband lusts after useless things. He sleeps beside you but he dreams of a box full of hardware. He is as faithless as Omkip and Koro and Pran, the second son of the Hhoon family from across the Faro."

"Dali-Roo is not faithless. He is sick"

"Thank heavens your poor father isn't alive to witness this. But if he were, he'd tell you that for a man to be faithless is normal at least. Lust for a robot is an abomination. Dali-Roo is perverted. I have ears. I listen. I have not heard the sounds of your lovemaking in twenty-six days."

"You spy on us? You count what we do in the middle of the night?"

"I count all right and that's not all. Do you think I haven't seen you go out in the night to that red-mouthed beetle gum addict? You come home with stains on your knees and your hands! My own daughter, satisfying herself like a cheap whore because her husband's in love with a piece of scrap metal."

❋ ❋ ❋

When Dali-Roo told Bancha he was but three sensors and a diode from his goal, it occurred to her he might get away with this, at least in the criminal if not the spiritual sense, and she allowed herself a respite from the worries that plagued her. She believed the strong potion he ingested every morning had protected him, not by stopping his thefts, but by making them invisible to his hawk-eyed supervisor—there was more than one way for a potion to work. She allowed herself a cautious optimism that her son would grow up with a father in the house. But that night, as she lay next to her husband under their sagging mosquito net, she dreamt that a huge red hand had slapped itself across her mouth. The feeling was so real, it woke her up, and opening her eyes, she saw Yanko hovering above her, an arm reaching under the net, his big stained hand covering her lips to keep her from crying out.

He motioned for her to follow him, and quiet as two grains of rice floating on a pond, they moved through the next room, where Yoi and Lopo slept on their straw mats. Outside, they walked fifty meters along the rutted road before Yanko spoke. "Good news, Bancha. Yesterday before our shift ended, I was called to the office and promoted to line supervisor. Starting tomorrow, I'll protect Dali-Roo."

Returning to her sleeping mat, Bancha curled herself against Dali-Roo like a nested spoon, her arm flung across his strong back, her long fingers loose on his chest, and slept as peacefully and as happily as she'd ever slept. Before dawn the next morning, her happy mood blended into a public jubilation, for loudspeaker trucks rolled through the village blaring recordings of Ayama Na's most famous rock stars and announcing a holiday. During the night, Queen Hova and King Mindao had produced a royal heir. Throughout the kingdom, citizens took to the streets to rejoice.

Before lunch, the piecework truck delivered backs, fronts, and sleeves to the houses where women stitched, and the women settled down at the government-issue sewing machines to produce commemorative T-shirts bearing the likeness of the infant prince. Long after sunset, the glow of small oil lamps still dotted the countryside. Twenty-seven cartons of T-shirts were piled by Bancha's and Yoi's machines when Dali-Roo patted his old ox on the side of its head, jumped on his motorbike, and sped off to work.

▨ ▨ ▨

Dali-Roo couldn't locate Yanko in the DECON room where, to prevent dirt and dust from contaminating the electronic components, line workers donned blue booties, white coveralls, and sterile face masks. Since Yanko had imbibed along with the heartiest revelers at the tri-village rice mill, Dali-Roo thought he'd probably overslept. If Yanko failed to show up on the assembly line by the two-minute warning bell, a floater would take Yanko's place for the day. With no extra mouths to feed, Yanko could shrug off a day's lost wages. Without his irreverent company, however, Dali-Roo would have to drag the workday up the mountain of time by himself.

At the warning bell, Ripdup stood at the station next to Dali-Roo's, but before Dali-Roo could lament his friend's absence, Yanko appeared, wearing an orange supervisor's vest. Above his face mask, Dali-Roo's dark eyes popped, for the two had spoken at the rice mill, and Yanko hadn't mentioned that he'd been promoted.

"Surprise," Yanko said when he passed Dali-Roo.

"Did you know about this yesterday?" Dali-Roo asked.

"The *purae* manager warned me not to tell in advance. Company policy."

"So's not swearing in the factory. So's not chewing beetle nut in the rest room. Since when does policy inhibit you?"

"Look who's talking," Yanko said and moved on.

At the start gong, Dali-Roo did his best to focus on his task so he wouldn't miss a connection, but whenever he could lift his eyes, he watched Yanko perform his new tasks. Yanko examined safety screens, pulled products for quality control, and slipped behind the component shoots to tally the inventory. Dali-Roo felt betrayed.

He and Yanko had grown up together, married the same year, and helped raise one another's houses up onto stilts. Both their wives had fallen ill with the fever on the same day. Dali-Roo had wept for Yanko when Yanko's wife died, and Yanko had rejoiced for Dali-Roo when Bancha pulled through. Together, they'd watched the drought doom their fields and together resorted to the long ride to the factory. In spite of occasional disagreements, mostly about the precepts, which Dali-Roo followed and Yanko didn't, each had the other's best interests at heart. Yet, Yanko had kept this secret from him. Did Yanko think Dali-Roo would envy him or begrudge him higher wages? Dali-Roo's eyes begged the clock to move faster so he could set this right with his friend, but at the mid-morning break, Yanko rushed through the door of the Supervisor's Lounge. Then Dali-Roo's eyes had to push the clock up the mountain to lunch.

When the lunch gong sounded and the men on the assembly line returned to DECON to shed their protective suits, Dali-Roo lagged behind to pull a lever at Kimree's station and slip a sensor into his pocket. Yanko lingered until Dali-Roo completed the theft and then disappeared into the supervisor's lunchroom.

▩ ▩ ▩

Lopo tickled the patient ox with the brushy tip of a dry banana leaf until the ox finally snorted, and then he tried to get the attention of his mother and grandmother who were too busy to play with him as they usually did. By noon, when Bancha and Yoi stopped to massage each other's backs and prepare lunch, Bancha had filled eight more cartons with T-shirts and Yoi had filled ten.

"Lazy girl," Yoi said, noting that her daughter's stack of boxes was shorter than hers. "You've been mooning over that red-mouthed adulterer who pulls you from your sleeping husband's side. I know where your head is."

Yoi set her knife on the chopping block and wagged a finger at her daughter. "Have you forgotten how Riieeku ruined her life?"

Bancha scraped steamed tarot root into a wooden bowl. "I'm sure you'll remind me."

"Instead of paying attention to her sewing machine, she daydreamed of her lover and sewed her two middle fingers together."

Ha! Bancha thought to herself, how predictable her mother was. And how incapable of understanding that Yanko's friendship for Dali-Roo ruled out anything but brotherly love for his friend's wife. All of Yoi's friends, like Yoi herself, were sharp-tongued gossips with loyalty to each other as thin as the skin on boiled rice water. Yoi didn't trust her friends any more than they trusted her and therefore assumed the worst of everyone else's friendships as well.

After their lunch of tarot soup and fried morning glory, instead of their midday naps, the women donned big straw hats and went back to sewing T-shirts to honor the prince. Lopo slept on a bamboo mat in the shade of a coconut tree, so enervated by the heat his eyelashes bare-ly flickered when the motor of a Lexus SUV suddenly quit in front of the house. Before the slim Japanese man with the oily skin and the scrawny Japanese woman with the angled hair climbed out, Bancha already sensed their contempt for her thatched house on its crooked stilts, for her sewing machine, for the cartons of T-shirts stacked in the dirt, for her naked child asleep under the tree, for the ox with the dry crusty eyes, for the barren rice fields flanking the house—everything that was the opposite of the world they represented. And yet, she intuited that their contempt for her might be an echo of her contempt for them, for the way the junky toy their factory pro-duced had corrupted her husband, for the havoc they were about to wreak on her life.

The heels on the skinny lady's impractical shoes sank into ox dung, wet from the SUV's air-conditioning runoff, and Bancha secretly rejoiced. These two fancy business people meant her no good.

Although Yoi was illiterate, they must have assumed her the head of the household. It was to her they handed the warrant to search the house and the shed.

▩ ▩ ▩

Because of the long days he'd toiled at the factory, Dali-Roo could tolerate incarceration in a prison with fetid air and unpleasant odors. Prior to the assembly line, he'd spent his days in the fields or in a thatch house the wind blew through, breathing air that had whipped through forests and tumbled across hills. In his first moment in the factory's sealed rooms, a homesickness for fresh air had risen in his chest like a hundred blackbirds startled into a rush of flight. His heart had pounded; he'd thought he might asphyxiate. But he'd gotten used to the sealed rooms and the strange artificial light. In his cramped jail cell, Dali-Roo didn't suffer from the bars or the walls. He suffered from his thoughts.

A man who respects the sacred precepts agonizes when he disappoints himself. During the humiliation of his daily thefts, Dali-Roo had tasted personal anguish, but now, with nothing to do except think, his failures as a husband, a father, and a friend never stopped torturing him. Pacing in his cell, he forgot any decent or useful thing he'd ever accomplished in his life and plunged to the assumption of a wholly despicable self. For days on end, the demons of lost virtue crushed his mind and his spirit.

When not pacing, Dali-Roo sat cross-legged on his thin straw sleeping mat, reviewing his life and concluding that if there had never been a drought, he might have arrived at the end of his days falsely believing himself an honorable person rather than an individual who thought only of himself. He considered his refusal of Bancha's desire to have another child not only selfish but also dumb, for why question whether or not his hectares could support two families when they couldn't support one. He thought of how he'd jeopardized Yanko's integrity, for Yanko knew of his thefts but, in light of their long friendship, kept quiet, risking his own favorable circumstance at work and in the next life. He thought about how much he missed Bancha in his arms and Lopo on his shoulders. How much he missed his rice fields and his faithful ox. He even missed his mean-spirited, sharp-tongued, carping mother-in-law. But to tell the whole strange, selfish truth, he missed the parts of AIBO he'd stored at his house.

To the legal aspects of his case he paid little attention. Technically the charge against him was petty theft but, as a practical matter in a country in need of foreign investment, justice could be harsh and swift for a trivial crime that impacted foreign enterprise. Dali-Roo wouldn't have regretted a death sentence. He deserved his fate.

When a guard shoved him along the hall to consult with his attorney, Dali-Roo expected he'd been assigned a public defender with alcohol on his breath. Nang-Sim, the chairmaker's son, as a result of the ineptitude of a drunk and incompetent public defender, had spent seven years in jail for stealing bottles from the Pepsi factory and selling them on the street. The man waiting for Dali-Roo in the consultation room, however, one Mr. Slupsoo of the private law firm Slupsoo and Son, smelled as clean as a brand new shoe. The younger Slupsoo, son of the elder Slupsoo, wore a black and white striped suit and a fancy silk tie. With his tall height, wavy hair and masculine jawline, he could be mistaken for a movie star. "Tell me your story," Slupsoo said, and after he heard it, he told Dali-Roo he'd been waiting a long time for exactly this case. "I can win it for you, and I'll take it pro bono."

"What's so special about my case? I'm a thief," Dali-Roo said.

"No, no, no," Mr. Slupsoo protested. "You're not a thief. You're a hard-working rice farmer who had to go to work in a factory to put food on the family's table."

"I stole from the factory," Dali-Roo said.

Slupsoo put a hand on each of Dali-Roo's shoulders and stared into his eyes. "AIBOs rolled off your assembly line by the thousands. You wanted one for yourself. That was perfectly natural. When you couldn't buy it with the money you earned, you were very, very upset. You stole parts from the factory because you couldn't help yourself." He released Dali-Roo from his grip and took a step back. "You see what I'm getting at?"

Dali-Roo shook his head. He didn't see what Mr. Slupsoo was getting at. Only Mr. Slupsoo could see because only Mr. Slupsoo knew that in a month's time, he would announce his run for parliament. Slupsoo, who had friends in the press, wanted to link his name to a cause the Ayama Nan countryside could get behind. He intended to establish a new legal precedent—the "AIBO defense"— seduction by a sophisticated foreign technology. His client, like scores of other subsistence farmers in this drought-stricken land, had been disconnected from the rice fields and forced to labor in alien ways. When such a man worked the fields, he kept a share of the crop he produced. In his world, that was fair. The disparity between producer and production at the factory drove his client mad. The "AIBO defense" would win votes in the villages and play in the capital, where suspicions ran rampant that foreigners were taking over the country.

"Desire for AIBO drove you to insanity. Wouldn't you say?" Mr. Slupsoo tried again, prompting a positive response by nodding his head.

"I wasn't insane," Dali-Roo said.

"But you admit you wanted to possess this robot pet above all else, right?"

"I guess so."

"In the supervisor's office, when you confessed, you knew you were doing wrong. But when you stood on the line and saw AIBOs rolling off by the dozens, you weren't yourself. You lost your mind, isn't that so?"

"Of course I didn't lose my mind. I'd thought for a while I wasn't myself, but in prison I learned better. When I stole, I was my truer self."

"What makes you think that?"

"Because I am a selfish man."

Mr. Slupsoo's eyes narrowed and then he laughed. "Well, Dali-Roo, that is an opinion you will keep to yourself. Understand?" Mr. Slupsoo snapped his brief-case shut and motioned for the guard.

※ ※ ※

"He's right," Yanko said when he visited Dali-Roo in the prison. "You were not yourself. Do what your attorney says and keep your opinions to yourself. Besides, what did you steal? A few grams of chrome? A few centimeters of wire? On the open market they're not worth a hundred *ghree*!"

"And what is a human?" Dali-Roo said. "Five liters of water? Ten grams of mineral? At the market, that wouldn't bring twenty-five *ghree*. Is that the worth of a human being?"

"*Ack chee mi yobat*! If you think you can compare the value of a person with the value of a toy for rich Americans, you are out of your mind! Your lawyer's a hundred percent right."

⬚ ⬚ ⬚

Dali-Roo's trial lasted a single day. In the morning, the nine person Sony legal team presented its case to the judge. Although Ayama Na's judicial system did not include trial by jury, the defendant had the right to be present, so Dali-Roo watched as the plaintiff's lead counsel introduced the stolen parts into evidence, each of which Dali-Roo had lovingly collected. An expert witness for the plaintiff rolled out a strip of indoor-outdoor carpet—AIBO's "preferred" surface, she said—and put the Artificial Intelligence Robot through its tricks. She described AIBO's six emotions, its five separate instincts, and its ability to learn through human interaction; all of which, in her opinion, demonstrated that Dali-Roo absconded with more than mere components. He stole intellectual property.

In the afternoon, Mr. Slupsoo put his client on the stand. The judge listened as the soon-to-be parliamentary candidate asked Dali-Roo if every day, before he left for work, he hadn't promised his wife and mother-in-law that he would stop taking parts from the factory. Dali-Roo said he had promised. He asked Dali-Roo if he'd drunk a strong potion prepared by his wife to prevent his stealing things that didn't belong to him. Dali-Roo said this was true.

"And every day you went to the factory believing you could resist, isn't that right?" Slupsoo asked.

"I suppose."

"But you found yourself powerless not to take a piece of the product, this AIBO we saw the plaintiff's expert witness demonstrate this morning. Isn't that so?"

"Yes, but I knew..."

Mr. Slupsoo interrupted his client. "No further questions, Your Honor," he said.

During cross examination, the SONY attorney asked Dali-Roo if he'd known it was against company policy for employees to take things from the factory.

"Of course," Dali-Roo said, thinking of the woman with the little pointed breasts. "They warned us in the orientation."

"Were reminders posted in the DECON room and along the assembly line?"

"Reminders were everywhere."

"Did you systematically plan to take all the parts you needed to construct AIBO for yourself?"

"I did."

"And you knew when you confessed you were admitting that you committed a crime?"

"Objection, calls for a legal conclusion," Mr. Slupsoo said.

"Sustained, you do not have to answer the question."

"I knew."

In his closing arguments, the ambitious Mr. Slupsoo used phrases like "humble rice farmer," and "driven mad by desire for an irresistible *Japanese* product" (emphasis his). Step by step, Slupsoo walked the judge through the AIBO Defense. "Your Honor, a man of the fields, such as my client, is so completely consumed by the desperate struggle to feed his family he doesn't have time to weigh ethical subtleties. Such a man hasn't developed a nuanced comprehension of criminal right and wrong. My client is a good person, a family man, a man who has never before broken the law but who, in the grip of his passion for this *Japanese* toy pet..." Slupsoo pointed at AIBO "...couldn't control himself. This is a textbook definition of temporary insanity."

▓ ▓ ▓

To be present when the judge delivered his verdict the next morning, Bancha left Lopo with Yoi and hitched a ride to the courthouse on the back of Yanko's motorcycle. Along with everyone else in the courtroom, she stood when the judge made his entrance, and tried to catch Dali-Roo's eye, but Dali-Roo's attorney had his big arm around Dali-Roo's neck so he couldn't turn his head.

When those in the gallery were seated, Mr. Slupsoo, who'd had a haircut the day before in anticipation of a photo op, whispered encouragement in Dali-Roo's ear.

The judge cleared his throat for an announcement. He told the assembled that overnight, the king and queen had issued a royal decree. He handed the bailiff a scroll to read.

Bancha listened hard to the many erudite paragraphs, none of which she quite understood, although, to be sure, the gist of the document came through to her with wondrous clarity. The king and queen spoke of their beautiful crown prince: two months old that very day and pronounced in perfect health by the royal medical team. To share the joy in their hearts, the king and queen had declared an amnesty for all prisoners in Ayama Na, unless they were accused or convicted of capital offenses.

"Case dismissed," the judge told Dali-Roo. "Go home to your family."

▓ ▓ ▓

Bancha and Dali-Roo, with Lopo on his lap, sat at the table in their kitchen while Yoi served the golden noodle soup she'd prepared especially for the homecoming of her jailbird son-in-law. Along with the golden noodle soup Dali-Roo drank hot green tea sweetened with sugar cane, the drink he'd preferred at breakfast, lunch, and dinner before his troubles sent his wife to the distant village for the bitter brew that had worked in such mysterious ways.

Dali-Roo believed prison had changed him forever. He would have predicted one couldn't live through what he'd experienced without becoming someone new. But in the middle of his first night home, imagining everyone asleep, he snuck outside, and by the light of a tiny oil lamp, examined the corners and floor of the shed, hoping to find a little piece of AIBO that might have slid out of the cardboard box when it was seized as evidence. Returning empty-handed to Bancha's side, he wondered how he could still crave an object that had inflicted so much suffering on his dear wife and child. Maybe the ambitious lawyer had been right. Maybe he was insane. Maybe, even without the royal amnesty, the judge would have found him innocent.

Before the sun came up, he heard the sound of a motorbike, and sticking his head out his window, saw Yanko unstrapping a metal box from the back of his bike. Dali-Roo's pounding heart jumped into his throat for he knew exactly what his friend, the assembly line supervisor, had access to as he walked up and down the assembly line.

"Welcome home," Yanko said, grinning a big red grin and handing the box through the window to Dali-Roo's eager hands.

Dali-Roo and Yanko completed the assembly in under two hours while Bancha and Lopo watched and Yoi beat her breast, cursing the day her misguided husband had made this abominable match for her wonderful daughter.

Lacking AIBO's preferred surface, Dali-Roo placed the "human companion" on a sleeping mat. At Dali-Roo's command, AIBO jerked itself forward and rooted for the little pink ball, which it found after three tries. Dali-Roo flipped it on its back and it righted itself the way it was supposed to. About this time, Lopo lost interest and toddled to a corner to play with his talking alphabet toy. He'd learned all forty-four letters in the months that Dali-Roo hadn't paid attention. *Na, ho, ve* he repeated to Yanko as Dali-Roo played with AIBO for another two hours, the operating life of the battery. Then Dali-Roo returned AIBO to its carrying bag and hooked its recharger to the generator his thoughtful friend had also supplied.

Dali-Roo entertained himself with AIBO day after day for a week and a half, until, on the eleventh day after his release from the prison, a sweet humectant aroma came in on the air. Within minutes silvery sheets fell from the sky. It rained so hard it washed the crust from the old ox's eyes and turned the Faro River from a bed of rocks and ruts to a swiftly flowing current. When the Faro overflowed and water puddled through the rice paddies, Dali-Roo put AIBO on a shelf and headed into his fields with his old ox to sow the seeds that would turn his hectares to a carpet of brilliant green shoots.

After the rice was harvested and threshed, after Bancha had visited Oiric Lun for a potion to insure the health of the new life developing in her womb, Dali-Roo noticed AIBO for the first time in months. There it sat, gathering dust on the shelf. How odd a thing it seemed. Why in the world, he wondered, would he allow it to take up space in a house that needed room for a new child. He lifted AIBO from the shelf, carried it to the Faro, and without a second thought, pitched it into the tumbling water.

Yoi, from whose eyes nothing that ever happened in her son-in-law's house escaped notice, hurried downstream and cast a net in the water. When she'd trapped AIBO, she pulled the net onto the shore and disentangled the webbing from the curled metal tail and the four metal paws. After setting AIBO free, she heaved it against a big rock until it broke into pieces. One by one, she threw the pieces in the river, all but the largest— the rustproof, ark shape of chrome that made up AIBO's curved back. This shiny piece the practical Yoi turned upside down and carried back to the house. For the rest of her life, she used it to store her bobbins and her many colored threads.

Skin Deep

Along with the manager assigned to her after she won the Miss Lake Sporee title in a local feeder contest, the lovely Song Li moved through the lobby of the Blue Orchid Hotel, site of the Miss Ayama Na Beauty Pageant. As they descended the wide marble staircase to the ballroom, Song and her manager passed the glass case that held the beauty queen's crown, two hundred pearls and twenty-five diamonds in a platinum setting. That crown, Song thought, could have fed, clothed, and educated the entire population of Lake Sporee for fifty years. She might have shared the thought with her manager but criticism of the king and queen, donors of the crown, was forbidden in Ayama Na, punishable, in theory, by imprisonment and even by death, although the royal family had never exacted the ultimate penalty. Then again, Song might not have volunteered her opinion even if it were legal to do so, because she recognized her judgment as cynical and clichéd, the outward manifestation of her inner conflict about participating in a beauty contest.

Sometimes Song made herself sick. If she couldn't be whole-hearted about this Miss Ayama Na thing, why had she interrupted her studies at Pin Dalie University, Ayama Na's premier institute of higher learning, to spend her days primping, lifting weights, and practicing for the talent competition? Why had she let her earnest manager, a former beauty contestant herself, waste the last four months on such a half-hearted, conflicted, neurotic pageant candidate?

On the flip side of the internal debate, Song yearned to wear that luxurious crown on her beautiful head and fly on a plane for the first time in her life halfway around the globe to São Paolo for the Miss Universe Pageant. In her nineteen years, Song had never traveled north of the Faro. Was it so greedy of her to want to see her own country and the rest of the world?

And yet, to place a higher value on beauty than on education, even in the short run, embarrassed and confused her, for she'd received two important international scholarships and a local future-teacher award, gifts a woman from an impoverished lake province family had no right to squander. As she put it to the beauty pageant recruiter who'd spotted her on campus, "Doesn't our country need teachers more than it needs beauty contestants?"

❈ ❈ ❈

"You? In a beauty contest?" said Vorapat Lin, the fellow student with whom Song walked across campus three times a week from Psychology to Democracy versus Totalitarianism.

"Ridiculous, right?"

"Certainly not," Vorapat said. "You're so beautiful, you'll win. You surprised me, that's all. You're the most dedicated student I know. But if you want it, go for it." Vorapat punched the air with her fist.

Go for it was exactly what Song wanted to hear. From the age of six, she'd never questioned the validity of her goals, but suddenly, her incessant studying nauseated her. Why should her entire life consist of an unbroken string of days in the same one hundred square kilometers, a student, then a teacher, forever in a classroom? Didn't her students deserve more from her?

"What more?" her mother yelled. "It's what's in here that counts." Su Li reached out and rapped her daughter's head. "And in here." She poked Song in the chest. "Intelligence. Heart. That's what makes a teacher great."

"How would you know?" Song said. She'd come home to compete for the title of Miss Lake Sporee. Home was a houseboat in a floating village not far from the mouth of the lake, a squalid kitchen and cramped bunk beds ruled over by a mother who hadn't attended school three days in her life, who worked morning to night cooking and mending nets for Song's father and brothers, whose stained and wrinkled hands smelled of shrimp and dried fish. The houseboat lapped up and down and moved in and out at the mercy of the weather, and in the dry season, it flowed with the whole floating village closer to the center of the lake, exposing garbage-strewn banks.

"A beauty contest! *Ack chee mi yobat.* Did you work for your beauty?" Su Li said. "Did you study for it? Did you earn it? It cost you nothing—this beauty. And nothing is what it's worth! Have you forgotten so soon what Chea predicted for you?"

Throughout Song's childhood, the itinerant fortune-teller, upon whom her mother relied, had paddled her skiff alongside their houseboat to trade fortunes for fish. "You," she'd said, pointing to a crisscross of lines in Song's palm, "possess a superior intellect. One day, you'll found a regional high school at the mouth of the river. Here, where the line thickens?—that's three generations of your students who will go forth to rebuild Ayama Na."

"I haven't forgotten. I just need some time off," Song said, explaining to her mother that even if she won the Miss Ayama Na contest, it would delay the start of her teaching by only a single year. Su Li opened the hatch in the floor and threw scraps of food into the crowded fish farm trapped under the houseboat. Song felt woozy as the fish swarmed and snapped, a return of her childhood fear of falling through the trapdoor. The fish farm was her mother's side operation and Su Li had used every *ghree* she earned selling the fish to purchase Song's school supplies. "Only one year," Song said. "One little year."

"One little year?" her mother mocked. "One little year? In one little year you can teach thirty children who will grow up to be doctors and businessmen, people who will make life better for everyone in Ayama Na."

"What about my life?" Song said. Beyond the open side of the houseboat's sleeping quarters, she could see the pitched bamboo deck where her mother had laid yesterday's catch out to dry.

"What about it?"

Song eyed her mother's sun-splotched skin, her strong calloused hands with their split and broken nails, her wide bare feet, soles the texture of dried cod. "Did you want to spend your whole life cooking for my father and my brothers? Turning and drying the shrimp they pull in? Opening that hatch to throw scraps to those disgusting fish? Didn't you ever want to breathe the cool mountain air? Or get your teeth fixed? Or smell like something besides a dead fish? Didn't you ever want to run away?"

Su Li lowered her voice to its most serious pitch. "When Chea saw your future in your palm, I understood my life. Did I want to be anywhere but here? Never!"

Mingling with the sharp odor of the fish drying on the bamboo deck, Song smelled the sewage-infested lake water, the fetid odor that had permeated her childhood, and she struggled not to retch. "Then you'll never understand how I feel," she said.

※ ※ ※

"See that stage, Song," her manager whispered as they entered the ballroom where the events of the pageant would unfold over the next five days. "Right there, the judges will crown you Miss Ayama Na."

They crossed to the buffet tables where other contestants and their managers helped themselves to sea urchin cakes, the national delicacy, and to the rest of the special culinary treats the chefs of the Blue Orchid Hotel had created for the twenty-five beautiful women vying for the title of Miss Ayama Na, one from each of the thirteen provinces and twelve from Pin Dalie, the capital city divided into twelve population sectors. Song discounted her manager's oft-repeated prediction that she'd win this year's pageant—the manager's job is to pump up the cadidate—and studied the competition for herself.

In the Miss Lake Sporee contest, Song had competed against local girls who lacked money for cosmetic dentistry or laser treatments for damaged skin. Here, she didn't see a single yellow tooth or pocked complexion.

And every contestant rose to Song's height—one meter, seventy-five. Yet, by the evening's end, Song's own comparisons of bone structure, posture, and extemporaneous speech assured her that she was as valid a contender as any woman here, with an equal opportunity to advance to the semi-finals.

If she didn't blow the talent competition.

Song had yet to perform her act in front of an audience and as recently as four months ago, had no legitimate talent at all. She'd never played a musical instrument or taken a dance lesson and had almost forgone the Miss Lake Sporee contest for want of an act. At the last minute she'd written three poems, slight works that she read with a quiet dignity that impressed the Lake Sporee judges, two men and a woman of limited education themselves. Her closest competitor, Siripa Sawangalu, who really did have talent— she could belt out a tune—was short and missing a tooth, so the poems had sufficed. But they wouldn't get her to the semi-finals in Pin Dalie.

For three weeks, Song's manager subjected Song to a trial-and-error process involving failed forays into dramatic presentation, singing, juggling, fencing, stand-up comedy, and tea ceremony. Then they got a lucky break and hit upon a talent for which Song had a genuine natural gift—she could throw her voice from over here to over there.

Although she mangled the more difficult consonants, and the strain of throwing her voice caused distortion in the muscles around her mouth and neck, her manager assured her that she could conquer these problems with hard work and a capable instructor. The next day Song's manager showed up at Song's studio apartment with Ayama Na's most experienced ventriloquist, Mr. Sun Soovai, and his ugly gnome-like knee dummy (techni-

cally, his automaton), Sonny. She also presented Lulu, a
dark-eyed, long-lashed, wooden knee dummy with full
rosy lips, an excellent open-shut mouth mechanism, and
special apparatus for batting her eyelashes.

Each day, after her predawn run through Pin Dalie's
streets, after her weight lifting routine at a Pin Dalie
gym, and after a meeting with her manager for her daily
weigh-in and interview practice, Song and Mr. Soovai
worked together in her apartment for three hours. He
coached her in breathing technique, including quick exhalation, open-shut mouth correspondence, near and far
calls, vocal substitution of the consonant *b*, work-arounds
for the impossible letter *p*, and specialty noises: including
man in a motorcycle accident and the extremely difficult
steam hiss, in which the tongue has to curl and press its
tip against the back of the upper palate.

By the end of the second month of their work, Mr.
Sun Soovai informed Song's manager that Lulu's speech
sounded almost entirely natural and that Song had elim-
inated her face and neck distortion. Mr. Soovai saw no
reason he and the manager couldn't begin to develop
Song's act for the talent competition. In addition, Mr.
Soovai reported that he and Song had forged an exceptional working rapport.

The latter remark, it must be noted, understated the
case, for although Song was ravishing, and Mr. Soovai
old, bald and married, during the fourth week of lessons,
the two had hurled themselves into a sizzling affair.

Sex between the master and his gifted protégée
reached intense and almost intolerably satisfying levels as
the lovers threw their voices to their dummies, parked on
chairs at the side of the bed, and their dummies shouted
back lovemaking instructions. "To the left," Lulu would
say at strategic points. "Tighter, tighter," Mr. Soovai's

Sonny would shriek at critical moments. The couple reveled in the thrill of performing for an audience, even if the audience was a pair of blockheads.

Song's manager, far from a stupid woman, guessed the shenanigans in the little studio apartment, but she chose to turn a blind eye, believing that Song's emotional involvement with Mr. Soovai would motivate her to work all the harder. Together, the manager and Mr. Soovai completed the script for Song's talent performance with the manager contributing bits she knew would please the judges and Mr. Soovai supplying ventriloquy techniques challenging enough to win the respect of professionals but not too risky for a novice ventriloquist. All in all, in the manager's opinion, a winning talent act and a triumph for her. She felt certain she was managing the next Miss Ayama Na.

To keep Song focused exclusively on her task, undistracted by affairs of the heart, Song's manager made a fateful decision—she banned Mr. Soovai from the Blue Orchid Hotel during the pageant week, leaving Song and Lulu to fend for themselves. A colossal mistake, as it turns out. For it must be noted that the relationship between a ventriloquist and his or her knee dummy can be one of extraordinary psychological complexity, and that such complexity is the norm, not the exception. Song's knee dummy, "the Lovely Lulu" (her designation in the act), was obviously—what could be more obvious?— Song's equal in intellect, but in the script Mr. Soovai and Song's manager wrote, Lulu speaks in the "little-girl voice" (a classic vocal style), bats her eyelashes, behaves the flirt, insists on partying, and rejects the serious side of life. Moreover, midway through the routine, to allow for a virtuosic display of ventriloquism technique, Lulu throws a temper tantrum (including the difficult steam hiss) when Song forbids her to buy a frilly sundress for a lawn party. To convince Lulu to abandon her quest for frivolous merriment, Song unfurls a poster of Queen Hova and explains to Lulu that before Queen Hova married King Mindao, she was the commoner, Hova Utai, who had applied herself to her studies and to professional work, and advanced to CFO of a computer corporation. In Song's manager's opinion, invoking the beloved queen's likeness at the conclusion of the act would bring down the house.

Lulu bridled at her silly part, and without Mr. Soovai's surveillance in practice sessions at the Blue Orchid Hotel, she departed from the script to vent her anger at Song. She berated Song for delaying her teaching mission for so shallow an enterprise as this beauty pageant and for allowing Mr. Sun Soovai and the manager to write the simplistic, degrading, misogynist tripe they were to perform instead of writing the act herself. "If you've abandoned your college classes to participate in some asinine beauty pageant," Lulu sneered, "at least lose the drivel and say something smart."

"But…"

"But nothing, Song. How can you stand by and let two intelligent women speak these idiot lines? Have you no respect for yourself or for me?"

Lulu became so argumentative, Song ended the practice session and would have abandoned future practice sessions altogether had she not felt it imperative to keep her breathing supple and her consonants sharp.

Under the circumstances, Lulu pressed her advantage. "So tell me Song," she said on their second day alone in the hotel, "what would your mother say if she saw you in bed with Mr. Soovai?"

"It's none of her business."

"None of her business? She paddled ten kilometers around the lake, rain or shine, to take you to school, never missing a day, not even when the fish swarmed and all hands were needed in the lake. Seven years in a row, you were the only child who had perfect attendance, and this is how you repay her? Abandoning your studies and jumping into bed with a fornicating letch old enough to be your grandfather?"

"You had a part in that," Song said. "You batted your eyelashes and coached from the sidelines."

"Ha. And I suppose it will be my fault when you give up teaching forever to become an Avon executive or throw your life away on an anorexic modeling career."

"Why do you hate me?"

"Hate you? I don't hate you. I want you to stop making excuses. You blame the recruiter for enticing you into the pageant. You blame your mother for not giving you a break from your studies. You blame me for your affair with that geezer. When will you take responsibility for yourself!"

"In a few days this pageant will end. I'll be back in school and you'll be in a box in my giveaway pile. I won't have to put up with another syllable from you."

"Back in school? I don't think so! You'll win this fiasco. They'll stick that ridiculous crown on your head and fly you to Brazil."

"Don't be absurd. This isn't Lake Sporee. This is the Nationals. Every one of my competitors is tall and has flawless skin. I'm not in contention."

"Enough of that nicey-nicey modesty crap. Be frank with yourself. Six of your competitors have obvious boob jobs. Miss Chon Giang has hives on her neck. And look at the coif on Miss Khamphoon—that woman's a shine junkie and a hair-product slut. Then there are the Misses

Pin Dalie, don't get me started. Sector Six is an idiot, she will embarrass the nation every time she opens her mouth; Sector Nine has an overbite; Sector Four is ten kilos overweight and can't keep her fat face out of the steamed coconut cakes."

"Stop it," Song screamed. "You're wicked and awful. You're a gossip. You used to be kind, but you've turned into a monster."

"Now who's hating who?" Lulu said.

That did it! Despite her desire to be a conscientious professional who practiced every day, Song stuffed Lulu in her case and shoved the case under the bed. For the next two days Song refused to think about Lulu and lost herself in the whirl of pageant events, photo ops with big shots, runway practice for the swimsuit and evening gown competitions, and the twice-daily rehearsals for the dance routine to be performed by all twenty-five contestants at the final ceremony.

Song also had private interviews with each pageant judge. She discussed international events with insight and handled personal questions with wisdom and aplomb. Asked why she wanted to be Miss Ayama Na, she spoke of her desire be a role model for the underprivileged children of the nation and demonstrate to them what a disadvantaged child from a poor province can achieve.

On the morning of day four of the pageant, a day devoted to the talent competition, before descending to the ballroom to perform her act, Song finally put Lulu on her knee again. She intended only to practice rapid exhalation technique and not let Lulu say an intelligible word, but as soon as Lulu opened her mouth, she berated Song for lying to the judge who asked why she wanted to be Miss Ayama Na.

"I did not lie," Song insisted. "I want every child who attends a floating school on a filthy stinking lake to look at me and see how high they can rise."

"Ha," Lulu said. "Six months ago, you couldn't name a single Miss Ayama Na, but you could name every teacher you ever had."

"Not another word out of you!"

"Why? Are you afraid of the truth?"

At that terrifying question, Song threw Lulu across the room. She landed on the carpet, arms and legs in a jumble, four meters distant. As fate would have it, Song had learned to throw her voice four meters six. From her twisted heap on the floor, Lulu yelled, "What the hell happened to you? This beauty pageant has turned you into a whore and a liar."

"Shut up or I'll get a hatchet and turn you into match sticks."

"Now you're a murderer too?"

The incident shocked them both. They stopped insulting one another and fell silent. Stunned, traumatized, and trembling, Song walked across the room and picked Lulu up. She straightened Lulu's skirt, smoothed her hair, and inspected her eyelash apparatus.

That afternoon, Song drew the eleventh spot in the talent competition, and she and Lulu stuck to the script exactly as written, including that most embarrassing "inspiration" of Song's manager, where Lulu leans over, kisses one of the judges behind his ear, and whispers a remark that makes him giggle and blush. The judges ate it up. When Song unfurled the poster of Queen Hova, every judge grinned from ear to ear. The judges awarded Song an overall talent score of 9.4 out of 10. Song's manager, whose own talent had been gymnastics, could hardly stop herself from leaping into the air and landing a somersault.

※ ※ ※

As the orchestra struck up the tune, the twenty-five pageant contestants step-kicked onto the stage, eight from stage left, eight from stage right, nine from the center, and executed the leg lifts, stomps, and cross-overs that propelled them around the performance space. After the dance routine, a full twelve minutes in length, the swimsuit and evening gown competitions would take place, followed by the selection of the five semi-finalists, each of whom would repeat her talent act in front of the TV cameras and the live audience. Finally, the judges would render their verdict and the host would place the crown on the new Miss Ayama Na's head.

At the pageant's expense, the contestants' families had been brought to Pin Dalie and put up in the Pan Pin Dalie Pacific down the street from the Blue Orchid so they could attend the final evening's events. As Song danced, she searched the audience for the family she hadn't seen since the weekend of the Miss Lake Sporee contest. When she couldn't locate her mother, her father, or her brothers, she reasoned it was shrimp season and survival came first. She did see Vorapat Lin, the classmate at Pin Dalie U. who'd encouraged her to "go for it." Vorapat sat three rows back of the press, which occupied the first two rows behind the judging tables. When Vorapat caught Song's eye, she gave her a punched elbow thrust, the Ayama Nan equivalent of a thumbs up.

During the dance sequence, the dancers took turns at center stage where they executed knee lifts and triples and tried not to bang into each other or fall into the huge blue orchid displays at the footlights and sides of the stage. Seven minutes into the dance, while at center stage for the fourth time, Song saw Vorapat Lin across the footlights highlighting paragraphs in a textbook on her lap. Finals week, Song remembered, and in spite of her breathlessness, felt herself sigh.

At last the dance ended and the contestants rushed to change for the swimsuit competition. As Song paraded down the runway, it sunk in that she was an audience favorite. Had there been an applause meter, her applause would have topped the scale.

Evening gowns followed, and then to kill time and build suspense while the judges deliberated, the pageant host showed film clips of behind-the-scenes pageant events, the highlight, footage of the "girls" awarding one of their own the Miss Congeniality Award. The prize went to Churi Pradub (Miss Batam Treng Province), arguably the least attractive woman in the competition. The audience watched Miss Batam Treng weep and hug her pageant sisters who'd voted to give her what Song had heard a nasty few refer to as the Miss Ugly Award.

Finally the moment arrived. The judges handed the pageant host the all-important envelope, and with great fanfare, the host announced the names of the five semi-finalists. Twenty unsung contestants slunk back to their lives of oblivion and regret while five joyful young women hopped up onto the platform.

Song had to feign surprise when the host called her name. Calmly, she looked left and right at her four competitors, among them that shine junkie with the crackling hair. Also on the platform: Miss Pin Dalie Sector Five, Miss Pouthvang, and Miss Kamp Ninh. Up close, Miss Kamp Ninh had mediocre posture and six ragged moles on her left shoulder. Miss Pin Dalie Sector Five had lopsided implants that would make her the laughingstock of Brazil. And Miss Pouthvang? Well, Miss Pouthvang's eyes didn't sparkle.

Song saw that she would win. It was just as Lulu predicted. She would wear the crown with the two hundred pearls and the twenty-five diamonds. King Mindao and Queen Hova would bestow their royal blessings at the Summer Palace, and Song would board the plane for São Paolo and the Miss Universe Contest. The trapdoor under the houseboat was opening. She was about to fall in.

Miss Pin Dalie Sector Five completed her talent act, a traditional Ayama Nan balletic dance. Although she executed the dance perfectly, the audience sagged. They'd seen enough dancing for one night. Song and Lovely Lulu were next.

Song walked to the middle of the stage and in one smooth motion unfolded her straight-back chair, glided onto its seat, and perched Lulu on her knee. From the start of the routine, Song's lips were supple, her hands quick, her consonants sharp, her breathing in synch, and her open-shut mouth correspondence corresponding to a *t*. Song and Lulu delivered their lines exactly as written, and the audience laughed at all the places Mr. Soovai and Song's manager had predicted they would. The end of the routine was coming up fast, that high point of audience satisfaction where, to teach Lulu a lesson, Song would unfurl the poster of the country's beloved queen. Song reached her free hand behind her, untaped the poster from its hiding place along a slat of the chair, unrolled Queen Hova's face, and raised it for all to see. She had to pause the act while the audience applauded their favorite Ayama Na royal.

When she resumed the act, Song held Lulu so tight she couldn't tell where Lulu left off and she began. It seemed to her that she and Lulu had merged into one person and were speaking with one voice, not two. "When

Queen Hova was still the commoner Hova Utai," Song said, pointing to the queen's picture, "she made a terrible mistake."

The audience became so quiet, Song could hear Lulu blink.

"She did?" Lulu said.

"Yes she did! She married a king and shut herself away in a royal palace, when she could have remained in the business world, helping to create jobs and opportunities for the citizens of our country."

"She could have continued as a role model for Ayama Na's working women," Lulu added.

"She deserted us," Song said. "Worse, she deserted herself. Now she's stuck in a palace."

"Women should be CEOs, CFOs, lawyers, doctors and teachers," Lulu said, "not idle princesses."

Song heard the gasps from the judges and the audience. Rising, she collapsed the chair and tucked it under an arm. With her other arm around Lulu's waist, she bowed to the audience and tipped the automaton so Lulu could bow too.

The nervous audience squirmed and whispered among themselves: Had the act truly ended? Was this a joke? Wouldn't there be a rescue? A redeeming punch line? The judges, aghast, conferred and shook their heads. The members of the press took advantage of the lapse in the proceedings to work their cell phones. Song's manager crumpled, her head in her hands. The handsome pageant host, busy offstage romancing a losing contestant (Miss Pin Dalie Sector Three) rushed toward the microphone.

From the edge of the stage, Song glanced for a last time at the audience, then vanished into the side curtain. This performance had come to its end.

The Artist's Story

Alan Jackman stopped midway across the bridge connecting Bungkotankang Street and the rest of Pin Dalie. Under him flowed the Pin Dalie River, as filthy as he remembered it, grimy and littered with trash. He peered along the riverbank in the direction the locals had pointed when he showed them the missing artist's snapshot, and there, a hundred feet to the west, down by the water's edge, stood Peter Faraway, gaunt and disheveled as he appeared in the photograph, beard ragged, hair long and matted, sunburned face as red as a fireworks flare. It was ten in the morning and Faraway was just waking up.

Jackman watched the artist struggle to untangle himself from a ratty old blanket and locate his Philadelphia Phillies cap. He pulled it from a dilapidated bamboo wagon loaded with homelessness stuff—motley clothes, bulging plastic bags, assorted bottles and spiral sketch-pads—and shoved it on his head. Then he climbed onto a wooden crate and began orating up the slope, spewing forth a tirade about monopolistic establishments that thwart personal initiative and rob artists of opportunities to survive in the world.

The regulars on the bridge, the amputees, beggars and pitiful children who shadowed tourists until they handed over a euro or an American buck, ignored Faraway—he was part of the scenery—but the tourists crossing on foot to Bungkotankang Street stared at this homeless American shouting up at them from a hot, humid fly buzz. A hundred degrees, maybe 110, and this guy had on heavy denim pants, a long-sleeved wool shirt, that battered baseball cap, a scarf around his neck. It made Alan Jackman hot just to look at him. It made him flush and sweat because lately Jackman felt like going nuts himself, and whatever had pushed Faraway over the edge—maybe it would push him over next.

For the past eleven months, Jackman and Faraway's younger sister, Nadine Faraway Barton, had been having an affair, Nadine cheating on her second husband, Jackman cheating on his wife of seventeen years. No happy ending Jackman could foresee. *Give it a rest*, Jackman thought, stowing his problematic USA life and crossing the rest of the bridge. He had promised the artist's sister he'd find her brother and bring him back.

Jackman turned left along the river side of Bungkotankang Street, the sleaziest street in the sleaziest sector (the infamous Ninth) of Ayama Na's capital. He stood on the pebbly verge and glanced down the slope as he started to descend, keeping Faraway in his line of sight. Although Jackman flew into Pin Dalie on business a few times a year and at night hung out in the Ninth, he never ventured to the deserted river side of the street. He stuck to Bungkotankang's crowded commercial side, buying pearls for his wife, jade for his mistress, and T-shirts for his two pampered daughters. Then he'd sit at a sidewalk café drinking *Yama Hi*, watching the pimps and prostitutes stake out their turf, watching especially the one-legged, redheaded whore who marched up and down the street, a red lacquered crutch wedged under an armpit, a tourist attraction all by herself.

As Jackman progressed down the incline, the thorny branches of the half-dead shrubs caught his pant legs. He picked his way through dusty brush and discarded junk until he reached the hard-packed sand and stood a few feet from Faraway. Absorbed in his tirade, the artist didn't seem to notice that he had a houseguest.

"Administrative insanity restricts opportunity," Faraway shouted. "Social mediocrity diminishes personal productivity. Sick conformists and fanatical influences oppress and degrade the artistic way of life. The establishment's devious laws force artists to live in humiliation and misery. Artificial rules and regulations conspire against creative freedom...."

The litany of complaint mystified Jackman because, in Jackman's opinion, Faraway had had it made. Some twenty years earlier, when Jackman and Faraway were still in their twenties, the Modern had purchased one of Faraway's paintings, an honor nearly unheard of for an artist so young. Not only that, Faraway's work hung in private galleries and he'd started to become a darling of art collectors. In other words, he'd been poised to bring in the big bucks. What the hell was he so disgruntled about?

As the artist railed against "greedy agents, know-nothing critics who'd co-opted definitions of art, and the soulless trends foisted on artists by the marketplace," Jackman almost glimpsed the logic of this wreck of a life. But after he'd listened to the same dozen sentences three times, Faraway just sounded nuts. All Jackman heard was the singsong drone of a psychological basket case.

Close up, Faraway stunk. Sweat, wet cloth, the metallic stench of the greasy white stuff he'd smeared on sores on his ankles and calves. Infected mosquito bites? Some jungle rot eating him from the inside out? Every time Faraway waved his arms or stamped a foot, the odors intensified. His body was like a compost heap, everything still green in him turning a steaming wormy black.

While he waited for the artist to take a breath and notice him, Jackman studied the tiny iridescent beetle exploring the edge of Faraway's beard, the grime sloshing in the creases of his sweaty forehead, the shivers regularly shaking a body swaddled for a brisk fall Philadelphia day. Nadine had it right: Her brother needed help. From the looks of things, he'd needed it for years.

Jackman gave a fake cough and the artist turned, his rheumy eyes taking a good ten seconds to register Jackman's presence. "Hello Peter," Jackman said, wondering if Faraway would remember him. Jackman hadn't aged the way Faraway had. Jackman still had his health and the tawny good looks he'd paraded around South Central High in Philadelphia, the thick, sandy hair and tan, lanky body that had attracted Nadine first time around. The artist's sister and Jackman had been high school sweethearts. Back then, he'd picked her up at the Faraway residence a couple of times a week, sometimes bumping into the brother with the sketchpad in his hands. It was possible Faraway would recognize him.

But Faraway didn't know Jackman from a hole in the wall. He stumbled off the wooden crate and ran the rant from the top again, poking his fingers at Jackman's chest, pulling on his T-shirt, exhaling sour breath in his face as he labored to make him comprehend how municipal controls crushed artists' wills, how the greed and egocentrism of dictatorial power killed artistic expression.

"OK, pal, I get it," Jackman said, backing away.

"Yeah? Explain it to me." Faraway lurched forward and grabbed Jackman's T-shirt again.

"Take it easy," Jackman said.

Faraway poked his hands into that teeming bamboo wagon, jimmied out a mildewed leather briefcase and worked on a zipper that had separated along half its length, his face dripping sweat as he tried to knit the teeth together so the thing would unzip, his swollen hands shaking, his fingers turning red. Jackman sat down beside him on the damp sand, took the briefcase between his knees and forced the zipper unstuck.

"Look at these," Faraway said, yanking out a handful of ragged file folders and shoving them at Jackman. Jackman leafed through the folders. The first held applications to officials in cities throughout the U.S. and the rest of the world seeking permission to paint the local scene and sell the paintings in public spaces. Every application had been denied, as had the appeals, more than a few stamped with insulting red. Next came the fines and citations—vending without a permit, vagrancy, loitering, sleeping where the wretched were prohibited from resting their weary heads. Finally letters, the originals of which Jackman figured must have ended up in the FBI crackpot files, correspondence with mayors, governors, the Secretary of the Interior, the Dalai Lama, his Holiness the Pope.

Your Holiness, Are you aware of the bureaucratic insanity artists endure in their quest to find a compassionate environment in which to do their work? As an artist of the world, in spiritual connection with other artists against an inhumane and controlling authoritative malevolence, I beseech you to....

Jesus, Jackman thought as he restacked the folders, hands weighing the municipal controls restricting Faraway's life, this guy's life is a train wreck. He recalled the postcards Nadine had fanned on the bed to talk him into retrieving her brother from Pin Dalie on his next business trip. Written in Faraway's increasingly degraded penmanship and overwrought syntax, the postcards charted his nomadic existence for the better part of a decade, tales of sleeping on a beach or in a metro, trading art for food with waiters at the backs of hotels, once even sitting in a jail cell for a week for setting up an easel on royal palace grounds.

"Frustrating," Jackman said and met Faraway's feverish eyes.

Faraway jumped up, grabbed Jackman by an arm and pulled him erect. "See. I want to paint for the man on the street. Not to make agents and galleries rich. And no one will sell me a twenty buck permit, because it's not about art, it's about who you can bribe, who you know, who you control and who controls you. Now do you get it?"

Again, it struck Jackman that Faraway could sound almost right. "Point taken," he said and patted the artist on his upper arm, shocked by the lack of girth under the flannel sleeve. While Jackman replaced the folders in the briefcase and tried to maneuver the zipper closed so it might possibly, one day, open again, Faraway reached for his drawing pad and his colored chalk and worked a quick sketch of Jackman, an uncanny likeness he allowed Jackman briefly to view and then retrieved so he could sketch an oversized heart inside Jackman's chest. Its lines were so animated the chambers seemed to beat. Inexplicably Jackman felt grateful, redeemed.

※ ※ ※

"Who you? Why you talk Peter Faraway?" The red-headed whore with one leg stood waiting for Jackman up on the pebbled path river side of Bungkotankang Street. Jackman noticed the small red hibiscus flower tattooed on her stump and stared at the black fishnet stocking and three-inch high heel she wore on her good leg and foot. A scent of perfume floated his way, a subtler aroma than he'd have given her credit for.

"What your name?" she said.

"Alan Jackman."

"Why you stare at leg, Jack Man. Not polite. You never see amputee before?"

Was she kidding? Until a few years earlier, landmines lurked everywhere. Amputees lined the bridges, stalked the outdoor cafés, loitered by tourist hotels. If you looked one in the eye, you ended up the Pied Piper of cripples.

"It's the stocking," he said. No apology necessary, fair game to stare at her. She'd let her picture appear in an Ayama Na tourist guide, its caption, "the Mayor of Bungkotankang Street."

"Stocking sexy," she said.

"Right." The adjective fit, despite her haggard eyes and weathered skin. He put her age at thirty-four or thirty-five, hair diverting attention from the ravages, thick curls dyed a deep shade of red, the mass fastened

carelessly at the crown with a cheap metal clip, wild ten-
drils escaping down her forehead and neck.

"You plan make trouble for artist?"

"The opposite. I'm a family friend. I've come to take
him back to the States and get him some help."

"Peter not need help from Jack Man. If Peter need
help, I help him. I his girl friend. He live here now."

"Well, it doesn't look like he lives very well. He's
filthy. He's skin and bones. He's starving to death."

"Peter eat good." She started to move. "He not starving. I prove to you."

Jackman had to rush to keep up with her as she crossed
Bungkotankang street—she walked that efficiently. No
leaning, no listing. The click of her heel alternated rap-
idly with the thump of the rubber tip at the end of the
crutch, and she negotiated the transition from street to
sidewalk with greater skill than he did. Reaching it first,
she held the door to a cheap fry joint open for him. The
waiters yelled greetings to her, calling her "Red," the
English surprising him when it registered. She pointed
to the drawings on the walls, clearly Faraway's work,
the same dynamic technique that had made Jackman's
heart beat on the sketchpad. In the paintings, Jackman
recognized the locals of Bungkotankang Street: the old
man with the long white beard who sold caged doves to
tourists to set free for good luck, the pimp with the flash
cards advertising improbable anatomical positions.

"Peter trade art for food," Jackman's redheaded,
one-legged guide said as she pushed through a swinging wall of vertical beads into a smoky kitchen. On the
way through, she ate a couple of fried shrimp off a plate
intended for a diner and called out something to the fry
cook that made him howl with laughter. His whoops followed them out the back door into the crowded market,

a maze of low-ceiled, neon-lit stalls that extended back from Bungkotankang Street as far as Jackman could see. She wove her arm through his to prevent hawkers pitching him, stealing his wallet, forcing on him Buddha statues, woven shawls, exotic eastern spices, or floppy-necked barbequed chickens. He's with me, the arm said. Her crutch swung up and down, pointing out Faraway's art on the sea of portable walls. "You think Peter not able get what he need?"

When they exited the market to the back alley, the glare of the sun blinded Jackman. It was high noon in Pin Dalie. His sight returned in time to see the redhead pull black-rimmed sunglasses from the deep scoop of her neckline and lift them to her face. The farther they walked from the market, the more the alleys narrowed, sunlight hard-pressed to shine in, but her glasses remained, their huge black lenses transforming her to a giant-eyed celebrity. She caught him staring again. "What you look at, Jack Man?"

"You," he said. As if she didn't know.

"You like what you see?"

He didn't answer.

"Forget it. I not do sex with Peter's friend."

Jackman let it go. He could mention he hardly considered an STD his preferred travel souvenir, but what was the point? He might need her assistance getting Faraway on a plane.

The smells intensified—grease, cardamom, rotting garbage. Rats darted between the dense ramshackle residences, structures crowded in jigsaw fashion, their crooked roofs jury-rigged in place, their coal-blackened smoke vents bent in weird angles to reach open air. He estimated they'd covered a quarter mile of alleys when the whore inserted a key in a door painted red. "Look for red door," he could imagine her instructing potential customers. When his eyes adjusted to the dim interior light, he made out a double bed, a small table, one chair, a gooseneck floor lamp. At the head of the bed, he saw a half dozen red satin pillows on the black silk spread, and across the foot, a red silk shawl that had been haphazardly flung there. A plank mounted on a sidewall held a basin of water and a scary propane hotplate. The redhead opened a door at the back of the room. "Bathroom at end," she said, pointing down a narrow communal hall. "Peter not filthy. Peter wash here."

What light existed filtered in through a tiny window on the alley, and in that light, the room glowed red. Red walls, softly textured and skillfully sponge-mottled, provided a backdrop for Faraway's paintings and drawings, many portraying the redhead herself. The redhead washing at the basin. The redhead asleep. The redhead draping the red shawl across her ample bare breasts. Jackman wondered how many pictures she'd extracted from Faraway in exchange for sex, baths, shelter in the rainy season, and how many she'd sold to maximize her investment in him. Jackman didn't believe the "girlfriend" story. The whore didn't strike him as someone who gave anything away.

She sat on the edge of the bed, crutch tossed onto the floor, good leg crossed over the stump. In the pale rosy light, with the rims of her sunglasses resting on her cheeks, and her legs carefully arranged, she appeared whole and unmutilated, as sensual as anyone in her line of work. Tempted to stare again, Jackman turned his back to her and walked toward the wall to examine the paintings.

"Peter make wall with rags. He build frames. He hang pictures. Room work of art. What you think?"

"Splendid," Jackman said, a cynicism in his tone he didn't intend, nervousness he guessed, her earlier supposition of desire on his part and the unanticipated physical intimacy undermining his confidence.

She indicated the room's only chair. "You CIA, Jack Man?"

He sat, his tall frame awkward in the too small chair. "What gives you that idea?"

"Answer question."

"Of course not."

"You lie to me, I kill you." She removed the sunglasses. Her eyes were narrower than he remembered. He didn't doubt she could arrange his death

"I'm not lying," Jackman said. "Why would the CIA care about Faraway?"

"CIA hate Faraway type. Want Faraway type dead."

"That's ridiculous. He's a homeless vagrant."

"You baby, Jack Man. You little child. You not understand first one thing about how world work."

"Explain it to me."

"Look what happen on Bungkotankang Street. People beg, people steal, people sell no need stuff, people buy no need stuff. This person no arm. This person no leg. Tourist no heart. Lock money in safe in hotel. Leave jewelry in big USA house. Bring few measly dollar bill to street. Peter not try sell something stupid. Not try buy something stupid. Not try protect self. Peter paint. Peter try make people see. CIA hate that."

She was smarter than he thought, analytical, self-possessed, capable of expressing complex thoughts in the English she'd picked up on the street. He'd failed to take her seriously, elitism on his part, the presumption that the notions of a whore in a ravaged country couldn't possibly count. Still, she'd pegged him wrong too. He wasn't

CIA. "Let's say, for argument's sake, you're right about the CIA. The CIA doesn't have to kill Faraway. He's dying all by himself."

"Artist not dying." She sounded definite.

"He has malaria and who knows what else. He needs medical care."

"Everyone in Ayama Na need medical care. Malaria not important. Malaria everywhere."

"What about the swollen leg? And the sores on his ankles? They're infected. He's on his way out."

"Show what you know. West people think malaria kill you. Or bird flu. Or broke neck. Or scab on leg. Or lose weight. Wrong. These things not kill you. *Djara-Aana* thing that kill you."

"*Djara-Aana*?"

"Not possible translate."

"Try."

She paused. "*Djara-Aana* mean *Unfairness of Life*. But this not good translation. *Djara-Aana* big thing. Different thing everyone, but same thing." She pointed to her stump.

"*Djara-Aana*?" Jackman asked.

"Right. Leg missing. Possible stump ruin me. But I fight."

"And Faraway?"

"Artist not allow sell painting. Possible this make artist bitter. Bitter kill you. Peter know this. That why he paint. That why he shout up sidewalk. That why I love him and why I consent be his girl friend. He fight *djara-Aana* like tiger in cage. You not understand this, Jack Man, because you stupid. You take Peter USA, you end up kill him. Go home. Leave artist here."

※ ※ ※

Every night, at one minute past midnight, Ayama Na Air Flight 67 leaves the Pin Dalie airport and puddle jumps to Thailand, a country with runways that handle transpacific aircraft. He and Faraway should have been on that midnight 737 to Bangkok, and then on a 7 A.M. flight to the States. At midnight, however, Jackman sat in the cocktail lounge of his hotel, the famous Blue Orchid in the center of Pin Dalie, elbows on a long black leather bar, watching the hands of a wall clock creep past the witching hour. Why weren't he and Faraway on Flight 67? Why hadn't he medicated the artist, poured him into a cab and kept him in a stupor until the plane took off? He had a vial of formidable pills in his pocket, a stash supplied by Nadine in case her brother balked, enough Atavan to keep Faraway asleep for a week.

After half a bottle of wine, Jackman felt woozy. He knew he was sloshed, but he recognized the queasiness for what it was and what it wasn't. It wasn't the alcohol. It was an encounter with his meaningless life. At least Faraway had gone nuts for reasons that mattered. Even half dead, Faraway had a serious agenda. The redheaded whore might not love him the way she claimed she did, but the artist's life had earned her respect, and Jackman, from the depths of his midlife self-loathing, envied him that.

Because who respected him? He peddled computer technology to governments of developing countries that should have used the money to build schools and pave roads instead. The stuff he sold would be obsolete before anyone figured out how to operate it. He'd rationalized for years that nothing got done in these graft-infested nations anyway and that foreigners who criticized or meddled could find themselves disappeared. Which is why when Nadine asked him to find Faraway on his next trip to Pin Dalie, he'd refused. He understood the risks of interfering in a place with rules you didn't comprehend.

But Nadine had waved the artist's picture in Jackman's face—a picture her brother had sent—and implicated him in a crime of neglect. "How can you refuse to help this man?" she'd said with such indignation, such a lack of irony, you'd think she hadn't waited ten years to act on the evidence that her only sibling had lapsed into extreme physical and mental distress.

"I'm in a different space now," she said when Jackman asked why the sudden desire for a rescue scenario. The new space had to do with some shrink she consulted for boredom and depression (conditions apparently unalleviated by Jackman in her bed) who suggested her self-esteem would improve if she prevented her brother from wasting his life.

And just who was it who was wasting a life, Jackman wondered. Faraway, who, with his earthly belongings piled in a wagon on the bank of a stinking river, made people look at the unfairness of life? Or a snake oil salesman who spent his downtime mixing margaritas in a fancy remodeled kitchen and tweaking his travel itinerary—not, mind you, to get back to the States in time for his daughter's dance recitals—but to get back in time for his weekly trysts with the artist's sister?

Why in the world would he bring Faraway back with him? So Faraway could live in a house with an electric garage door opener? So he could spend the next twenty years dropping apple cores down a garbage disposal? So he could have cocktails with people who had never experienced a moment of *djara-Aana* and still had the gall to think themselves miserable?

He'd leave Faraway right where he stood and depart in good conscience. And as for Nadine, he'd tell her he'd found her brother dead or living happy as a pig in shit with a wife and three kids. Maybe that would keep her from going ballistic and telling his wife they'd been fucking at the Hyatt every Wednesday for a year. Tomorrow night, he'd be on Flight 67 by himself.

And yet, Jackman thought, Faraway must have wanted to be rescued or he wouldn't have sent his sister a photo of his emaciated, red-faced, feverish self. He wouldn't have kept her informed of his whereabouts for ten years. Nadine was right. That photo was a cry for help, evidence Faraway wanted to be found and brought back. So far Faraway hadn't told Jackman any different.

Then again, Jackman hadn't asked.

▦ ▦ ▦

At 4 A.M., Jackman stood on the bridge looking out along the beam of a flashlight he'd borrowed from the Blue Orchid Hotel. It didn't surprise him not to see Peter Faraway down there on the riverbank. Jackman knew where to find him.

The whore had left the red door half-open, as if she expected him. From beyond the threshold, Jackman looked in. The artist sat in the chair, the gooseneck floor lamp arced over his shoulder, a paintbrush in his hand, a spiral sketchpad in the cone of light on his lap. The whore lay on the bed, eyes closed, body covered to the chin with the black silk spread, her hair, loose from its clips, fanned out around her face like an aerial shot of an actress floating in a swimming pool or on a calm glassy lake. Jackman swung the door wider and stepped in.

Immediately, the whore slid herself up against the red satin pillows and pivoted off the bed, the short filmy see-through thing she wore falling to the top of her red satin underpants. Seeing her high firm breasts and smooth flat abdomen, Jackman reevaluated her age, lowering his estimate a decade. In Pin Dalie, you wised up fast or you begged on a bridge. She could be twenty-five.

"Nadine is worried about you," Jackman said.

The artist worked with a skinny brush and a few jars of watercolor, putting the finishing touches on another picture of the redhead asleep. At the mention of his sister's name, he flipped the page of his sketchbook and exchanged the brush for some sticks of colored chalk. A few moments later, he held up Nadine. He'd gotten the hair color wrong—she'd become a strawberry blonde since he'd last seen her—but he'd drawn her smile exactly right. Insincere and cocked to one side.

"She'd like to see you," Jackman said.

"Tell her to visit me."

"Why don't you visit her?"

"Misery. Greed. Conformity. Monopolistic establishments that eliminate opportunities for artists to succeed in the world." Faraway leaned sideways to scratch an inflamed, oozing sore on his ankle.

"She sent a plane ticket for you." Jackman indicated the blue and white striped edge of the airline envelope protruding from his pants pocket.

The redhead hopped to the end of the bed, lifted the red silk shawl and arranged it over her shoulders. She retrieved her crutch from the floor and pointed it at Faraway. "He not going anywhere, Jack Man."

"I'm not asking you, I'm asking him."

"I'm not going anywhere," Faraway said.

Faraway wasn't thinking straight, let alone thinking for himself. "Your foot is purple and inflamed," Jackman said, his tone calm, steady, reasonable. "You have a fever. You're probably septic. You could die here."

"I'm not dying."

"I think you are. Have you taken a good look at your ankle?"

"People not die from sore on leg. I already explain, Jack Man."

"Don't give me that *djara-Aana* voodoo crap. He needs serious medical care."

"You make fun me, Jack Man? You think I not scientific person? You think you know what best for him?"

"Absolutely, I do. I'm taking him home so his sister can get him the appropriate help."

"You fulla shit, Jack Man." She pulled herself tall, the red shawl flowing behind her. "And his sister bitch. We send picture and letter. I take picture myself and Peter write letter. Ask money to fix Sector Nine medical clinic. Instead, what she send? She send you, Jack Man."

"What letter?" Jackman took a step closer to Faraway. "Nadine didn't get a letter. She got a picture. Period."

"You not believe me, Jack Man? You think I make letter up?"

"I'm not asking you. I'm asking Faraway." Jackman turned his back to her and tried to make eye contact with Faraway, but the artist didn't look up. He was working on the sleeping redhead painting again, concentrating on her hair, outlining its curls so her face appeared nestled in twisted red branches.

Jackman heard himself shout. "Faraway. Answer me. Did you send your sister a letter?"

Nadine had first shown him the photo in the 399-dollar-a-night suite that the Hyatt on the Delaware reserved for him every week, a suite he paid for in cash (whether or not he used it) so it didn't leave a paper trail. She told him the photo had arrived in an otherwise empty envelope postmarked Pin Dalie. She told him it was a photo that spoke for itself.

Jackman knew the whore was telling him the truth. No contest, Faraway's whore was more honest than his. Wiring money or sending money with Jackman wouldn't have satisfied his whore's project specs—she required a rehabilitated artist to parade around Philadelphia. Jackman felt his anger at her in the roots of his teeth. Suddenly Nadine was crystal clear to him. She was a woman who wouldn't help a fly find a pile of shit if there wasn't something in it for her.

"You want see copy of letter, Jack Man?"

"Not necessary." He turned so he faced her again.

"Maybe artist sister send money, Jack Man, and you keep for yourself."

She was insulting him for the sport of it. "Wrong," he said.

"How I know you not thief?"

"Same way I know you sent the letter."

She mulled that over, her expression indecipherable. "Okay. Sister no help. How about you, Jack Man? Why you not go bank machine and give money for clinic. Construction not cost so much here—45 million *ghree* build new clinic. That nothing to you."

Did she really believe that in America you went into the back yard and plucked money off the oak trees? At the current exchange rate, 45 million *ghree* came to 225,000 dollars, give or take—roughly half the price, in real estate speak, of his "spacious 5 BR 3BA stone colonial on a wooded quarter acre."

"How about it, Jack Man?"

"I can't finance a clinic. I have a wife and two children." She didn't know the half of it. The summer camps, the private schools, Heather's SAT tutor, Morgan's ballet lessons, her anorexia, her therapy bills. The goddamn kitchen remodel. He pulled out his billfold and flipped it open to a snapshot of his daughters.

She tipped her head and studied the photo. He'd taken it a year ago. Heather and Morgan in the refurbished kitchen, both of them leaning against the counter, their elbows on the newly installed granite.

The redhead had it right. Nadine was a bitch and he was full of shit. If he weren't full of shit, he would mortgage his house, leverage his investments, and send 45 million *ghree* to her for the Sector Nine clinic. If anyone could put money into hands that would use it right, this woman could. Better yet, he'd bring the funds in himself. Then he'd climb on a soapbox on the riverbank, and for the next ten years of his currently good-for-nothing life, he'd shout uphill to the tourists on Bungkotankang Street to empty their wallets, withdraw their bank accounts, and even out the planet's *djara-Aana*.

He would stand out there in the blazing sun, day in day out. Hot, hungry, thirsty. Skin burning. Throat sore from shouting at the tourists on the bridge while they gawked back at him with pity or disgust. Jackman figured he'd last on that riverbank about fifteen minutes.

"I respect family," she said. "You give 25 million *ghree* for clinic. Keep rest for wife and skinny girls."

"When we get back to the States, I'll send a donation," Jackman promised. "And after Faraway gets on his feet, I'll bring him back here." Jackman meant what he said. He had no intention of letting Faraway become Nadine's pet. He'd accompany him back to Pin Dalie himself. "I'll take care of your artist, you have my word."

"You take care artist? Ha. That funny, Jack Man. You not able take care wipe artist's ass."

All at once, Jackman hated her. He detested her condescension, her lethal disregard for common sense, especially, he detested her disrespect for him.

"You want to die here?" he shouted at Faraway. "Because that's what will happen to you, you know."

Visibly agitated, the artist jumped to his feet and leafed backward through the sketchpad, turning pages as fast as he could. He missed what he looked for and started again. When he found the picture he'd made of Jackman at the riverbank, he lowered the sketchpad to the table, and while Jackman watched, the artist leaned down hard with a black stick of chalk and drew an X through Jackman's heart.

The hot flush of humiliation started at Jackman's scalp. His eyes stung. Who were these two to judge him? To tell him he was full of shit? To cross out his heart? What did a depraved whore and a crazy homeless bum know about his life? Did they know he stayed married for the sake of his kids? Did they know he flew 70,000 miles a year to provide for his family? He didn't need abuse from these two. He grabbed the airline ticket from his pocket, ripped out the open ticket in Faraway's name and flung it on the bed. "For all I care, Faraway, you can rot here. And trust me, you will."

He turned to exit, then turned back for a last word to the one-legged, redheaded she-devil of a whore. "If he dies, you have no one to blame but yourself. I wash my hands of both of you."

She called after him as he rushed down the alley, "So, what else new, Jack Man?"

The Cut the Crap Machine

At his clinic visits, the doctors told Um Ta to avoid letting the sun beat down on his head. They'd snap their fingers and warn him he could die just like that, especially if it got so hot paint flaked off statues. From his table outside the dim-sum joint on the corner of Sankatdongkam and Keararat Streets, the elderly playwright watched flecks of gold fall from the plaster elephants beside the restaurant's entry arches, but he'd lived through seven years of forced labor in the clay fields and wasn't about to pamper himself. A glance at the amputees begging across Sankatdongkam Street reminded him what real misery was. Or he could envision his wife and son in their unmarked graves somewhere in the murderous countryside, but that was another story, one he didn't figure he'd live long enough to write.

He pressed the palms of his mottled hands against a tall glass of *White*, a milky concoction touted on bus benches throughout Pin Dalie as the equivalent of an ice bath, but he rarely lifted the drink to his mouth. He was preoccupied with the young playwright across the table, his collaborator on the first new play in Ayama Na since the insane coup that eradicated ninety-nine percent of the country's artists and intellectuals. Lu Kang sat there swigging beer, chain-smoking cigarettes, and eating as if he were trying to fill a bottomless hole in his gut.

"Ten *purae* months and this is what we have to show for it?" Lu Kang scowled at the manuscript on the table, its pages shaded by a bottle of fiery red chili paste. Beer slid from the corners of Lu Kang's lips and oozed down his chin as he flipped the thumb of his good hand in the direction of the flaking gold pachyderms. "*Purae* sentimentality of yours! Play's as phony as those elephants over there." His good hand grabbed two more dim sum bowls from a tray that a skinny teenage waiter swooped toward their table.

In spite of the insults Lu Kang heaped upon Um Ta day after day, Um Ta maintained a benevolent silence and a generous attitude toward his hot-headed young collaborator. Before the coup, Um Ta had been the country's premier playwright, the highly acclaimed winner of important national awards; he didn't have to prove to himself that he could write a hit play. On the other hand, when Lu Kang's career was cut short, he'd been a fledgling theater student with a single campus play to his credit. Embittered and in no mood to waste energy on manners or respect for his elders, Lu Kang grabbed a chicken's foot from a dim-sum bowl and noisily sucked the skin off its toes. "Every compromise I let you talk me into makes me want to puke. This thing is shit!" He reached forward and pounded the manuscript so hard the chili paste jumped.

So vast were the collaborators' artistic and philosophical differences that, with opening night only nine weeks away, a three-act play that should have been in rehearsal for a month existed as nothing more than the rough draft of the first two acts, a total of sixty-three pages that the playwrights had forced themselves to crank out only by scheduling their actors for a preliminary reading of acts 1 and 2. This reading was scheduled to take place after the collaborators finished their lunch.

Ten months earlier, when King Mindao expressed a desire for a new play to inaugurate the reopening of the Pin Dalie Cultural Center (the royal family's latest philanthropic endeavor), the king's researchers identified Um Ta and Lu Kang as the only playwrights who'd survived the country's bloody talent purge. They'd found Um Ta in a factory sewing slippers ten hours a day for an American superstore chain and Lu Kang working a crane at a hotel construction site, steering with his good arm and stepping on foot pedals to maneuver the beam.

"The read-through might surprise you, *allifa*." Um Ta said.

Lu Kang flinched at the Ayama Nan word for *my son*. "Cut the crap, Um Ta. If you're hoping I'll agree with your irrelevant ideas, you're even more pitiful than I imagined."

In his famous years, Um Ta had declined all requests to collaborate, although collaboration was a tradition of Ayama Nan cultural life. He'd told himself he feared losing his unique artistic vision, but in the clay fields he'd understood the truth. He'd been haughty, competitive, and loathe to share credit, also stingy and emotionally ungenerous, withholding approval from his fellow playwrights, his students, and most everyone else, including his only son, who'd died before Um Ta could make amends. His son would be three years older than Lu Kang had he lived. Sometimes, Um Ta felt as if he floated over Lu Kang, hovering just above the earth and just below death, stealing extra months so he could complete his two works-in-progress—the three-act play and the rehabilitation of his cynical young collaborator. If he were generous, giving, and patient, and if he lived long enough, he believed he could teach Lu Kang a few things worth knowing about how to create a major theatrical work.

In the magnesium mines east of the Faro, Lu Kang had lost his parents, a sister, a brother, an aunt, two uncles, two nephews, and a right arm. He had no use for Um Ta's ideals or his idiot character arcs. Lu Kang grunted as he sucked the wrinkled yellow skin off another scrawny boiled chicken's foot. His large, crooked teeth gripped the puckered yellow flesh and slid it along the metatarsals, then he spit the little bones onto the manuscript in a display of contempt.

Every day, for the last ten months, the two had worked together in a hot trailer on the theater construction site with two-handed Um Ta, the de facto typist, sitting on a folding chair, plucking the keys of an antiquated Dell PC while Lu Kang paced back and forth, railing against every tender or soft-hearted word Um Ta wanted to write and fighting for his unremitting view of man as immoral and opportunistically cruel.

Lu Kang shoved a steamed bun in his mouth. The red-edged gray pork and spongy white dough broke apart and churned between his teeth. He was coarse, but also, in a rough way, he was handsome—lips full, eyes deep, skin as swarthy as a dried pomegranate peel. A big man, he ate and drank and caroused like a tiger let out of a cage, roaring, hungry, and so alive with desire that, despite the empty sleeve that dangled from his right shoulder, whores would have given him their favors free if their pimps hadn't had a thousand eyes on the street. The play's leading lady had been in Lu Kang's bed since the day of the casting call, held just after the playwrights completed act 1, an act since rewritten three times.

"You know what I think of this speech?" Lu Kang flipped the manuscript to the last page of act 2—page 63. "Of this whole *purae* scene?"

Um Ta sighed. He knew.

"Here's what I think of it!" Lu Kang ripped page 63 from the staple and crushed it in his fist as he shot to his feet. He leaned toward the gutter and tossed the crumpled wad into the coursing swill of Pin Dalie's underserved lives.

Pungent and garlicky aromas from the oily kitchen rode on the back of the exhaust fumes from Keararat Street as the traffic light turned green. Suddenly Um Ta couldn't breathe.

"You look like shit. You dying on me?" Lu Kang said.

"And trust you to finish the play?" Um Ta gasped at the effort of so many words. In Um Ta's dreams, the manuscript appeared as a beast constructed of disparate animal parts: a baboon with a vulture's wings, a tiger with a pigeon's tail. The war over every word had produced a hodge-podge of inconsistent personalities and contradictory motives, part farce, part social satire, part serious human drama. Um Ta lifted the glass of *White* to his lips, hands trembling their habitual tremor, bony fingers barely covered with skin. He'd long ago found it too fatiguing to eat.

"Good riddance to this *purae* oozing puss pocket on the history of Ayama-Nan theater," Lu Kang shouted to the gutter as page 63 floated away. With a cocked elbow in Um Ta's direction, the national gesture of disrespect, Lu Kang took off for the theater.

Um Ta tucked 2,000 *ghree* under a dim-sum bowl, rescued the rest of the pages, and got slowly to his feet. Before he'd taken three steps, he felt the familiar tightness in his chest and the sharp pains in his ruined knees and hips.

※ ※ ※

In the years when a literate populace had been alive to think about such things, Um Ta had been considered the father of modern Ayama Nan theater. He'd pushed the stage beyond elaborately costumed religious and mythological subjects and traditional dance extravaganzas to small-scale psychological dramas in which ordinary people wrestled with contemporary problems. To continue the trend he'd started he'd proposed to Lu Kang, as protagonist for their new play, an elderly barber who would learn to cope with the senseless deaths of his wife and child as he interacted with the equally bereaved customers who came to his barbershop.

Lu Kang despised Um Ta's approach, although as a fledgling playwright, it had been an approach he'd admired. (His student play, an intimate dissection of a teenager's rebellion, sowed ground Um Ta had plowed.) In the aftermath, however, he considered history irrelevant and insight and interpersonal relationships a waste of time. Vigilance in the present was what mattered to him, the exposure of corruption at the highest levels of Ayama Na's self-styled democratic government. As a main character, he argued for a corrupt, avaricious, and brutal politician.

"Our country is a nation of burdened consciences," Um Ta said, "We owe it to the dead to make sense of that."

"Cut the crap, Um Ta. The living don't think about the dead, except to rejoice that they aren't among them."

"A character on a stage can illuminate everyone's personal struggle with their own survival. A play can provide an audience catharsis."

"Leave me out of it. You're talking about yourself. You'd make our nation's corpses grist for examining your conscience."

"And you'd write as if a country filled with smoke never suffered a fire. "

"You'd spend three acts telling burnt people they're charred."

"I'd try to discover how a person—and by extension a nation—can prevail over loss and move on."

"*Ack*, here it comes. Our little barber will learn once again to experience love."

"I don't rule that out."

Lu Kang issued forth a mocking laugh. "Cut the crap, Um Ta. Love is just greed by another name. It's the desire to be loved in return. There'll be no love in our play!"

In the compromise, however, Lu Kang allowed Um Ta a love interest in exchange for Um Ta's allowing him the protagonist of his choice—a man he named Praphan after a harsh ruler of the seventh century. As Lu Kang conceived him, Praphan would be a crooked member of parliament who, along with other crooked politicians, purchased young girls from impoverished families for use in brothels they secretly owned.

Into Praphan's sordid life, Um Ta would bring Daranee, the aging daughter of a highly placed magistrate, a plain girl that Praphan would woo and marry for access to her father. In spite of his faults, Daranee would love Praphan with all of her heart.

"Go ahead," Lu Kang said. "Write your mush. It'll let me expose love for the delusion it is. I'll prove no such emotion exists."

"We'll see, *allifa*," Um Ta had said.

* * *

A pair of cantilevered teak bridges arched across a dry, pebbled lake bed to the half-constructed "floating theater," the centerpiece of the Pin Dalie Cultural Center. When filled, the artificial lake would provide a habitat for a thousand orange koi and thirty-two native species of fresh-water plants. From the middle of the lake, a theater would appear to float, an illusion supported by dozens of fourteen-meter pylons sunk deep into the earth. After crossing the westernmost bridge, Um Ta walked through the space destined to be the lobby and entered the theater on the orchestra level, while up on the stage, the ten actors he and Lu Kang had cast for their play arranged chairs in a semi-circle. Intense sunlight beamed through the theater's unfinished roof, a lattice of boards and open space that offered little relief from the fierce July heat.

Um Ta took a seat in one of two temporary chairs set halfway between what would ultimately be the orchestra and the loge. Lu Kang, in the other chair, ranted to himself and ripped the final page—page 63—from each copy of the script. This act of sabotage on Lu Kang's part violated the collaborators' hardest-fought compromise, a three day battle that had left Um Ta exhausted. In Um Ta's judgment, without the speech on that page, a soliloquy in which their protagonist—Praphan—sees himself as a scoundrel and is transformed by the insight, the play became nothing but a mean and heartless screed and lost its claim as a serious work of art.

Um Ta had won that battle by agreeing to Lu Kang's demand that every single character in the play operate from motives that were deluded or mean. Um Ta knew he'd gotten the better of the bargain, for in permitting the speech, his young collaborator had bartered away his darkest conceit, the immutability of man's evil nature. Still, Um Ta hadn't expected Lu Kang to renege on the deal, and for the play's and Lu Kang's own sakes, he wouldn't allow it. He turned to Lu Kang. "What do you think you're doing?"

"Saving us from ridicule."

"We had an agreement. I expect you to honor it."

"Why should I?"

"Because, *allifa*, that's what civilized people do."

"Civilized? Cut the crap. There's no one on this *purae* planet who fits that description, least of all me." Lu Kang ran onto the stage and distributed the mutilated scripts to the cast.

This wasn't over yet, Um Ta thought. Patiently, he collected the detached pages from the floor. He'd leave them on the actors' chairs during the break when Lu Kang, man of large appetites, would go outside to smoke or disappear with the play's leading lady for an amorous interlude in their office-trailer behind the dining hall. Scowling at Um Ta, Lu Kang returned to his seat.

The play commenced.

❖ ❖ ❖

(A brothel. Characters, half naked, converse while getting dressed.)

ANONYMOUS BROTHEL PATRON: So, Praphan, tell me. When will I meet your beautiful fiancée?

PRAPHAN: Tomorrow, at the engagement party. And when you meet her, I warn you not to stare at her ears. They're hardly her best feature. *(laughs)*

ANONYMOUS PATRON: Clearly you've made an excellent choice for a bride, my friend. With a wife with big ears, there's no need to holler when you want her to meet your demands.

PRAPHAN: So true! But Daranee's ears aren't big. They're shaped like a tree fungus. *(gnarly gesture with hands)*

ANONYMOUS BROTHEL PATRON: I see. Then, if you don't object, I'll keep my eyes on her breasts.

PRAPHAN: Object? Why should I? But if you stare at her breasts, you'll see nothing, for she's flat as a sea urchin cake.

ANONYMOUS BROTHEL PATRON: *Ack chee mi yobat.* I am beginning to understand where it is I should look.

PRAPHAN *(raises eyebrow)*: And where is that my friend?

ANONYMOUS BROTHEL PATRON: At her father's influence.

(loud laughter from both men)

If Lu Kang, from whose pen this dialogue had tumbled like water over a waterfall, had had his way, he'd have made every dialogue in the play a similar revelation of despicable character. Hearing the scene, Um Ta recalled their painful writing process, for Lu Kang initially assumed all plot decisions could be his. As he saw it, in the rest of act 1, a reporter would confront Praphan with evidence that he owned whorehouses in which child sex slaves regularly succumbed to sexually transmitted infection but, instead of publishing the politician's dirty deeds, the journalist would try to blackmail him. As the act closed Praphan would order his thugs to find the journalist who'd gone into hiding.

Um Ta acceded to Lu Kang's act 1, biding his time, keeping firmly in mind the lessons he needed to teach. But, as Lu Kang began dictating the first scene of act 2, in which the journalist was to be brutally tortured and killed, Um Ta stopped typing and asserted himself.

"Your protagonist is too degenerate," he said. "The audience won't relate to him. They'll stop listening."

"Cut the crap, Um Ta. Everyone's degenerate so everyone will relate. It's as natural for a person to be degenerate as for a snake to eat rats."

"Everyone is not degenerate, *allifa*. Take yourself, for example. Day after day, you work with me on the play as if your life depended on it, engaging in philosophical argument, developing plot, refining structure. It's no small thing to live and work as an artist."

"Cut the crap. I write because I covet admiration. I want people to listen to what I have to say."

"People listen when characters exhibit dimension and depth. People listen to troubled souls, not stick figures with single agendas," Um Ta said. Lu Kang balked, but when Um Ta discoursed on the subject of suspense Lu Kang agreed to leave the reporter's fate a mystery and shift the focus to Daranee.

⬚ ⬚ ⬚

On stage, the actors finished their reading of act 1 and were ready for a break before beginning act 2. As they began to disperse, Lu Kang motioned for the leading lady to wait.

The leading lady, however, had other ideas. She ignored him and walked out on the arm of the leading man.

"*Purae famuta*," Lu Kang swore under his breath. Jumping from his chair, he shoved it with his powerful foot, kicking it clear across the orchestra and into the loge. At the same time, he ranted to Um Ta about the failures of the simpering worm they'd hired to play Praphan. Squeaky voice, pretty boy face, stature of a midget. Were we out of our heads? The part requires, he said, a tall man with cruel eyes, not a pipsqueak mooning around the stage like a stoned Buddha statue. Lu Kang's insistence that they fire this actor on the spot and cast a new Parphan resulted in a heated discussion that occupied the collaborators until the cast returned, depriving Um Ta of the opportunity to distribute the missing page of the manuscript. Um Ta, however, reminded Lu Kang of the king's displeasure over their late production schedule, and managed to protect a perfectly adequate actor from losing his job to an author's jealous whim.

As usual, Lu Kang and Um Ta settled their disagreement with a trade-off. In exchange for allowing the actor to remain, Lu Kang would lecture him publicly on how to do his job.

"Stop squeaking—lower your vocal cords, for god's sake. Put some arrogance into that moronic expression on your face."

"I thought I...."

"Cut the crap. Just do what I say."

The actors eyed one another, and act 2 commenced.

(Stage left, an ostentatious living room in the house where Daranee lives with her father, the Judge, and her younger

*twin sisters; stage right, a lush garden behind the house. Action
begins in the living room.)*

FIRST TWIN: *(looking at Daranee's new diamond ring)*
Four carats!

SECOND TWIN: *(laughs)* Must be the going rate to buy a
judge these days.

DARANEE: *(vulnerable and sad)* I know I'm not as allur-
ing as either of you. I'm twenty-eight and plain and
men don't notice me. I assure you I'm not blind to the
reasons Praphan came into my life. Still, he chose me
when he could as beneficially have chosen one of you,
for you have the same influential father I do.

FIRST TWIN: What a fool you are. Praphan knew we'd
reject him. Haven't you noticed our suitors lined up
at the door?

DARANEE: Perhaps it's his handsome face, tall stature,
and good manners that attract me to this man. Or
perhaps it's my feeling that I'm old and this is my last
chance, but what does it matter when I'm powerless
to extinguish my feelings for him?

FIRST TWIN: Handsome face? Good manners? He's slick,
unctuous, and insincere. You should get out more,
Daranee, you know that? For your advanced age, you
are dangerously naïve.

SECOND TWIN *(to the other)*: Unfortunate, her lack of
suitors, don't you agree?

❖ ❖ ❖

After her sisters leave the room, Daranee remains to
await Praphan's arrival. She studies a glossy photo of her
betrothed and, in a touching soliloquy, reminds herself
that handsomeness and height are superficial accidents

of fate, not virtues one ought to fall in love with. But she convinces herself she discerns positive qualities in Praphan and concludes that if she honors his goodness she will foster its growth.

DARANEE *(staring at Praphan's photo while pacing back and forth in front of the window that opens to the garden)*: From now on I will devote all of my energy to resurrecting what is most noble in this flawed and damaged man I love. With patience and effort, the beauty of his soul will match that of his face and physique. For what is man if not a form in flux, striving to better himself, whether he knows it or not? By judicious praise, I will addict him to honesty and render him incapable of lying to anyone, least of all to himself. In the end, his good actions will increase his own happiness and benefit our scarred and humble land.

Um Ta got to write Daranee's "introspective drivel" in exchange for Lu Kang's authorship of the dialogue between her twin sisters as they stand in the garden and listen to her speak.

(in the garden)

FIRST TWIN: She has retreated from all good sense. A woman in love can't see the truth.

SECOND TWIN: Can't see the truth or doesn't want to see the truth? Did you miss the contorted self-delusions that allow her to think well of herself?

FIRST TWIN: She really believes her love can improve him.

SECOND TWIN: Cut the crap. She doesn't love him. She wants to look in a mirror and see a generous and tender human being, the one person in Praphan's world who can change him. What she loves is her image of herself.

FIRST TWIN: But don't you pity her? She's aging and desperate.

SECOND TWIN: She should have utilized the plastic surgery centers when she was young, as we did. With prettier ears and breasts that fill C-cups, she wouldn't need to lie to herself about goodness in an evil, callous man.

FIRST TWIN: You're right. Daranee will have no one to blame for her disappointment but herself. Perhaps, though, we should restrain from adding to her pain with our ridicule.

SECOND TWIN: Now who wants to love an image of herself as the benevolent twin?

First Twin: Perhaps I am kinder than you are.

SECOND TWIN: Cut the crap. I know better. You and I, my dear, are genetically identical.

(The sisters disappear from the stage as the handsome future groom enters the living room where his future bride is waiting for him.)

PRAPHAN *(rushing to Daranee, kissing her hand)*: My darling fiancée, forgive me for being late. Difficult issues detained me.

DARANEE *(smiling brightly)*: No matter my dear. Come, let's go into the garden and perform a walking meditation among the flowers and trees to clear your mind and celebrate our happiness.

PRAPHAN: Dearest, let's sit right here and have a drink while we wait for your father. I've brought him a box of the finest cigars.

DARANEE: He won't be home for at least an hour. Come, let's go outside.

PRAPHAN: No, dear, I need a drink. I've many heavy thoughts to erase. My enemies, greedy men whose activities I oppose, have accused me of vile acts. If you hear rumors of me, I beg you ignore them. I have no time to focus on maintaining a spotless reputation. I must put my energy to ridding Pin Dalie of its criminal element and helping the common people. Some men have evil in their nature and are up to no good.

DARANEE: Of course I'll ignore rumors, Praphan. I know you to be a man in whom goodness runs deep. Come. A walk will provide greater clarity than alcohol. It will enable you to see into the heart of these men who wish you ill and then you'll know better how to deal with them.

PRAPHAN: *(He moves to the bar)* Everything in the garden is too pretty my dear. How will a garden help me see into the heart of evil? *(He pours)*

DARANEE: Are not the rose with its thorns, the bee with its sting, and the red ant with its bite waiting to ambush us in the garden, my dear? Are not dead blossoms visible everywhere to quicken our sorrow?

PRAPHAN: Neither the rose, nor the bee, nor the ants have intent to harm. The distress they cause is unintentional. It's in the nature of what they are.

DARANEE: But haven't you just said, dear, that the evil men do is in their nature? Please explain to me how, in your wisdom, you make the distinction.

PRAPHAN: In the garden there is no subterfuge. Flora and fauna cannot make false accusations. In the street, there are premeditated lies.

DARANEE: You are wise and what you say is true. But your answer leaves me with disquiet. Do you mean if you did not love me, you could pretend you did, and if I were not clever enough to unmask the lie, you would go unpunished for stealing my heart?

PRAPHAN: You have nothing to worry about on that score.

DARANEE: You could lie about that too, darling one.

PRAPHAN *(laughing)*: We have reached the hallway of the hundred mirrors.

DARANEE: Come with me to the garden, Praphan, where you will be with the bee, the rose, and the ant—all without artifice, all to be accepted and loved for what they are, as I love you.

The dialogue for the twins, written solely by Lu Kang, had been read by the actors with confidence, but the dialogue for Praphan and Daranee, written by both playwrights, with conflict over every line, confused and confounded the actors at every turn. They looked to Um Ta and Lu Kang with questioning eyes and read as if unable to decide if their characters ought to sound malevolent or kind, self-deluded or wise, or if the scene should be played straight or for laughs. Um Ta didn't know the answers to these questions himself and he cringed as the actors read, marking his copy for revision.

The next scene, in which Praphan and Daranee marry, didn't fare any better for it too had been written by the playwrights together. At the wedding, for which Daranee's father, the Judge, has spared no expense, a greedy priest who accepts a bribe from the groom to extol the groom's virtues (Lu Kang's contribution) nonetheless expresses wise and subtle truths about marriage (Um Ta's contribution). Then the bride's twin sisters and the groom's criminal cohorts engage in repartee that attains the height of indecency in its mockery of marriage (Lu Kang again).

In the next scene, the wedding night, the groom, touched by his bride's virginity (Um Ta's idea), nonetheless rushes to the bathroom to phone his friends on the cell phone and tell them of the plum he has plucked from the Judge's garden, fully ripe (Lu Kang). Daranee, meanwhile, lies in their marriage bed reminding herself of her husband's essential humanity (Um Ta).

The next week, Praphan returns to the brothel. Marriage clearly hasn't altered his carnal behavior (Lu Kang), except that now he comes home to a wife who pours his drunken, reeking body into bed, removes his shoes, massages his feet, all the while waxing poetic about his importance to the nation and the potential significance of his work as a public servant (Um Ta).

Difficult as it had been, in light of the playwrights' cross-purposes, to write these scenes, the arguments over the scene that ended on that ripped out page 63 had been worse, for originally, Um Ta had wanted Daranee to die in this scene.

"I'd sooner spend my next five lives as a worm," Lu Kang had said, jumping up and down in the trailer where they'd worked, "than allow the characters, through all of act 3, to mewl over the meaning of her death and make a martyr of her, while Praphan moves through the stages of grief to some hypocritical personal salvation." Moreover, Lu Kang admitted he needed Daranee in the next act because she was a weak and self-deluded fool, easy for other characters to abuse, a vehicle to express the nightmarish version of humanity he'd acquired in the mines.

In the end, after weeks of wrangling, Lu Kang agreed to Daranee's death in childbirth as a dramatic device, but he would not allow it until the very last minute of the play. In exchange for the delay, Lu Kang allowed Um Ta to write that speech on page 63—the one he'd ripped from the scripts.

The actors were reading page 61, on which Praphan meets with his "business associates" in a rubber plantation to exchange sensitive information best not said aloud in a building that might be bugged. As they discuss profits and losses and the necessity for the bartenders at their silently owned brothels to water the drinks, their bodyguards pat everyone down for wires and guns. Then one of the corrupt politicians announces that a snitch of his—a drug addict who hangs around the fly-infested eateries on Sankatdongkam and Keararat Streets—has discovered the hiding place of the reporter who is blackmailing Praphan. The thugs ask Praphan if they should fix it so the reporter "is never a problem again."

On page 62, Praphan asks for a moment to himself. He wanders off to a secluded area while the other men joke about his newly acquired "delicacy." Alone, under a muted spotlight, a troubled Praphan paces back and forth and, in a soliloquy on page 63, shares his private, complicated, and as Um Ta has written them, entirely nuanced thoughts.

The actors were about to complete their reading of page 62. It was now or never for Um Ta to get page 63 to the stage. If he hesitated for one additional second, with his halting gait, by the time he reached the actors, they'd have closed their scripts, pulled cigarettes from their pockets, and re-inhabited their own lives instead of their character's. With ten copies of page 63 in his hand, Um Ta struggled out of his seat and stumbled toward the stage.

At the steps to the stage, he heard Lu Kang grunt with displeasure and, from the corner of his eye, saw his young collaborator spring from his chair, his one good arm extended in his direction.

Um Ta hurried to keep ahead of Lu Kang, bones grinding on bones in his aged hips and knees. He could feel his legs weaken and his heart skip beats. At the stairs, his knees failed him and he fell backwards, left foot twisting under the right. He heard a crack as he landed and felt a searing pain between his left ankle and knee, a knife-like stab that lasted only an instant because a far more intense pain replaced it, a crushing pain in his chest. His gaunt face contorted and his eyes closed with the weight of the mountain on his lungs. When he reopened his eyes, he saw Lu Kang's big swarthy face directly above his.

"I'm dying," Um Ta said and knew it was true.

"Cut the crap, you're not dying. You broke your leg. We'll carry you to the clinic."

"It's not my leg, it's my heart. Don't move me. I want to die in the theater." He could barely whisper.

"Don't you dare die on me. You can't. Not yet!"

Um Ta fought for breath.

"No," Lu Kang yelled. "We have work to do..." Lu Kang's face was a centimeter from Um Ta's shoulder.

Dimly, Um Ta saw the actors encircling the two of them.

"I saw you trip. I almost reached you in time." Lu Kang's voice cracked.

Um Ta felt moisture on his shoulder, and realizing he was feeling the young playwright's tears, managed to lift a hand to Lu Kang's cheek.

"Damn you, hang on," Lu Kang said, holding the frail hand in his. "You don't trust me to finish this play by myself! Remember?"

Um Ta gathered the last of his strength to whisper into his collaborator's ear. "Cut the crap, *Allifa*, of course I do."

Lu Kang grabbed the pages Um Ta's hand still clutched and pulled one loose. "Read," he said, holding page 63 out to the actor who played Praphan, the man he'd envied and wanted to sack.

"Now?" the actor said. "You want me to read at a time like this? What's the matter with you?"

"Damn you. Read or your fired."

PRAPHAN: *(to himself, soberly)* What is this unfamiliar feeling in me? I, who expect nothing but the most repulsive motives from everyone including myself. Why should I feel this queasiness in my belly at the thought of ordering the reporter's death? Too much salt cod and beer at lunch? *(starts to pace back and forth)* Or Daranee? There is no way for Daranee to learn of the reporter's murder. And even if she did, she couldn't link it to me, so why worry that my ordering his death will diminish me in her eyes? And what do I care what she thinks? What matters is staying out of jail. *(beat)* Yet I hear in my head all my wife says about me. As I fall asleep at night, I replay her words regarding honor and service to my country. Why are her sentiments so often with me? Why do I think of them at this very moment? *(rising agitation)* If I've disdained everyone's opinion, why would I consider hers now? People never change. They are stupid or cruel and without a choice in their character. *(Pauses, faces audience, lifts foot to a log.)* My business partners await my decision, but what shall I tell them? For the first time in my life, I don't know my own mind.

The Blanks

The Demon Kings must have been testing Kenchoreeve Pranaranasam, Ayama Na In Depth's most experienced tour guide—how else to explain his encounter with the Blanks? Soured on life, bent out of shape by ugly divorces, disgusted that their second marriages (to each other) had turned even uglier, Philip and Elise Blank had holed up for years in their big house with their big screen TV, reclusive and nursing their grudges. These two go-nowhere social misfits would never have crossed Kenchoreeve's path had not the Demon Kings, in their desire to win Kenchoreeve back, inserted into Philip and Elise's cranky psyches the uncharacteristic urge to travel to exotic far-eastern lands.

Darkly handsome, intense and earnest, Kenchoreeve Pranaranasam held up a sign with block letters spelling out "Mr. and Mrs. Blank" as the passengers disembarked from Ayama Na Air's Flight 262, a Boeing 717 that puddle-jumped every afternoon from a neighboring country to Pin Dalie Airport and back. Blithely unaware of the Forces of Evil challenging him, the thirty-five-year-old tour guide expected an ordinary airport meet and greet—he'd reassure the Blanks that their hotel was one of the city's finest, relieve them of their bags, and usher them outside to the air-conditioned van which Lien-Lo, his driver, had double-parked at the curb. In turn, he'd get to watch the Blanks relax the way all his clients did when they realized they were in his capable hands.

What Kenchoreeve didn't expect was that Philip and Elise wouldn't notice or care that he was competent, courteous, and smart or that they would treat him as though he didn't exist. But Philip and Elise Blank really were the tourists from hell, world class annihilators of anyone else's right to be treated with respect. Mean expressions pasted across their sweaty faces, they approached the customs counter shouting at each other as though they were still at home in the privacy of their marital apocalypse.

"Fuck you Philip," she shouted at him.

"Kiss my ass Elise," he shouted at her.

When he was a younger, more impetuous fellow, easily aggravated and without perspective, Kenchoreeve might have bailed on the Blanks. He'd have pulled out his cell phone, called his boss, and threatened to quit on the spot if Mr. Rookai didn't reassign these two to someone else. There were dozens of tour agencies in Pin Dalie, Ayama Na's capital. The political turmoil in the country had ended, Americans were flooding in, and thanks to his father, who'd been a language professor before the mayhem commenced, Kenchoreeve had superb English language skills. With his straight white teeth, abundance of energy, and nearly unaccented English, he could have strolled down the block from the offices of Ayama Na In Depth to Best Tours For Less and landed another tour gig in seconds. A couple of years ago, he probably would have done exactly that. Unless, of course, the tourists in question had the smell of big money about them, in which case he'd have plastered a phony smile on his swarthy face and grinned his way through the stint, unctuous, flattering, and angling for a humongous tip.

For the past two years, however, since the birth of his twins, Kenchoreeve Pranaranasam had been working on himself, endeavoring to cultivate wisdom and compassion, cleaning up his degenerate life, and struggling to perform his work with honor and integrity. No longer did he leave Ayama Na In Depth's clients in the lurch, but rather tried to see the good in them and give them a vision of his lovely, gentle country—a nation so much older, wiser, and sadder than theirs—that would lodge in their hearts and change them for the better. Moreover, when he couldn't offer a genuine smile to the tourists he served, he didn't smile at all. He was done being a whore for tips.

In other words, Kenchoreeve Pranaranasam was in the throes of a conversion to Virtue, exactly the condition that drove the Demon Kings mad. His resolve made them want to puke up their evil guts. From their viewpoint, down in the Netherworld, every soul that struggled toward Virtue tipped the balance of the planet in some stupid and sappy direction. The Demon Kings needed Kenchoreeve (and everyone else) to act from their basest instincts so humanity would collapse and the Forces of Evil could inherit the Earth.

"So what's it here—a hundred degrees?" Philip said as he plopped down his suitcase and scratched the crack in his ass.

Pin Dalie Airport's arrival and departure terminal was a single large room with doors open at each end and an inadequate air-conditioning system, always overwhelmed. Kenchoreeve handed Philip a bottle of ice water from his shoulder pouch and reached for Elise's bag.

"Hey what're you doing? Don't carry her bag. She can carry her own. You carry mine."

Kenchoreeve took Philip's bag in his other hand.

"Listen, if we're going to get along, I come first, understand?"

"Isn't he charming?" Elise said.

"Your van better be air conditioned." Philip's voice was so loud, Kenchoreeve took a step back.

"It is," Kenchoreeve said as he led the tourists he was destined to serve outside the terminal to the van at the curb.

"Good. Or your agency would have to give me a refund." Philip spoke to his back.

"Give him a break, Phil. He doesn't know you're just kidding. Maybe he's never been a tour guide for a couple of hedge fund managers before."

"Why don't you just shut your big mouth and get in the van."

※ ※ ※

Normally, when Flight 262 arrived on schedule, as it did that afternoon, Kenchoreeve followed the company itinerary and had Lien-Lo drive to the planned sightseeing stop on the way to dinner. After ascending a winding road up a hill to a monastery that overlooked all of Pin Dalie and climbing an additional forty-four steps on foot, tourists would find themselves staring at a pure white Buddha statue, fifteen feet tall, hands in the offering position. At the graceful iron railing in front of the statue, his clients could see breathtaking views of the tour's coming attractions: to the east, the capital city with the green and gold cupolas of the Royal Palace dominating the skyline; to the west, the skillful restorations of the magnificent ancient cities that had put Ayama Na on the tourist map.

But Philip wasn't about to climb forty-four steps. Philip was hungry. He needed to eat. So Kenchoreeve instructed Lien-Lo to skip the Monastery of the Offering Buddha and drive the twenty-one kilometers from the airport straight to Pho Nac Lam, the well-lit, linen-napkin-clad tourist restaurant in Pin Dalie's Sector Seven.

It didn't surprise Kenchoreeve when the Blanks didn't speak to each other on the drive to the restaurant, but it did surprise him when they didn't say a single word to him. Usually, on their first drive through the thinning forests and sprawling factories of Ayama Na's outskirts, his clients craned and twisted their necks right and left, asked questions, and listened with rapt attention as Kenchoreeve explained local agricultural problems and the infusion of foreign capital responsible for the new roads and hotels under construction along the route. But Philip and Elise, in their travels through the neighboring countries, must have seen enough diseased teak trees, sprawling cell phone factories, and creeping commercial ventures, for they spread themselves out in the van's middle seats, heads flung back, eyes lidded, open mouths gulping inverted snores.

"Are they as bad as a I think?" Kenchoreeve whispered to Lien-Lo in their native tongue. Far more educated than Kenchoreeve but without his language skills, Lien-Lo had been Kenchoreeve's driver for the seven years he'd worked for Ayama Na In Depth. An architect before the country's political traumas, Lien-Lo was the same age Kenchoreeve's own father would have been had he lived.

"They're a challenge," Lien-Lo said.

Kenchoreeve glanced back at the Blanks, splayed out behind him and felt his spine grow cold with an icy chill that seemed to come from a cruel and sunless world. If Lien-Lo, with his hard-won detachment, categorized these two as a challenge, they could do him in. Every time the van hit a rut in the road, the Blanks jolted out of their comas for a second or two, grumbling and growling, burping and farting, until they crashed again. Finally, in front of the restaurant, as they stepped out of the van, Kenchoreeve heard their voices again.

Philip maneuvered out first, groaning with the effort of unbending his long legs. "What's taking you so long," he called to his wife, still in the van, hunting for something in one of her bags. Philip patted the round gut hanging over his pants. "I'm starving to death."

Kenchoreeve checked himself from thinking the ugly thoughts he used to think when his rich western clients uttered that expression. As if they had the slightest idea what starving to death meant. Stop it, he said to himself—an attempt to interrupt the image that came to him next: his emaciated father, at age forty-five, lying on his funeral pyre.

"Give me a break!" Elise shouted out the open door of the van. "You just ate on the plane."

"You call those hockey pucks food?"

"He's talking about sea urchin cakes, your national delicacy," Elise called out to Kenchoreeve, her tone a complex combination of the messages she wanted to convey—conspiratorial cunning, as though she and Kenchoreeve were in this together, dealing with a precocious but difficult child, and pride in herself for having read up on Ayama Na's cuisine in *The Lonely Planet*.

"I don't care if they're the national jock strap. They taste like hockey pucks," Philip said. "And would you get the hell out of that car!"

"I'm looking for the cameras. I'm not leaving them in the van."

"Didn't you hear him? He said the driver would stay with the van. Leave that stuff there."

"I'm taking the digital. You want to lose two thousand pictures?"

"Do you see that? Do you see what I have to put up with? What did you say your name was...Kimchee? Isn't that some kind of cabbage thing they serve around here?" He laughed and stared hard at Kenchoreeve, waiting for him to laugh too. Kenchoreeve lost his focus and regressed to grin.

Down in the Netherworld, the Demon Kings prodded each other with the tips of their pitchforks and chuckled. So far so good.

⊠ ⊠ ⊠

"Let's talk about this itinerary," Elise said the next morning in the van. They'd begun the drive to the Royal Palace, a cluster of jewel-encrusted buildings, including a massage school and a temple with eighteenth century frescoes, maintained by the royal family in opulent splendor. Elise held the three sheets of paper topped with the Ayama Na In Depth letterhead that Kenchoreeve had put in her hand at the airport. The itinerary itemized three days of activities, hour by hour, from pickup to drop-off. "Listen," she said. "You have to cross this afternoon's arts and crafts shops off the list. And ex out the Artisan Village thing on the schedule tomorrow. I couldn't care less how they make paper umbrellas or that shiny black shellacked crap. I didn't spend twenty-four hours on a plane to buy stuff I can get at the Cost Plus in Great Neck."

"Fifty percent cheaper," Philip said with his mouth full of Red Vines he'd pulled from Elise's daypack.

"Right," Elise continued, chuckling at her husband's remark. "We didn't sign on with Ayama Na In Depth to see salesmen at work in some junkshop. We want to get to know how the real people of Ayama Na live."

The real people? The real people sold things so their families could eat. How did it get more real than that? "I understand," Kenchoreeve said, feeling his resolve slide into a pit of black. Already, he was experiencing serious *patchukai-lem*—reliving red-hot contempt for the tourists he'd guided. In Kenchoreeve's opinion, people who gawked at his country had an obligation to shop. It was the price they paid for the right to treat Ayama Na as if it were a human zoo or a third world theme park.

"Good. That's settled. No shopping," Elise said.

Philip snickered. "Sorry, Kimchee, there goes your kickback!"

"Philip, that's disgusting!"

"Elise, what is your problem? He knows I'm joking. See, Kimchee, that's what I'm talking about. This ball buster has been crushing my nuts for twenty years. She never lets up. This is the story of my life. I have migraines. I have ulcers. She's trying to kill me."

"And," Elise said, ignoring her husband's insults as if they were the background music of her everyday life, "I'm not riding on an elephant. No e-le-phant. Is that understood?"

"Good news for the elephant," Philip said, shoveling more Red Vines in his mouth.

Kenchoreeve skipped the commentary he'd normally deliver to help his clients better appreciate the Royal Palace: the lineage of the royal family, the reality of their influence. He reached over and upped the van's A-C setting from 21 to 27. Let these two stew in their own bitter sweat.

The Demon Kings, keeping close watch, erupted in merriment at the tour guide's insurrection, evidence that the old Kenchoreeve Pranaranasam was but a scratch below his new moral surface. To remind themselves of the prize they were winning back, they played videos of Kenchoreeve's behavior prior to his renovation. They watched him imbibe intoxicants late into the night and show up at his clients' hotels on subsequent mornings hungover and unshaven. They stomped their feet and hooted as he seduced the teenage daughter of a perfectly decent couple from Dubuque on a trip to the Northern Forests. And they doubled over with laughter when, to answer tourists' questions about historic monuments and great temples, he concocted facts out of thin air. How could they have let this nasty piece of work nearly slip from their grasp?

It was carelessness, that's what it was—complacency on the Demon Kings' part. When Kenchoreeve vowed to be faithful to his wife and an inspiration to his twin sons, the Demon Kings told themselves they needn't worry about an indolent tour guide who refused to believe in Samsara or the Sacred Precepts and who, in consequence, had to practice Virtue solely for its own sake. What were the odds of his succeeding at that? They'd turned their attention to more significant scoundrels, abusive priests and crooked politicians, for instance, and by the time they noticed Kenchoreeve again, Virtue had pushed its way in. Now, thanks to Philip and Elise, they could relax. It would take a Buddha to find the good in the Blanks. Kenchoreeve Pranaranasam didn't stand a chance.

※ ※ ※

The next morning, when Philip and Elise were late descending the carved teak staircase that led from the guest rooms of the Pan Pin Dalie Pacific to its sumptuous lobby, Kenchoreeve found himself wishing they'd spent the night vomiting or marching back and forth from the bed to the bathroom so they'd have to bow out of the day's tourist activities. The night before, at dinner, the two had gobbled down foods cited by every Ayama Na guidebook as absolute *no-nos*, including raw salads and gooey custard desserts. Unrefrigerated for hours and incubating germs, those custards turned into bacterial cultures that Kenchoreeve, himself, would never have ingested. Please, he thought, let them be ill.

He acknowledged the lack of compassion in his wish, but if the fates granted him this day's respite, he'd redouble his efforts to find the good in these two. He swore to this on his sweet young sons' innocent heads.

Then there they were, the gleaming teak spiral staircase creaking under their weight. Philip, with his balding dome and his paunch and his nasty expression, came into view first, and ten steps back, hauling her heavy daypack bulging with guidebooks and cameras and snacks, huffed and puffed Elise, rushing to catch up, her pale blue eyes staring out above her wide, flushed cheeks. Philip marched to the breakfast buffet as it was being cleared, shouting to the waiters, "Hey, where you going with that?" He grabbed a banana and stuck it under his arm, then filled his hands with sweet rolls and spicy steamed buns.

"Get some for me," Elise shouted across the lobby.

"Get your own," he shouted back, and Elise put down her daypack and, as fast as her she could, rushed across the lobby to the Pan Pin Dalie Pacific's feeding trough.

As Kenchoreeve watched the two shove sweet rolls and unpeeled fruit in their mouths while hoisting themselves into the van, it seemed to him that Philip and Elise could drink the filthy brown water that ran in the city's gutters without getting sick. It was as if some alien force protected their bodies from liver diseases and the intestinal parasites to which the most careful tourists succumb. Meanwhile, Kenchoreeve's stomach flipped and flopped, sweat beaded on his forehead, and although he hadn't eaten in eighteen hours, if he had to guess, he'd be the one telling Lien-Lo to pull over so he could squat behind a bush at the side of the road.

Then he figured it out—it was fear doing this to him, not fear of the Blanks, but fear of himself, of regressing to the amoral individual he once was. There was so much noise to contend with, both inside his head, where his former temptations taunted him, and inside the van, where these two beached whales cleared their blowholes with every breath, that if he didn't struggle to remind himself of his goals, he'd soon be drinking himself blotto and fornicating with prostitutes.

To grab hold and do his best for the Blanks, he decided to deliver the scripted commentary and his learned embellishments, whether they heard him or not. "Today's first stop, a fifth century temple, has been declared a UNESCO World Heritage Site," he said to no one because no one was listening.

Lien-Lo looked at him with a raised eyebrow.

"Built by Jalamandu the Second, this extraordinary complex represents the height of Ayama Na's artistic and cultural achievements." In the last two years, Kenchoreeve had studied every fresco, frieze, and statue of this incomparable national treasure. As Lien-Lo drove, Kenchoreeve discoursed on the temple's history and outlined the religious influences of the statues and shrines his currently narcoleptic clients would soon witness for themselves.

Shaken awake when Lien-Lo opened the door, Philip slid out, unkinked himself, and took a quick look around. Elise followed, camera dangling from her neck, bottle of water in her hand. The magnificent temple loomed across the moat a few yards in front of them. "Jesus," Philip said, "More old rocks? I'm sick of this shit! I'm getting back in the van."

"You didn't come all this way to sit in a car. This is one of the seven wonders of the world," Elise said.

"I've seen enough temples for one lifetime. I'm staying right here. I'll talk to Leno."

"Lien-Lo doesn't speak English," she said, "and you don't speak Ayama Nan. That'll be some conversation."

"Oh yeah? Shows you what you know. Hey, Leno." Philip waited for Lien-Lo to face him and when he did, Philip said, "Oogle boogle oogle google boogle," paused for a breath and repeated the gibberish.

"See? Look at that," Philip poked Elise. "Leno here's smiling. We understand each other, don't we Pal?"

"Philip, do you think you're funny?"

"You know what's the matter with you, Elise? You have no sense of humor, that's what. Besides that, you're a moron."

"Could you say that a little louder so everyone in this parking lot can hear what a sweetheart you are?"

"See, Leno, see what a humorless bitch I have to live with?" Philip climbed back into the van and lit up a cigar as Elise and Kenchoreeve walked toward the bridge that led over the moat to the temple. They returned before he took his last puff. Elise had snapped photos from ground level, declined to climb the steps to the towers or the frescos, and decided it was too hot to tromp around to the back of the temple. Kenchoreeve realized that she was lost without Philip, actually in a rush to get back to him. What was the matter with her? Why did she remain with him?

"It was great, you should have come," Elise said as Lien-Lo handed her a fresh bottle of water from the cooler. The van stunk of cigar smoke.

"Yeah? If it was so terrific, how come you're back so fast?"

"It's hot out there."

"I knew this would happen. I knew it. It's really stupefying how dumb you are. You hate heat and you pick countries to visit that are smack in the middle of the equator. Are you too stupid to read a map?"

"You wanted to come here. You said you did."

"Like hell. This whole vacation was your idea. It's costing my children their inheritance and now you're too hot to sightsee? You give me heartburn. You got antacids in here?" He threw the daypack at her.

She reached in, extracted a bottle of pills, and threw the bottle at him. It bounced off the door and hit the side of Kenchoreeve's face.

"Not a problem," Kenchoreeve said, smiling maniacally and rubbing his cheek. *Ack chee mi yobut*, he'd kill for a drink.

※ ※ ※

In the pre-dinner break built into the itinerary, Kenchoreeve Pranaranasam resisted that drink, although the Cho Phat bar, around the corner from the apartment building he lived in with his wife and twin sons, tempted him as it hadn't in the previous two years. He could feel how that cool beer would slide down his throat, past his tonsils, and into his gut. But after Lien-Lo dropped him off, he hurried up the three flights of narrow stairs to his flat and played with his wonderful boys until the van returned to pick him up.

Dinner with the tour guide, included in Ayama Na In Depth's package each night, was the highlight of the Blank's day and the low point of his. Every time he entered a restaurant with them, he exceeded Mr. Rookai's food allowance by at least fifty percent. They'd insist he order extra dishes, wrestle each other for the steaming bowls, and not shut their mouths until they'd eaten the last shred of fish and grain of rice. Meanwhile, Kenchoreeve would sit there, losing his appetite, miserably picking at egg curds, and trying not to add to the aversion polluting his mind.

As the van approached the Pan Pin Dalie Pacific, Kenchoreeve closed his eyes and rubbed his temples, fortifying himself for the ordeal ahead. When he opened his eyes, Lien-Lo pointed down the road, where Elise plodded along on the shoulder. Having wandered beyond the Pan Pin Dalie Pacific's sanitized zone, she was threading her way through ugly city litter and ragged piles of canine excrement. She carried nothing with her—no purse, no daypack, no water bottle.

Lien-Lo halted the van alongside her as she started across the street to avoid a trio of ravenous dogs fighting over a chicken carcass that had spilled from an upended garbage pail. Back of her shirt soaked with sweat, oily beads of perspiration glistening on her forehead, she gestured the van away and kept walking, but when the mangiest cur let out a vicious growl and bared its teeth at her, she climbed in. She grabbed a tissue and blew her nose.

"It isn't safe for you out here alone, Elise. Where were you going?" Kenchoreeve said.

"For a walk. Where do you think?" Her tone was defiant, but her vocal cords squeaked. She'd been crying.

"Is everything all right?" Kenchoreeve asked.

"I'm locked out of my room."

"Ah. I'll speak to a desk clerk. She'll give you another key."

"I don't need a key. Philip's in the room. Figure it out."

Kenchoreeve felt a sudden jolt of chivalry kick in, a desire to protect her. That schoolyard bully didn't scare him. "I'll phone him from the lobby and tell him it's time for dinner?"

"I wouldn't do that if I were you. He's temperamental."

"Well then. We'll go to dinner without him."

"Of course not," she said. "What fun would that be?"

Kenchoreeve and Lien-Lo exchanged glances.

Elise saw the look that passed between them. "You don't understand."

"What don't we understand?"

"You don't understand anything." She thought for a moment. "You two are off the hook. Night's over for you. See you tomorrow."

Kenchoreeve should have run up those stairs to his apartment again, but when Lien-Lo drove away, he rounded the corner. The blue and yellow neon *Yama Hi* sign in the Cho Phat window winked at him, and while he stood there, coils of cigarette smoke reached out the open bar door and lassoed him in. Before he knew it, he was on a barstool, feeling sorry for himself.

Virtue? Where had it gotten him? Confronted with a challenge in the person of Philip Blank, his benevolent attitude had shriveled and collapsed. He hated Philip Blank. Period. End of story.

He wanted a drink. And when good and drunk, he would phone Mr. Rookai's sexy sister-in-law and see what he could arrange for the rest of the night.

"*Yama Hi,*" he said to the bartender, intending to obliterate all recall of his renovated self. And of Elise, of her anguish and her brave smirk as she exited the van and walked into the lobby. He and Elise—undone by Philip Blank.

What would Elise do? Sit at the hotel bar all night the way he sat here? Or worse—would she wander again into the dark ugly streets?   Couldn't he at least have made sure she was safe tonight before abandoning her and hitting the bar? He had connections at the Pan Pin Dalie Pacific, the young female desk clerks who invariably flirted with him and suggested aloud that he cheat on his wife. If he asked a favor, they'd assign her another room for the night—off the books and gratis, so Mr. Rookai would never discover that his premier tour guide had broken Ayama Na In Depth's crucial fourth commandment: Never interfere with your clients' interpersonal fights.

Kenchoreeve dialed Lien-Lo. He needed a ride back to the Hotel.

▩ ▩ ▩

The bartender remembered the big woman with the loose pink shirt and the curly blonde hair. She'd belted down three vodka gimlets, eaten a bowl of complementary peanuts, and then crossed the lobby toward the staircase. Kenchoreeve needed to see for himself that Philip had let her into the room.

As he walked up the stairs, he could hear Philip's loud voice screaming a firestorm of vituperation that both appalled and fascinated him. Although Elise tried to hold her own, she was no match for her husband's fierce and withering intelligence. As Kenchoreeve stood outside their door, transfixed by their insults, the conversation abruptly became about him.

"You picked this ridiculous tour company. It's your fault we're saddled with this idiot tour guide."

"He's trying his best. He's following the itinerary," Elise said.

"Yeah, well he's not doing jack for us. I told him I was sick of these fucking rocks, and what's on tomorrow's agenda? Three more piles of rocks and the National Museum of Rocks and Sticks."

"They're world-famous tourist sites," Elise said. "What in god's name do you want to see?"

"How the fuck should I know? This is his country. He's the expert. Let him tell me."

"We bought the Asian Treasures package. He's doing what we're paying him to do."

"You're as big a fool as he is. We're not paying him to follow an itinerary. We're paying him to keep us happy. That's what we bought!"

"Nothing makes you happy, your royal highness."

"At least you've finally got the form of address right. Now get out of my sight."

"Where do you expect me to go?"

"Who cares? Stay in the bathroom or pull the blanket over your head. I'm sick of you."

The last thing Kenchoreeve heard, as he fled down the stairs, was Elise sobbing her heart out.

⊠ ⊠ ⊠

Nights in Pin Dalie were hot, dark, humid, and permeated with sour slum smells, but Kenchoreeve decided to walk the nine kilometers back to his apartment to clear his head. As Lien-Lo drove away, Kenchoreeve tried to recall a single client in the last two years who had criticized his work even mildly, let alone with the vehemence Philip did, and he couldn't think of one. Many, in fact, e-mailed his boss praising his skills. He always followed the itineraries Mr. Rookai cranked from the computer for Ayama Na In Depth's clients. Two days? The Five-Temple Package; three days, the Seven-Temple Package; four days, the Ten. A shrine here, a monument there, a few shopping ops, a museum in the middle—fill up the hours, keep the route logical, don't waste gas. You think *ghrees* grow on trees around here? Mostly, it worked, or if it didn't, the tourists he served, polite and appreciative, kept their complaints to themselves. But clearly, he'd failed the Blanks. Bored with his country, frustrated with him, they'd been reduced to amusing themselves with cruelty to each other.

Philip was right—he hadn't done squat for them. When Philip refused to get out of the van at the sightseeing stops, Ayama Na's number one tour guide hadn't given so much as a moment's thought to revamping the itinerary to account for idiosyncrasy, inclination, or personal taste. Kenchoreeve looked at his watch. He still had a full day left as the Blank's tour guide. He'd do right by them, itinerary be damned.

Kenchoreeve didn't return to the bar. He went home and slept in his bed next to his wife. Down in the Netherworld, the uneasy Demon Kings redoubled their efforts.

⬚ ⬚ ⬚

"Today we're going to Lake Sporee," Kenchoreeve told Lien-Lo early the next morning.

"But Mr. Rookai..."

"Don't worry about him. I let him know the new itinerary," Kenchoreeve said, bending the truth to his higher purpose. He'd left Mr. Rookai a phone message, explaining the change in plans and reminding him of the motto emblazoned on the Ayama Na In Depth brochure. "We Aim to Please." Then he shut off his cell phone so Mr. Rookai couldn't call him back.

Mr. Rookai never included Lake Sporee on an Ayama Na In Depth tour. The narrow dirt access roads, deeply potholed and strewn with debris, played havoc with Ayama Na In Depth's expensive air-conditioned vans. But if Kenchoreeve had to repair the vehicle at his own expense, he didn't care. He owed the Blanks this trip. They wanted a slice of life, he'd give it to them. At the lake, he'd rent the least dilapidated skiff in the row of docked skiffs and instruct the skipper to motor slowly through the shallow inlet toward the center of the lake, passing along the way sun-darkened, rough fishermen in bare-bones rowboats, hundreds of them, hunched over nets or casting their lines. As the skiff motored past the columns of crude floating homes, naked children would wave from the decks or hold up strainers they'd dipped into the stinking water to show off an anchovy or a couple of shrimp they'd managed to snag. On the houseboats, barefoot women with deeply weathered skin, busy drying yesterday's catch, would turn the fish their husbands pulled in. The skiff would pass the floating school, a floating market, a floating general store and the Blanks would see for themselves the precariousness of this existence—food, shelter from the elements, and the bare necessities of life eked out day after day through unrelenting hard work. Kenchoreeve wouldn't bore the Blanks with a single spoken word. Silently, they'd observe the hardships of his most impoverished countrymen's lives, and moved at last by this poignant land, they'd return to America improved versions of themselves.

All this seemed inevitable as he walked home from the hotel in the dark of night. In the morning, however, Kenchoreeve weighed the venture's downsides. He discounted as a minimal inconvenience the stench of the water, the litter and sewage, but he had to acknowledge the savage mosquitoes and treacherous flies at this time of year. He'd warn the Blanks in advance and spray them with insect repellent—the highest concentration of DEET in the anti-bug arsenal.

"Biting insects?" Philip said.

"How long did you say it takes to get there?" Elise asked.

"Was this your brilliant idea, Elise? Did you put him up to this? Or did the genius figure it out all by himself?"

"It was my idea," Kenchoreeve said, his mind refusing to take in what was happening here, believing for an instant that Philip was complimenting him. "You've tired of relics and expressed a desire to see how the real people of Ayama Na live."

Elise's laugh was nervous. "You can't tell me everyone real in this country lives on a houseboat, can you?"

Kenchoreeve felt poisonous snakes wind around his ankles and calves. "Who do you think the real people are?" he said.

"Well, I think..."

Philip interrupted. "I'll tell you who the real people are, Kimchee. They're you—that's who. How 'bout we find out who you are?"

It was outside the powers of the Demon Kings to put words in people's mouths, but Philip Blank had reached perfection all by himself. Under the best of circumstances, Kenchoreeve bristled when his clients pried into his life. Americans were the absolute worst—they needed to be your friend, as if friendships could be struck in three or four days, as if they could know you in that time or take the measure of your happiness and suffering. Inevitably, they asked about his marriage, his kids, his childhood, his siblings, or most offensive of all, about his parents and their lives. In his recent virtuous years, to remain kind and courteous, he'd think the phrase "cultural differences," and assume his clients thought buying a tour package entitled them to ask their guide questions the citizens of Ayama Na wouldn't dare ask one another.

In the seven years he'd known Lien-Lo, for example, Kenchoreeve had never asked him what he'd done to survive his years of forced labor in the fields and mines or why he'd lived when Kenchoreeve's father had died. It was none of his business. People did what they had to do to get through those unspeakable times.

As for the Blanks, if they didn't want to go to Lake Sporee and see the fishermen's lives for themselves, he'd follow Mr. Rookai's itinerary to the letter—three piles of rocks and the museum of rocks and sticks. And he'd be damned if he'd answer a single personal question.

"So Kimchee," Philip said, "Let's see who you are."

"Many consider the first temple on today's itinerary the best restoration in the tenth century complex," Kenchoreeve said. "We will approach this small gem of Ayama Nan architecture from the east entrance to get a clear view of the famous three-headed lion."

"First question," Philip said. "How much do you hate Americans?"

"What kind of thing is that to ask?" Elise said. "You think he's going to tell you he hates you?"

"Yeah, okay, she's right. For once in her life. I'll re-phrase the question. Kimchee, what's your opinion of that motherfucker Henry Kissinger?"

Kenchoreeve bit down hard on his lower lip. "The monument you will see in a few minutes was built by Jalamandu the Third to honor his son, slain on the bat-tlefield. Carved of pink sandstone..."

"Hey, I asked you a question," Philip said.

The snakes coiled around Kenchoreeve's ankles slith-ered to his kneecaps and tightened their grip. "I have no opinion. I'm thirty-five. I was a child then."

"I bet your parents went through some kind of hell. Maybe they didn't bother to mention it."

"Our country invited the Americans to come in and help."

"Is that what they teach you to say in Tour Guide School?" Philip turned to Elise. "He thinks he's com-promising his tip if he tells the truth. He doesn't realize I tip people bigger who despise that fascist pig. You think Kissinger was a fascist pig, don't you Kimchee? Isn't that what you think?"

"Jesus, Philip, give him a break."

"No. You give me a break, Elise. For once, I'd like to hear these guys admit how America screwed them over and how much they hate us. I'd be grateful for some honesty around here."

"Our country thanks you for your generous foreign aid," Kenchoreeve said.

"Which your corrupt government skims right off the top." Philip waved his hands at the thatched-roofed huts the van was passing on both sides of the road. "Where's the electricity? Where's the indoor plumbing? I bet ninety-five percent of the money that flows in here disappears before it's ever logged in."

Kenchoreeve turned to face front, a fire inside him. A thousand snakes hissing.

"I think you made him uncomfortable," Elise said.

"That's what's wrong with you, Elise. You assume everyone's as ignorant as you. You think he doesn't know what I'm talking about? You think he doesn't read a newspaper or a history book? Trust me, he understands graft and corruption. The greed at the top in this country makes that cocksucker on the third circuit bench look like Thomas Jefferson. Uncomfortable? Don't give me that shit. Grow up, would you please. It's a relief for him to have it out in the open!"

"I'm just saying..."

"Well just stop saying. I heard enough out of you. You're as big an idiot as my idiot brother. That's the story of my life. I'm outnumbered by fools."

"You're sick, Philip,"

"I'm sick? No, you're sick. I've been waiting for years to hear something intelligent come out of your mouth."

"We're here," Lien-Lo said in halting English.

"Well, what do you know? Another country heard from. Look who speaks English." Philip flung his head back and closed his eyes. "Do me a favor, don't wake me up until this useless trip is over." In thirty seconds, his snores filled the van. To Kenchoreeve's ears, they sounded like pitchforks landing on the roof of the car.

⊞ ⊞ ⊞

To return to the Pan Pin Dalie Pacific, Lien-Lo took a route he usually avoided. He approached the city from due North, through the sleazy Sector Nine where rag-clad beggars lined the streets and bridges, hoping to extract a few coins from the vehicles that inched by. Among the indigents, you could observe the tragedy of the mines— one-armed amputees, one-legged on crutches, no-legged in wheelchairs, their skinny cupped hands outstretched and clutching the air.

While Philip slept, Elise stared out the window. "Oh god," she said, a hand flying to her mouth. "You have to see this." She poked Philip until he woke from his stupor. She pointed out the window. "Look at this. Oh god, I can't stand it."

Philip forced himself from his slouch. "Hey Kimchee," he said after viewing the scene, "The bimbo here is sensitive. It bothers her to see people without arms and legs. What're you going to do about it?"

Kenchoreeve twisted in his seat until he stared straight into Philip's eyes. "I'll give Leno a stick," he said, "and send him ahead to shoo away the cripples. Anything to please you and your lovely wife."

The stunned look on Philip's face lasted only a second before it changed to a smile. "Now you're talking, Kimmie. You see, Elise? What'd I tell you? This guy hates us. Finally we're getting what we paid for—Ayama Na in depth."

Horrified at his disrespect of a client, Kenchoreeve said, "There was no excuse for that, Philip. I apologize."

"Why?" Philip said, putting a hand on the tour guide's shoulder. "You don't have a single thing to be sorry for."

"See," Elise said gently. "See what a good person he is? That's what you didn't understand. Now do you get it?"

※ ※ ※

In fact, Kenchoreeve did get it. Suddenly he understood what he'd never understood before. He understood that Elise loved her husband because if she didn't love him, if she let herself hate him, her hatred would be a bottomless pit. And he understood that two years ago, he—Kenchoreeve—had made the same choice with the people he guided. For who, in this demon-infested life, was truly worthy to be loved? And yet, because the alternative destroyed your soul, you had no other choice. If Kenchoreeve followed the trail backwards, he could blame the Americans for his father's death, for his mother's paralyzing depression, for his brother's malaria, for the dengue fever that killed his youngest sister and her unborn child. He could loathe and despise every American he ever met. They were spoiled, soft as mush, blind to history, full of themselves. They were gawkers, false moralists, and deluded about the meaning of friendship. If he had a *ghree* for every American who invited him to look them up and even to stay with them when he came to the States, he'd be a millionaire by Ayama Nan standards, but he still wouldn't have the plane fare to New York or L.A. Had anyone ever offered him that? He'd never even traveled to Ayama Na's neighboring countries where his jet-lagged clients with money to burn, ran around sightseeing like bug-eyed simians.

At least Philip didn't patronize him, didn't want to be his friend, and didn't care what Kenchoreeve thought of him. Between them was a business contract. Nothing else. In the end, maybe Philip Blank was the least hateful American he'd ever met.

* * *

In the morning, when he picked Philip and Elise up for transfer to the airport, he had the odd thought that Philip's belly, bursting the buttons on the stained yellow and white striped shirt hanging over his pants, was like the belly of the Chinese Buddha that stared out of the glass windows of Pin Dalie's souvenir shops. At the terminal, at the moment of parting, he shook Philip and Elise's hands and spoke words he meant. "It's been good to spend these three days with you."

Elise said, "Likewise," and Philip said, "Yeah, right, who gives a shit," which made Kenchoreeve grin.

"What're you laughing at?" Philip fished in his pockets. He stuck a crumpled wad of *ghree* in Kenchoreeve's hand. "The moment you've been waiting for," he said as he turned and walked away. Elise, as usual, brought up the rear, struggling to catch up to her husband of twenty years.

Kenchoreeve watched the two of them move through the gates, people stepping aside in their wake, reminding him of the joke a computer salesmen from Texas he once guided told him when Lien-Lo drove past an ox asleep in the mud: Where does a ten ton rhinoceros sleep...

When all that he could still view of his latest clients was the top of Philip's shiny bald head, he still could hear him baiting Elise. "Hey, genius, get over here. Whaddya doing? You want to miss the plane?"

Smiling, Kenchoreeve opened his fist and straightened the *ghree* Philip had put in his hand. Philip had given him the exact tip suggested in the guide books, not one *ghree* more or less—the equivalent of three dollars a day, splitting the last day's tip in half because Flight 253 departed at noon. Kenchoreeve hadn't felt this light in years. It occurred to him to celebrate with a beer. But he wouldn't do that. He was scheduled to meet Flight 252 when it returned later that afternoon with his next set of tourists, four retired kindergarten teachers from a suburb near Memphis. *Ack chee mi yobat*, they'd bore him to death.

⊞ ⊞ ⊞

Down in the Netherworld, the abashed Demon Kings shouted and fumed. Whose big idea were Philip and Elise anyhow? Oh wretched judgment, oh over-played hand. Confused and baffled, the Demon Kings knew defeat—their loaded gun had fired blanks. The Earth still tilted in that sappy direction. Would that they had picked as their agents of Kenchoreeve's downfall a carload of polite, soft-spoken hypocrites.

"Damn, damn, damn, damn." The Demon Kings breathed the word on their fiery breaths. Damn those two. Worse than useless, that's what they'd been. The Demon Kings couldn't bear the sight of them for a single additional second. With a snap and a fizzle, they cut the Blanks loose.

⊞ ⊞ ⊞

"Good trip," Elise said, wedging herself into the plane's seat.

"Yeah," Philip said, patting her knee. "I have to give it to you. You did a lot of work putting this vacation together. Where we going next?"

"How about Antarctica?"

"Sure, why not. First we roast, then we freeze to death. You got any other brilliant ideas?"

"People say it's gorgeous down there. Totally peace-ful. You cruise out of Tierra del Fuego."

"Swell. A week of eating penguin meat."

"Tastes like chicken, dear."

"Can't be worse than these hockey pucks. What is this shit?" He stuffed a sea urchin cake between his teeth.

"That's what I love about you, Philip, you'll eat anything that fits in your mouth."

"You know what I love about you?"

"What?" She looked at him expectantly.

"Give me a week, maybe I'll think of something."

"Fuck you," she said, laughing.

"Kiss my ass," he said, not unaffectionately.

"When we get home, remember you asked."

"Promises, promises," he said, eating the last of his sea urchin cakes. Then he reached over and speared two of hers.

A Ruined World

L ong ago, Mi-Moona surrendered to the inevitable and stopped forbidding her son to run. He ran anyway, and every time she pointed a finger at him and issued her injunction, she suffered regret. Didn't a kid have a right to run wild even if his lungs burned and his legs screamed on the tiniest hill?

At the sound of Zori's labored breaths, those oxygen-starved gasps Mi-Moona heard as he rounded the bend, she dropped his wet T-shirts back to the basket and leaned in his direction. When she saw his blue-tinged lips, she reminded herself that freedom was his birthright as surely as the thing that was killing him. Otherwise she would have tied his puny body to the laundry pole so he'd outlive the ten years the city doctors predicted for him.

Zori's words caught on his breath as he wheezed out the single horrifying sentence that sent Mi-Moona's thoughts spinning in a different direction. This stinking tribe, she mumbled, as she tucked him under a muscular arm and ran with him past the next fourteen dwellings, each a two-room hut as primitive as hers—rough logs raised upon stilts, a pitched metal roof, and in the dank space between the floorboards and the earth, chickens and scrawny dogs scratching the dirt. As she rushed past the yards they blended together, littered with candy wrappers, half-melted crayons, cracked pencil stubs, the refuse of gifts to the tribal children from the truckloads of tourists hauled up the mountain to witness these innocent, unspoiled lives.

"Vee!" Mi-Moona yelled, her left arm still hoisting her son, her flat bare feet slapping the steps as her big legs tore up the stairs to the village shaman's house, a dwelling like the rest, although the yard was cleared of trash and the chickens and pig obviously well-fed, not because the tribe accorded this shaman respect but because her house stood first inside the village gates and the Ayama Na tourism bureau paid to let tourists fondle her potion jars and ask their dumb questions, such as how the change from a wandering life to this sedentary one had affected the tribe. As if they couldn't see for themselves the women grown fat, the scraggly tobacco fields pushing up spindly plants, the old men dribbling red betel gum juice onto their chests.

The elderly, white-haired V-47, like all the women of the tribe, like Mi-Moona herself, wore a garment as loose and floppy as the leaves at the top of a tobacco plant, billowing and expandable, although unlike everyone else's, V-47's was pure white, befitting her status as…what? A tourist trap, Mi-Moona thought, unwilling to grant Vee more status than that, although some fifty years earlier, she'd been the forty-seventh disciple of Fundabas Vee, the country's legendary aboriginal faith healer.

It is a fact that tigers no longer roam the exhausted forests of Ayama Na. The last ancient male died of old age and discouragement two decades ago. But Mi-Moona's only child imagined the woods alive with striped cats. Still, when he told V-47 what he'd seen at the river, she had reason to take this dreamy child at his word. The three retraced his steps, picking their way through jutting forest branches until they could see the yellow-green meadow and the insignificant trickle that at a lower elevation would join with other insignificant trickles to become the mighty Faro River.

Seated on a rock, head filled with who-knows-what fantastic conquests, Zori waited while V-47 and his mother descended to the bulge in the stream. Mi-Moona wouldn't let him revisit his discovery, but she feared that for the rest of her son's truncated life, he'd see in his mind's eye the sticky black hair on the bruised little head, the skin gray as a thunder cloud, the feathery eyelashes clotted with sedimentary muck, and the ropy thing sprouting from its belly button that must have looked to a six-year-old boy like a bleached river eel or a slimy white water snake.

By the time they ascended to the village again, a crowd had gathered, suspecting the object Vee had climbed down to fetch. "*Guhrse*," V-47 said, gesturing the word with her free hand—shooing them away as she waddled into her house to prepare the murdered infant for its ceremonial passage. At dusk, she led the tribe across the tobacco field and into the northwestern woods where a clearing had been carved from the pines for funeral pyres. V-47 placed the swaddled child atop the altar and kindled the fire that would obliterate the latest proof of her tribe's savagery.

V-47 required that the tribe witness the cremation in its entirety, every man woman and child, minus the thirty-six men who, in exchange for government subsidies, worked in Pin Dalie on a construction site for twelve months at a time, leaving thirty-six wives to satisfy themselves with other women's husbands and skinny teenage boys, infidelities that risked stoning and banishment. And risked as well, if luck wasn't on their side, the need to do away with the evidence of their adulterous meanderings.

Mi-Moona stood with Zori and Pol, her husband of ten years, a tawny, intelligent, cynical man, blistered by the futility of the tobacco fields. The harmonic grunts of Vee's sorrow chant rang through the night, evoking in Mi-Moona intense sorrow for the child's death, but also intense fury at how routine these funerals had become, this one for the twelfth infant murdered in this village in the last twenty-four months.

The stench of burning flesh fouled the air, but many in the gathering had already resumed their thoughtless everyday attitudes, gossiping and smoking as if at a party. Mi-Moona's older sister, Lo, with whom Mi-Moona had been on ugly terms as long as memory itself, stood amid a half dozen of her tribal women friends, a flock of overstuffed hens, their bodies adrift in their gigantic striped caftans, smoking cigarettes, whispering and swigging cheap government rum from an earthenware jug they passed hand to hand. While Mi-Moona watched, her sister clucked at a remark someone whispered to her, likely some rude crack about sex or a slanderous lie about Mi-Moona herself, for Lo's friends knew Lo thrived on talk of how Mi-Moona overprotected her child or didn't protect him enough, or how falsely humble she was or how she'd once again displayed her superior airs. These women with their network of gossip and spies surely knew who the murderer of this infant was.

"Look at my sister," Mi-Moona whispered to her husband who nodded and spat on the ground.

Lo strutted with impunity, above suspicion. Lo's husband, a quiet man who stocked and dispensed supplies at the tribal depot, slept beside her every night and loved her with a steadiness that mystified Mi-Moona, although to be fair, she would admit that Lo was an excellent mother to her daughter, Aleeta, and a better cook than any other woman in this lazy tribe.

And what of V-47? Self-righteous, deceitful in her condemnation of the crime, she had it in her power to discover the identity of the murderer, everyone knew that. Instead she chose ignorance, for if she chose otherwise, she'd have to act, and punitive action carried the potential for the rebellions and tribal splits that had occurred in other tribes when traditional authority clashed with popular desire. If Mi-Moona ever discovered the identity of one of these baby killers, she'd tell V-47 and everyone else, and V-47 would have no choice but to act. Mi-Moona promised herself that.

Off to Mi-Moona's side, at the margin of the clearing, a few teenagers laughed. Were these adolescents taking bets on when the next lifeless bundle would turn up? Or weaving their questions into lyrics for their makeshift pickup bands? *What you big ladies hiding in those big floppy dresses? Which one you staining rags with goat's blood to throw the Vee off the track? Which one you faked your monthly bloody messes? Which one you broke this here baby's little neck?*

Lyrics. That's what infanticide amounted to in this contemptible tribe that Mi-Moona's uncaring father had married her into, smug at securing for her a husband from the same tribe he'd five years earlier married her older sister into, ignoring the animosity between his daughters, ignoring the warnings of his wiser-but-weaker wife, may her soul return to a better life, who had begged him to think twice.

At least, Mi-Moona thought, the animosity hadn't passed to the next generation. The cousins, her son Zori and Lo's daughter Aleeta, were friends and when V-47 finally let everyone go home, admonishing them to sleep in their own beds, Zori and Aleeta walked across the tobacco field hand in hand.

The next morning Aleeta appeared at Mi-Moona and Pol's door, but instead of coming in to play with Zori, as she usually did, she invited Zori to play at her house.

"Zori can't go to your house without me, you know that," Mi-Moona said gently. Mi-Moona wouldn't let Zori visit his aunt without her, a rule that exacerbated the bitterness between the sisters. Lo vowed Mi-Moona could never again set foot in her house until she let Zori come there by himself—an impasse that had lasted for many months.

"My mother wants you to come too," Aleeta said. "She's making festival cakes."

Mi-Moona considered the invitation as she packed rice and yams into a pail for Pol's lunch. Perhaps Lo's rancor had used itself up.

"Don't go," Pol said. "It'll end like it always does between you two and I'll have an angry wife in my bed tonight."

Mi-Moona ignored his advice, and when she entered Lo's house, she kissed her sister's palm, a tribal gesture of respect from a younger female to an older one and, in this case, a deliberate peace overture.

The cakes glistened on the scrubbed wooden counter in Lo's greeting room. In their native tribe, too high in the mountains for tourist trucks, the men were industrious and the women talented. To make these cakes, which she and Lo had eaten at celebrations throughout their childhood, required hours of labor, a task no women of this tribe would undertake.

Spread in rows, the white-bordered black discs steamed, their soft centers congealing. Her sister added cakes to the cooking pan, one at a time, completing a third row and starting a fourth.

Once, in anger, Lo had smashed a festival cake on Mi-Moona's dress. The occasion had been Lo's own wedding. Mi-Moona had remained in the shadows to avoid seeking recognition for herself on Lo's marriage day, but Lo had accused her of the opposite motive, of obscuring herself to enhance her importance. "Where's Mi-Moona? Why isn't she dancing?" Lo had screamed at her when she'd found her, repeating the questions she claimed every guest had on their lips. In her envy, she'd grabbed a festival cake and ground it into Mi-Moona's skirt with her fist.

The first row of cakes had cooled enough for the children to eat, and Lo called them in from the yard. As Zori came through the doorway, Lo crushed him to her, enfolding him in her large arms. Mi-Moona would have liked to greet Aleeta with a similar ardor but she and Aleeta had adopted the habit of acknowledging one another only with their eyes, both of them wary of arousing Lo's envy by displaying feelings for one another, even out of Lo's sight. The tribal population lived on top of one another, and Lo had loyal spies.

Aleeta's character—her compassion, her caution, her stoic suppression of her own natural leanings—had been shaped by her mother's needs. Mi-Moona knew the signs.

"Help yourself, " Lo said to Mi-Moona after the children ran back outside. As Mi-Moona leaned toward the counter, she looked hard at her sister. Dark circles ringed her eyes and a strange yellow color had seeped into their whites. How would she feel if Lo died before they'd spoken of the bonds that united them—their mutual disappointment in their father, their sorrow at their mother's untimely and sudden death, their disgust with the indolent women of this tribe?

Mi-Moona almost reached out to Lo, but the moment passed. Lo turned and patted another cake into a perfect round shape in the pan over the fire. Mi-Moona praised the festival cake. How light it felt, how perfect its shape. Could she have the moment back? Would her sister turn and meet her eyes?

Mi-Moona took a bite and an unwelcome astringency assaulted her tongue. From where she sat, she could see out the doorway that the cake also tasted bitter to Zori who discretely dropped chunks to the ground, using the edge of his big toe to push sand on the crumbs.

"Aleeta looks well," Mi-Moona said, sounding trivial to herself. She tried to swallow the mouthful of dough.

"Why shouldn't she? I take care of her. Are you suggesting something different?" Lo popped the cap off a bottle of warm Coca-Cola.

"Of course you take care of her." Mi-Moona sighed. Here it was—the habitual unreasonableness on her sister's part, Lo dissecting her sentences, searching for excuses to be angry at her.

Mi-Moona took another bite of the cake. It drew the flesh inside her mouth to a point. Her sister, who could cook and bake with her eyes closed, had forgotten the sugar. A mute fear tugged at Mi-Moona's heart. "Is something wrong?" she said. Did her sister want a rapprochement before her death? Is that why she'd invited her here?

"What makes you think that?" Lo snapped.

"You seem distracted. You forgot the sugar."

"So, you are the expert now? You make these cakes better than I do?" Lo plunked two mugs on the table and filled them with the fizzy Coca-Cola.

Mi-Moona never made festival cakes. She knew better than to compete with Lo in the kitchen or anywhere else. Her sister had no idea the lengths Mi-Moona and everyone, including the children out there gamely eating or burying the bitter cakes, would go to avoid upsetting her. "You pick apart my sentences to see how you can twist my thoughts," Mi-Moona said. "You imply I want to hurt you. I came here with good intentions. You misinterpret me willfully."

"You're the one with the will. You ruined my wedding. Do you think I will forget that in this lifetime?"

"Enough about that wedding," Mi-Moona said. Lo nursed her grievances until her version of events, like weeds in a garden, smothered every useful plant. This was a subtlety about herself Lo never grasped. "I do nothing to hurt you. You only want to believe I do," Mi-Moona said, wondering if her words were true.

"You do nothing? In front of the whole tribe, you show me disrespect. You let Zori go to the river himself but you won't let him come to this house without you. Why is that?"

Mi-Moona dropped the rest of the cake on the table. "You ask me to explain? Then suffer the explanation. I let my child go to the river because the dangers of the river are nothing compared to the dangers here. In the stream are only water worms, eels, typhoid germs, and the possibility of drowning or finding a dead baby. But in this house, there's a woman who can't control herself. Since you hate me without reason, how do I know what you would do to my son?"

"You think I would harm hurt Zori?" Stung, Lo's eyes filled with tears. She crossed her arms over her huge chest.

Mi-Moona didn't respond. She'd said what she had to say.

"Why did you come here if I'm such a risk to your son? Take him and leave. Get out of my house."

In the yard, Zori stood in the protective embrace of Aleeta's arms, the children shielding each other from their mothers' loud and poisonous words. Mi-Moona took Zori's hand, but before she walked down the path, she put an arm around Aleeta and kissed the top of her head.

▨ ▨ ▨

Lo didn't look in Mi-Moona's direction as Mi-Moona walked away. She judged, by the length of time and the fading footsteps, when her sister and her nephew had traversed the curve and passed out of sight. Then releasing a long-held breath, Lo put her face in her hands and wept. The tips of her long fingers rested in her eye sockets while her palms, cupped under her jaw, pressed upward to stifle the sounds she feared she'd emit. Her heart felt sick of itself, tortured, and unmendable, and she expected she'd bray like a wounded, dying horse if she parted her lips. The sounds that escaped her clenched jaw approximated the yips of the chickens in the yard protesting empty water dishes. Her sister had no idea what she'd endured. No one did, not even her patient husband, Sose, from whom lately—and possibly for all of their marriage—she'd felt such a terrible distance.

She found herself listening for Mi-Moona's footsteps, craving Mi-Moona's return, even though she'd just evicted her from her house. Why did she long for Mi-Moona? Mi-Moona was the cause of her despair, the strongest link in the chain of her suffering, but aside from Mi-Moona, there wasn't a single woman in this tribe who recognized that she hurt. Her so-called friends weren't friends so much as acolytes, in awe of her energy and the skills she possessed. They fawned over her because they knew she'd one day take V-47's place. Even Sose, who should have understood, preferred detachment to the difficult struggle that might have saved her from herself. As the moments passed and with them the likelihood of her sister's return, the ache inside Lo intensified, the agitated fear that she could no longer bear the burden of her self. To whom, in her stubborn pride, could she turn? To whom could she confess? She listened for Mi-Moona's footsteps, but heard only the chickens' beaks pecking at pebbles and the soft rustling noises of Aleeta gathering the crayons and papers she and Zori had scattered.

Lo dried her tears with her baking rag and beckoned to Aleeta, at the same time sitting back in the hard wooden seat, spreading her ample arms and legs and loosening the fabric between her knees so her daughter could step into the angle of open limbs. Lo pressed Aleeta to her, stroked the child's hair and rocked her slim body back and forth, the feel of her in her arms calming her a little, enabling her to breathe, for in addition to her great love for this child, Aleeta represented every unselfish act of Lo's life. Aleeta justified the awful thing she had done. Never would Aleeta have to watch a newborn feed from her own mother's breast or hear a father *uuurfing* sweet baby talk at anyone else. Never would Aleeta witness a younger sister steal a parent's affection. Lo had seen to that.

The remains of Mi-Moona's festival cake lay on the table. Lo plucked it from the tabletop, crumbs tumbling onto Aleeta's hair as she took a bite. The sharp taste stung her gums. Mi-Moona had accused her of having forgotten the sugar and Mi-Moona had been right. Lo pushed her mind back through the cooking sequence: She'd awakened before dawn and tiptoed outside to mash the soaking taro root. She recalled adding the plantains, but not the sugar, for even after the sun had come up, the hot breath of her midnight guilt still wracked her thoughts. Her mind had broken in pieces—bits of dreams, bits of myths, the real and the unreal swirling and unfocused.

She pressed Aleeta closer to her, at the same time grabbing the rag she used to dry her own face. She let the wad of festival cake—a bitter lump she couldn't swallow— fall from her mouth into the rag's folds. "Did you eat a whole cake, Aleeta?" She felt Aleeta nod against her chest. "Did you like it?" Another nod. These nods made Lo's heart ache.

Lo smoothed Aleeta's hair from her face so she could kiss her forehead. Then she pulled her close again and sat that way for a long time, realizing only when Aleeta tried to turn her head, how suffocating her embrace must be. The sun had climbed to the middle of the sky and under the metal roof the heat in the house had become intense. They should have been outside, under a tree, sleeping the midday sun away, but Lo couldn't bear the scrutiny of her neighbors' eyes, the strength she'd have to pretend, the way she'd have to force her bright red lips, always glossed, always shiny, into that thing other people called her smile.

"Sit here," she said, releasing Aleeta and indicating another chair at their table.

Perspiration glistened on Aleeta's forehead and heat-reddened cheeks and her flimsy shirt was soaked with sweat. Lo pushed the glass of warm cola Mi-Moona had left untouched toward Aleeta. "Aunt Mi hid herself on my wedding day, did I ever tell you that?"

Aleeta gulped the dark fizzing liquid and peered at her mother over the edge of the mug, her small eyes watchful under their thick stubby lashes, her rippling black hair, loose and unkempt, tumbling over her low brow, framing her dark complexion, darker than Lo's, as dark as her father's, her hair also falling loose over her shoulders onto a childish chest, one as yet without any pubescent maturation that Lo could discern. Aleeta was not a beautiful child. She had Sose's coarse features, squat face, and short neck, but her intelligence, her patience, her soft husky voice added up to something every member of the tribe recognized as compensatory and exceptional.

Lo rose from the table and swept the festival cakes, one by one, from the counter into a small wooden pail, smashing them with the flat of her hand, each broken cake reconnecting her with her anger at her wedding. When the cakes were cleared, her hand was as sticky and stained as it had been after she'd smashed a cake onto Mi-Moona's skirt fifteen years earlier. The cake crumbs filled the pail. Later, she'd feed them to the dog and the chickens and throw the rest into the swill for V-47's overfed pig. She grabbed another rag to wipe her stained hands. "Your aunt claimed she wanted to make herself small and unnoticed so I'd get all the attention, but hiding made her the person in everyone's thoughts. Do you understand?"

Had Mi-Moona meant well at the wedding? The thought entered Lo's mind, but she brushed it away. She didn't want her daughter to feel love for her aunt or take her side. She wanted Aleeta to feel about Mi-Moona the way the rest of the women in this tribe felt. Even before Mi-Moona married Pol and took up residence among this tribe's women, Lo told stories about her sister designed to leave an impression of Mi-Moona's *abuva luph*, the holier-than-thou attitude disdained throughout tribal culture, so that when Mi-Moona joined the tribe, her deference toward Lo and intentional humility, both of which might have earned respect, would reinforce Lo's insinuations that Mi-Moona considered herself superior to everyone else, too haughty to party, too indifferent to cultivate friendships.

"What do you think of what Aunt Mi did?" Lo wanted to hear Aleeta criticize her aunt, but when Aleeta said, "Aunt Mi should have known hiding wasn't good," a stone hit Lo's heart from a direction she didn't expect. It wasn't relief she felt, but shame—a suspicion that her own mistrust and envy had corrupted her daughter's good nature, or worse, forced her to lie.

And for what? What sense did it make for her to work so hard to discredit Mi-Moona when she had so many attributes Mi-Moona lacked? Abundant personal magnetism, ambition, the ability to carouse yet keep herself sensible, qualities that had led V-47 to instruct her in the medicinal uses of herbs, in midwifery, and in tribal rituals so she could ascend to leadership after V-47's death. Why did none of this console her or keep her from needing to prejudice Aleeta?

"No matter what Aunt Mi did at your wedding, you married the best man in this tribe," Aleeta said.

Startled, Lo reminded herself that Aleeta, who adored her father, didn't know how she envied her sister's marriage. No one knew how thoughts of Pol excited her and how Sose bored her in bed every night. Although Pol thought himself better than everyone else, bragged, argued with the old customs, mocked traditional remedies, invoked his foolish "science," and reeked of *abuva luph* himself, whenever Lo spied the red welts of love on her sister's neck and breast, as she'd spied them that morning, two fresh red splotches on the collar bone, a thousand snakes writhed inside her.

Mi-Moona always triumphed! Even in having an ill child her sister had wounded her. The villagers treated Zori as if he were a reincarnation of a Buddha himself. When Zori ran through the village, a dozen voices called to him to slow his pace, a dozen hands patted his shoulder. Mi-Moona was pitied and considered a martyr because she bore this child, because her future held such a great sorrow.

"Aleeta," Lo said, "you will never suffer as I do."

"I won't, I promise."

"No, my jewel. You misunderstand. I promise you."

It occurred to Lo to go further, to confess to Aleeta what she'd done for her, to assign to her, in spite of her age, the wisdom to absolve and the power to forgive. Lo stopped wiping the stains from her hands, dropped the rag to the table and raised her eyes to her daughter. Skinny as a blade of grass, Aleeta sat there chewing on a fingernail, her eyes downcast, her nervous knees tap-tapping, and it struck Lo that she was looking at a child, that parents shielded children from the shocks of life, not the reverse. She pointed to the door. "*Guhrse*, my precious girl, go find a spot to play that's cooler than this one."

Still sticky with her mother's sweat, Aleeta ran down the back path that would join the path to her aunt's doorstep, a dangerous destination, but she didn't know where else to go with the terrible thing she knew. For months when she stood in her mother's arms, she'd felt a kick against her own body, thrusts from inside her mother's skin. This morning, while her mother held her tight, the kicking thing had vanished and she knew what her mother had done.

The children of the tribe, residing as they did in close quarters, were hardly ignorant of intercourse, pregnancy, and birth. Little ones feigned sleep or awakened in the night to animal-like grunts across the sleeping room. In the moonlight that came in through the thatched walls, they saw their parents big bodies stuck together, a vision acknowledged, like other phenomena of tribal life, in the teenagers' lyrics. *Hey little sister, what'd you see in the starlight? Hey little brother, did your PoPo dip a stick in the sugar cane last night?*

Aleeta's young legs carried her swiftly past the tobacco drying house, past old widow Ratana's, past the rusted looms (leftover of a failed weaving project the queen had initiated in this tribe years ago), past a house where the father worked in the city, past old Tong who stood on his top step chewing betel and humming to himself, ran until she reached her aunt's house. Her Aunt Mi and her cousin Zori were both sound asleep, lying on a sleeping mat unrolled in the shadow of the roof overhang. Mi-Moona's left hand rested lightly on the hip of her son whose labored breaths Aleeta had heard three houses away. She squatted next to them, waiting for them to wake up, one fist on the dirt to balance herself, the other hand feeling for the swelling in her left breast, the flower bud secret her mother didn't suspect.

Zori's scrawny brown and white mongrel opened an eye and took a look at her before scratching itself and rolling over. Zori's lashes fluttered. Her aunt didn't stir.

A heavy feeling in Aleeta's abdomen, deep inside where she imagined her womb to be, signaled to her the approach of her womanhood. *Twwwaaan-go, boom, tw-wwaaan-go boom; you a woman yet Aleeta or you still a little girl?* When she squatted or ran, or even when she sat still, something syrupy sometimes leaked from her, and when she touched herself between her legs, her fingers came up coated with transparent stickiness. The older girls said this meant her fingers would soon come up red. She moved her hand from her chest and slid it inside the thin strip of shorts between her legs. She looked at her fingers. Not a woman yet.

She was hot; she was sleepy; the world blurred and the still-a-girl carried her troubles into sleep with her. The next thing she knew her aunt was stroking her hair and murmuring in her ear, "You were crying, little one." Aleeta tasted the salt at the corner of her lips and saw Zori, off to her side, watching her with worried eyes. Seeing his sweet look of concern, knowing he would die, and that more babies would die, and that more stars would go dark in the sky, Aleeta leaned against her aunt and soaked her aunt's shoulder with tears.

"*Guhrse*," Aleeta heard her aunt say and turned to see Manit watching from the adjacent yard, her breasts huge, her lips crimson, her coiling bracelets throwing off ominous sparks. "*Guhrse*," her aunt repeated, and Manit shuffled away. Manit was her mother's friend and, certain she knew where Manit was going, Aleeta shuddered and gripped her aunt's arm.

"What is it?" Mi-Moona gathered Aleeta to her and Aleeta wished she could remain in her aunt's embrace forever, her anguish frozen in time, the secret unsaid, her disloyalty to her mother a decision not yet acted upon.

"Zori," Mi-Moona said, "go kill five tigers for me. I hear them growling in the woods."

Always when Aleeta came to this house, it was to play with her cousin, but Zori left without complaint. He chose a long stick from his pile of special sticks, his warrior weapons, and waved it at Aleeta as he walked along the path. Aleeta knew that as soon as Zori moved out of his mother's sight, he'd break into a run. If she were his mother, she'd never take her eyes from him. She'd make him sit still. She wouldn't let him spill the bitter berry tea—V-47's remedy for a sick heart—in the bushes across the path the way her aunt did. She pictured Zori as an adult under her care, lying on a bed, alive but gasping for breath. How could you know what was right? "If you had a secret that could hurt someone to tell, would you?" Aleeta said.

"I'd tell someone who cares about you as much as I do." Mi-Moona led her into the house, sat her at the table, and fanned her with banana fronds tied into a feathery bundle. "What do you want to tell me?"

"My mother knows who killed the baby Zori found at the river."

"Sweet one, she always knows. The women of the tribe trust your mother. They confide in her."

"This time, I know too."

"How do you know?"

"I felt it."

"What do you mean, you felt it?" Mi-Moona stopped fanning. She put her hand under Aleeta's chin and lifted her face.

Aleeta had no choice but to look into her aunt's eyes, eyes beginning to comprehend and narrow with rage.

"Before, when she hugged me, I felt it. Today, I didn't feel it any more."

"When who hugged you?"

Aleeta knew her aunt knew.

"Who?" Mi-Moona demanded.

My mother. Aleeta didn't utter a sound. She moved her lips in the shape of the words and her aunt watched her lips accuse her mother of murder. Mi-Moona removed her hand from Aleeta's chin and Aleeta's head, suddenly as heavy as a winter melon, dropped to the table. She thought she might never be able to lift it again. She had ruined everyone's life.

"You were right to tell me," Mi-Moona whispered, her whisper cracking like the rocks in an avalanche. She let the fan fall to the floor as she moved behind her niece. Aleeta felt her aunt's hands clasp her shoulders. "You were right, you were right," Mi-Moona repeated, sounding to Aleeta as if she were trying to convince herself.

The two remained that way, the child slumped forward in confusion and sorrow, her head on the table, every fiber in her waiting while her aunt kneaded her shoulders with an angry strength. When footsteps sounded on the path, Mi-Moona lifted her hands and rushed outside. Aleeta followed her out the doorway and tripped down the steps into her aunt's waiting arms, and although she buried her eyes against her aunt's breasts, Aleeta would swear to herself for the rest of her life that at that moment, she could see one of Zori's tigers rounding the bend, mouth open, teeth bared, ready to strike. She heard the roaring in her ears, felt the tiger's hot breath on the back of her neck, and knew that she was about to die a terrible death.

"What did you do," she heard her aunt say, and when she opened her eyes and turned her head to see who her aunt had spoken to (she already knew, of course she knew), there was her mother stomping across the yard, fierce and proud, bright red lips parted, a head taller than Aleeta remembered her.

"Give her to me." Lo attempted to pull Aleeta from Mi-Moona's grasp.

"Get back in the house." Mi-Moona pushed Aleeta behind her and at the same time pushed Lo in the other direction, catching Lo off balance, sending her flying to the dirt on her elbows and knees. Lo rose quickly, one knee scraped and bleeding, and came at Mi-Moona again. Aleeta, on the top step, stood with hands covering her mouth, watching Mi-Moona fight to keep Lo from rushing the steps. Mi-Moona turned Lo around, pinned her arms behind her, and tried to force her to the ground, at the same time spitting away her own hair that had loosened from its combs and come to bother her mouth. Lo kicked backwards at Mi-Moona with her bare feet until Mi-Moona was forced to release her. Free, Lo grabbed a handful of Mi-Moona's hair and pulled so hard Mi-Moona shrieked.

As the sound pierced the air, chickens scattered, feed dishes overturned, the tribe's forty-one dogs all howled at once. A dozen elderly men, too weak for work in the fields, and at least a half dozen women, four with wailing babies in their arms, appeared at the perimeter of the jousting space. The sisters stopped clawing at each other, gasped for breath, and stared at the crowd. "*Ghurse*" Lo shouted. The second "*ghurse*" was softer. She was out of breath.

Mi-Moona grabbed Lo's arm and half-led, half-dragged her up the steps, pushing Aleeta ahead of them until the three tumbled through the door and the greeting room to the sleeping room, the room best shielded from the eyes of the hill tribe's prying troublemakers. Mi-Moona dipped a cloth into the nighttime drinking water and tossed it at Lo so she could wipe her bleeding knee. Lo sat on the mat, panting with exhaustion, wiping her leg. Breathing hard, Mi-Moona stood and watched her.

Across the room, Aleeta sat on Zori's sleeping mat, neutral territory, unwilling to be claimed by either her mother or her aunt. She sat cross-legged, hunched over, arms around her legs, hugging them close to her body, making herself small and unnoticeable.

"Why, Lo, why? You could have given the baby to me. I would have raised her. I would have loved her." This was her Aunt Mi asking her mother why she murdered her baby, whispering her question because this was nobody's business but theirs, whispering it through a rush of tears because she wanted a baby and her sister had thrown one into the river like a dead frog. Her Aunt Mi slid to the sleeping mat, sobbing. Her mother sat wiping blood from her oozing knee.

Who would tell what to whom? Aleeta wondered. And after the telling, would V-47 call the tribe together and in front of everyone, send her mother to wander the mountains for the rest of her life? Would she never see her mother again? Or would Vee, to teach the tribe a lesson, make an example of their family and throw her and her father out too?

"Why? Tell me why, Lo. How could you do this?" her aunt pleaded.

Her mother didn't answer. She twisted and untwisted the bloody rag.

"She did it for me," Aleeta said. Her aunt looked at her, confused. How stupid her aunt was. If she, Aleeta, could see into her mother's envious heart, how was it that her aunt couldn't? "She didn't want me to be jealous of a younger sister and suffer the way she does."

"Is that it Lo? Is that true?"

"I protect Aleeta. I take care of her. I keep her from hurting."

"You think she's like you?" Mi-Moona said. "Don't you know your own daughter? She's not like you. She's like me. She wanted the baby you killed. She would have loved her younger sister."

"You and your *abuva luph*. You dare to think you know my child better than I do? She would have hated her sister the way I hate you. Go tell V-47 what I've done for my daughter. I'm proud of it. And I'd sooner wander the mountains for the rest of my life than remain in this tribe with you."

"I'll tell Vee nothing. Day after day, you'll see me looking at you, my eyes accusing you of murder."

"It's my eyes that will accuse you. You let your son run wild through the woods when you know running will kill him. And when you've sent him to an early funeral pyre, Pol will leave you. He hates his own tribe. He'll move to the city and you'll be left here, without a husband, without a son, without a friend in the world."

"Pol and I will go to Pin Dalie together. I'll be rid of you. You'll die here, in the middle of this foul stench of a tribe, exactly as you deserve."

The two continued to shout in poisonous whispers, to call each other names, to accuse each other of murder, to speak of insults and injuries dating back to the days when they were little girls. Each predicted the other would return as something awful—a fish who lays eggs in the water and swims away, a millipede, a silly white tourist lady, a filthy old sock. The more they argued, the stupider

they got; the stupider, the uglier, the more tedious and
boring.

Aleeta had no sympathy for either of them. She
wouldn't care if they turned into worms and slithered
away. She had nothing to fear from these two. She could
have been anywhere or dead for all they cared—that's
how busy they were hating each other.

She stopped listening to them and listened instead to
the world outside. She heard a truck, and then heard an
engine cut. A few dogs barked and little children shouted out excited greetings. She could imagine the children
running toward V-47's house at the gates of the village,
hands outstretched, waiting for westerners to fill them
with coins, sugary candy, and Crayola crayons in the new
day-glo colors.

Aleeta had learned to speak a few words in the language the tourists spoke. "Hello," "Thank you," and
"Have a nice day," and she understood some words the
tourists used when they talked to each other about her.
"Serious," they called her, and "intense." Sometimes she
was asked a question that the guide translated and which
she answered: about school (There was a schoolhouse for
tribe kids on this side of the mountain, she said, and she
went there a few times a month), and whether or not
she'd like to visit America. She would nod and point to a
calendar on the wall—each page a scene from the United
States. It was July and what she pointed to lately was a
fireworks display.

Aleeta felt as if her body had chosen that moment
to transport her to adulthood and she lifted herself and
looked sideways at the space under her, afraid she'd see
a wine-colored stain on Zori's sleeping mat. Often these
days, she feared her womanhood would start while she
played in the field or ran to meet a tourist truck, feared it

would catch her off guard in front of the older boys who stared at girls' legs for telltale signs. *Aleeta Aleeta, now you dripping with red. Now your PoPo can sell you to a big hairy KaGooNa for a donkey and a pig. Before he sell you out of here, gimme a taste of the honey in your honey basket.*

Never. She'd never let a boy or a man near her, not a boy in the village, not a husband, never. When her father made a match for her, she'd run away. She'd figure out how to go to America and when she got there she'd find that tourist lady who told her she looked like a smart girl and should attend school every day. She'd ask if she could live in the lady's house in return for feeding her chickens every morning and putting water in her dogs' dishes and leftover scraps in the pig's swill. She'd sweep the steps clean fourteen times a week and cook festival cakes for the lady's special occasions.

She wouldn't change her mind about getting married, either, because if she did she'd end up with a child, and she'd never risk that. For her child might turn out like Zori, with a sickness that would end his life before he grew up. Or it would be a cruel child like herself, a disloyal child who would betray her own mother. Or a child who would grow up jealous and make terrible trouble. Or grow up to let her son fight tigers in the jungle even if fighting tigers would stop his heart. Or her baby would end up a stooped old man dribbling red betel juice onto his wrinkled, caved-in chest. Or an old fat shaman who was supposed to be smart but didn't do anything right.

Never. Never, she thought, over the sound of her mother and her aunt's meanness to one another. Never. She'd been sad for a long time and in this ruined world, it was a sure thing that if she had a baby, whatever else her baby turned out to be, it would be even sadder.

North of the Faro

It seemed to the starstruck Khun do-Chi, as he strolled through his village with a rolled up movie magazine in the waistband of his skintight jeans, that he'd suffocate if he had to remain in Ayama Na one additional minute when every single day the film industry in the bordering country catapulted a far less talented guy to a blazing marquee. Deep within, Khun felt wild and free, and he couldn't, he wouldn't, spend a lifetime of Mondays through Fridays at hotel construction sites pouring wet cement, and a lifetime of Saturdays and Sundays bent to the earth on the family hectares, a rusty scythe in his calloused hand.

It was late summer and Khun do-Chi, fifth child (third son) of five boys and three girls, had paid his dues to the sweltering season, perspiring alongside his father and brothers in the arid fields, walking on homemade stilts at his two youngest nieces' birthday celebrations, cutting and inlaying fifty pink marble steps in Pin Dalie's latest tourist hotel. Khun do-Chi, twenty years old, had obligations to himself. With a final bow to his aging parents and kisses for his many nieces and nephews, he took off on foot through Ayama Na's fields, walking north toward fame and wealth.

And why not Khun do-Chi's face in that movie magazine? Not classically handsome, but with its long pointy nose, dark piercing eyes, and hairline already beginning to thin and recede, the perfect face for a character actor. In fact, Khun do-Chi looked like an Asian version of John Cazale, the late great actor who'd played Fredo Corleone, brooding eldest brother in *The Godfather* saga, a trilogy Khun and his friends revered. He'd scrutinized the first film so often he could recite the English by heart, playing Vito, Michael, Sonny, Kay, Connie, Fredo, and the rest of the beloved parts for the amusement of his siblings, his construction coworkers, and his friends. And better yet, he could ad-lib the film's dialog to rev up the monotonous events of his boring uninteresting stultifying life. "Today we settle all family business," he'd say at the market as he paid for his bagful of longan candies. Or to his mother's seventh child (fourth son) who'd raised his voice to Khun at the construction site, "You are my younger brother and I love you, but don't ever take sides against the family again." The laughter of his appreciative audience—his fellow slab haulers—fell on his ears like rain on a desert animal expiring of thirst.

And as for Ai, the boring uninteresting monotonous girl his parents had chosen for him, daughter of his father's third cousin's best friend, to make his feelings unmistakably clear, every time his parents spoke her name, he'd shout out in Michael's Italy voice, "No!

Appolonia! No," and follow that frantic warning with
a car explosion, sound effects courtesy of the fulminat-
ing pockets of his vastly expressive mouth and lips. His
brothers and sisters would howl with delight while his
father, tired of his third son's disrespect, would chase
him around the dirt yard, shouting and wielding a short-
handled broom, scattering the roosters and rousing the
pig.

Kuhn's parents desired his happiness. They consent-
ed to his adventure—he would leave anyway, they knew
that. But they also believed that loneliness eroded the
pleasures of a fancy life. So they asked the local shaman
for a blessing that would diminish Kuhn's ability to catch
a producer's eye and lead him back to them.

The journey to the neighboring country on foot, at
Khun's average pace, required nearly a month—it was
hot, humid, dangerous terrain, where undiscovered landmines lurked underfoot all the way to the mountains, and
when he reached them the air would cool, but the climb
would be tough. There'd be hill towns on the ascent for
food and shelter, but on the descent into the neighboring
country he'd have to sleep in caves, scrounge for berries,
and fish the streams.

Khun could have hopped a bus or booked a flight
on Ayama Na Air using construction money he'd saved,
but the walk had been advised by a fortune-teller he'd
consulted in Pin Dalie. She'd told him it would give him
gravity, help him conquer his fears, and bridge his past
and his future. He understood the trek as a way to honor
his quest for a different life.

The monks of previous generations had walked hundreds of miles through far denser forests than these puny,
disappearing timberlands he'd traverse, journeys of many
months, even years, overnighting in caves, begging alms,

braving the tigers of the jungle and the yet more dangerous tigers of the isolated mind. In his wandering month,
Khun hoped to taste their solitude, to achieve the complex intensity of actors like Al Pacino, Marlon Brando,
Robert Duvall, and of course, of his doppelgänger, the
late great John Cazale, men with postures as expressive
as coiled snakes and eyes that radiated the patience and
cunning needed to survive. He desired these attributes
for himself and he could imagine how, after his first big
show-biz success, he'd describe his solitary trek to his
interviewers when they asked how one so young could
have acquired so much depth.

On the day he left, he admonished his family not to
expect word from him until he'd crossed the border, but
on the sixth day out, Khun returned to his village in a
long wooden box, stone cold dead. As he'd trudged along
the dirt road leading to the mountains, he'd been struck
by a motorcycle and thrown forty feet, head smashed
against a rock.

The pain of this loss would have destroyed his mother
had she not had a safety valve for her grief—eruptions of
anger that spewed forth like geysers on a regular basis,
explosions of pure fury targeted at a woman she'd never
met but considered an enemy. The woman was Rianna,
the palm reader and clairvoyant Khun had visited in Pin
Dalie in his after-work hours, the person who'd foreseen
his success as a movie star. It was she who'd encouraged him to bridge his old life and his new with a walk
through the countryside, forest, and mountains.

Khun do-Chi's mother, crazed with loss, hated Rianna
as she'd never hated anyone, even her sneaky eldest sister-
in-law. What right did this stranger have to insert lethal
ideas into her son's head?

⊞ ⊞ ⊞

On the evening Khun do-Chi's body arrived at his mother's house, the woman his mother hated, oblivious of the tragedy, ate supper as usual with her husband and then carried her folding table from her ground floor flat to the corner she'd occupied for twenty-two years. There she lit her candle, set out her money box, and unfolded two chairs. To reach that corner, Rianna passed the half dozen other fortune-tellers who populated Prinsala-sakaphorina Street, known throughout Pin Dalie as the Street of Intuitive Powers. The line of people waiting to see Rianna was twice as long as anyone else's.

Her first client of the evening was a thirty-four-year-old childless woman who wept, "My three sisters, my four sisters-in-law, and every one of my friends have children." Her hand clutched her chest as if to keep pieces of her broken heart from flying out.

Rianna recognized that envy had doubled this woman's grief. "You are destined to be the most beloved aunt of your nieces and nephews," she told her. "Go home. Help your sisters and your sisters-in-law, get to know their children well, counsel them, play with them, let yours be the shoulder they cry on, guide them to educate themselves for professions, tell them how much you expect from them. The future of our nation depends on your efforts." Hearing these words, the barren woman's tense hands relaxed and her crying ceased.

When Rianna was a child, her grandmother had recognized her clairvoyant talents and had chosen her from among her fourteen granddaughters and grandsons to carry on her psychic traditions. She taught the seven-year-old what the hands could reveal—the general rules of thumb length, finger idiosyncracies, and the intricate road maps etched in the palm. At ten, Rianna could look at the hands of her cousins and tell her grandmother that Li would live to be more than a hundred, that Cha would have three sons, and that Emno was too headstrong for his own good. Once Rianna became proficient in hand analysis, her grandmother proclaimed this knowledge, in and of itself, trivial, all but meaningless in fact. Even the most foolish readers could interpret finger lengths and end zone bends, she said, and anyone who relied on these indicators did their clients no good.

Then Rianna's grandmother taught her to know emotions. But, two years later, when Rianna could distinguish five kinds of sadness, ten degrees of anger, and three levels of desire, and could distinguish between guilt and shame, and envy and jealousy, her grandmother minimized these talents too.

Anyone who pays attention to physical clues, she said, tightness of a voice and minute shifts of facial muscular tension, could decipher emotions. This ability did not distinguish great psychic readers from their less talented counterparts or from common street charlatans. The great psychics had personal wisdom and the courage to consider the circumstances of a client's life when giving advice, regardless of what the palm foretold or the individual felt. "Be brave," she said, "and you will do no harm. Clients who are not ready to take your suggestions will go to that fool in the next town who will tell them what they want to hear, even if it ruins their life. You tell the truth."

The next person at Rianna's table was a young mother with a baby in her arms who explained that, the year before, all she'd wanted was to marry, leave her parents' home, and start her own family, but now that she had what she'd wanted, she felt her youth had fled and she cried herself to sleep every night.

When she worked, Rianna often saw images that informed her advice. She would gather herself into a deep state of focus, one in which her self disappeared, and envision her clients' roles in their family and country. But as she concentrated on the young woman before her, a commotion occurred in the vicinity of her table.

Looking up, she saw that the line of people waiting for her had parted to let another of the street's palm readers through. It was Cheebah, a large woman in ornate, fringed garments, arms ringed with bracelets made of cheap multicolored metals, who pushed her way past the line and rattled toward Rianna's table, breathless and so excited she could barely speak.

And so the news of Khun do-Chi's death reached Rianna from the gloating lips of her noisiest, gaudiest sidewalk competitor. Cheebah had learned young Khun's fate from her sister-in-law, whose niece, by marriage to her second husband, shared the same native village as the wife of Khun's eldest brother. Cheebah delivered the news of Khun's accidental death as if it pained her to speak of this tragedy. With a flurry of flowered handkerchiefs, she waved her jangling arms about her head in distress and even managed to produce a tear on her painted cheek, although it was obvious she was delighted to deliver news that could cause Rianna to plunge in the street's esteem.

The rest of the palm readers and soothsayers gathered round and exhorted Cheebah to silence herself, grabbing her arms to drag her back toward her own table so they could spare Rianna her rival's envious presence. Rianna saw what the others saw—the pure theater of Cheebah's grief. But for Rianna, Cheebah was the tiniest tickle of a meaningless feather. A hurricane was roiling inside her, and Cheebah didn't add up to one breath of its wind.

Rianna's mind was flung about, buffeted and battered by terrible and destabilizing questions. Had she done this? Was she the agent of Khun do-Chi's fate? Heartsick, she snuffed out the candle on her table, refunded the *ghree* she'd collected from the distraught young mother, abandoned the money box, and pushed back her chair.

"No one will blame you, Rianna!" Cheebah called after her as she moved down the street toward her flat, putting her on notice that she would foment exactly the opposite sentiment as soon as Rianna passed out of sight.

How she made it to her flat without collapsing, Rianna couldn't have said, for she couldn't feel her heels or her toes or the soles of her feet. Once inside the two unadorned rooms she shared with her husband of twenty-five years, she lurched through the larger room that served as living room and kitchen, stumbled into the bedroom, and flopped onto the low sleeping mattress. Light-headed and sweating, she lay on her back, eyes open, trying to collect herself. Never before had anyone suffered as a result of her advice, let alone lost his or her life.

She stared at the ceiling's yellowish plaster, the bright bare bulb, the dingy brown stains above the small stool where her husband, Haak, sat every morning and every night to put on or remove his shoes, the first or last cigarette of the day drooping from his pinched skinny lips, its smoke coiling above his head and staining the ceiling. They'd moved to this small, ground floor flat six years ago, giving their former, larger flat, ten blocks north, to their daughter, Mala, when she and her husband had a daughter of their own. Another pain stabbed her, her suffering that Mala so rarely visited or invited them to visit her, so rarely that their only grandchild was a stranger to them. Was this her fault too?

On her way into the bedroom, Rianna had passed Haak sitting at their worn mahogany dining table reading the paper, his rimless bifocals, as usual, halfway down his skinny nose, his head tilted back so his eyes could peer through the reading zone. He had looked up at her, suspicious. At this hour of the night, the house was supposed to be his.

Now Haak appeared at the bedroom door. "What's the matter with you?" he said, the newspaper in his hand flat against his leg, a finger marking a page. "Are you sick?"

"Tired," she whispered. "Closed early." She stated this as if it were a simple fact, but it was the first time in twenty-two years she'd come home without giving advice to everyone in her long patient queue.

"Well, I need the bed in an hour," he said and turned to walk back toward the table in the other room.

Hot a moment before, now Rianna shivered. She grasped the white blanket from the vicinity of her feet, slid it up and over her flat red shoes, her plain black slacks and her starched white blouse, and held its satin edge under her chin with two fists as a sleeping infant might.

She didn't move. If she moved she'd break. She required all her energy to control her mind. Khun do-Chi. Khun do-Chi. She tried to think of him, not of her guilt, but Khun and her guilt were inextricably linked. She tried to remember that this was his tragedy, not hers, but she couldn't feel pure grief for him because she grieved as much for herself.

He'd come to see her once a month, sliding into her chair, his long expressive fingers flipping a thousand *ghree* into her money box. *Do you renounce Satan?* he'd say, mimicking the priest at the baptism of Connie's new baby. *I do renounce him*, Rianna would answer in heavily accented

English, and Khun would reward her with sparkling eyes and a grin, amused and touched that she'd watched *The Godfather* for his sake. She could almost hear his laugh and for a split second she forgot he was dead. The pain of remembering forced a moan from her lips.

She had considered herself, and knew others did too, responsible and sensible in the work she did. Had Cheebah not interrupted, Rianna, in counseling the dissatisfied young mother, would have pointed to a line in the young woman's palm that indicated her life would be long and the percentage of that life she'd spend raising her child limited and bearable. She'd have pointed out, as well, unequivocal signs that her client had the fortitude to see the sacred task through.

Khun, on the other hand, as one of eight offspring, wasn't needed to work the farm or care for his parents. He could strike out, bid for fame, bring honor to Ayama Na. Talented, funny, hardworking, able to take direction, he had a genuine chance to succeed in the neighboring country's film industry. Her task was to encourage him and give him an edge—give him depth, tolerance, humility, and confidence in himself. The idea of a long solitary walk to the border had come to her because she had a gift for the right idea, sometimes even for the perfect idea, and when she suggested the walk as a transition between a traditional life and a modern one, he seized upon it as if she had given him a jewel. Wasn't it an idea she would have seized upon herself?

And wasn't that her crime—interjecting what she herself wanted into his life?

Lying on her bed, she saw what she'd done. Who was it who'd wanted to be wild and free? She'd suggested to Khun what she coveted, a long walk away from an imperfect life. She'd failed to empty herself of herself, and as a consequence, her client was dead.

But his excitement had been genuine, his lifeline strong and unbroken, signifying he could take risks and overcome challenges. Didn't that corroborate her advice and assure his safe passage? No. No, it didn't. Palms were useless, her grandmother had taught her that. Another moan escaped her dry lips. She slid from the bed onto the floor and lay with her face pressed into the square of carpet at the bedside. The fibers that pricked her mouth tasted of dust and smelled of her husband's feet. Who was she, her own life a shambles, her husband needing the bed from eight to ten every night to consort with his concubine, she coming home from the corner to sleep on rumpled sheets impregnated with the odor of another woman's sex, her only daughter so disgusted she protected her own child from contamination with their marital hypocrisy—who was she to think she could tell other people how to conduct their lives?

She was worse than Cheebah, who envied her. Cheebah was a joke with her incense, her rattling copper and silver baubles, encased in the trappings of psychic power in a futile attempt to authenticate her phony skills and weak intellect. Cheebah would tell her clients what they wanted to hear, affirm their follies, exalt poor character traits, encourage their desires to run away when they should stay, or to stay when they should run away. Cheebah could do no harm, for she and her advice were dismissable. But Rianna, with her plain clothing and her seriousness and her deep focus, she was the menace, the one who could disrupt and disturb. Did she think she could protect the people she launched into new lives? Did she think she had the power of Vito Corleone?

Worse, she had never subjected herself to her own medicine, never focused her gaze upon her own life, never read her own palm, never visited someone who did what she did to learn her own character or for what she should strive.

But to whom could she turn? The other women on the street were less talented than she. Some were slaves to the palm, some young and unseasoned, and some, like Cheebah, petty and insignificant.

It had been rumored for decades that a supremely gifted clairvoyant resided in the mountains north of the Faro River, spending her time alone, walking for days or sitting for hours on a rocky crest surveying the valleys below, but no one Rianna knew had seen her or pinpointed the hill tribe she revisited for supplies. She might well have been nonexistent, a rumor or legend that once initiated, acquired an enduring mythical status. Two years ago, however, this clairvoyant had been the subject of an article in *Celebrity*, the Ayama Nan equivalent of *People Magazine*. The reporter, who claimed to have shadowed her for five months through the highest mountain passes, referred to her as Zho, the letter in the Ayama Nan alphabet that, like *X* in English, connotes a mysterious presence. Despite omissions that would confirm her identity, such as photos or maps, the magazine account had a certain authenticity for Rianna who could relate to the description of the trance-like, hypnotic state of the psychic when she focused on an individual who came for advice.

Still, the article could have been a hoax, a ruse to sell magazines, Rianna knew that, but she put 2,000 *ghree* and a few packets of crackers in her pocket and walked past Haak and out the front door. She turned in the direction opposite the corner with the table she'd abandoned, glancing back once at the objects of her misguided life. Her sidewalk table and her corrupt money box had claimed a young man's life. She vowed never to return to them again. And as for Haak, far from missing her, he'd be pleased to have exclusive use of their bedroom round the clock.

It was a moonless night. After Rianna crossed the bridge over the Pin Dalie River, the city lights faded and the darkness deepened around her. As the urban asphalt gave way to narrow dusty unpaved roads that cut through the country fields, the earth's fungal odors mingled with the rotting aftermath of the season's dry rice harvest. From the low-hanging leaves of the Po trees, fruit bats floated eerily, and some of the potholes alongside her feet seemed big enough to conceal jungle beasts. At midnight, after four hours of walking, the rains came, and by the time they stopped, her dripping clothes clung to her body and country muck covered her flat red shoes.

The sun was a hot white line beneath its own glow on the eastern horizon when Rianna reached Khun do-Chi's village. She'd walked fourteen hours straight and her toes had bled through the caked mud on her shoes. "Where do the do-Chi's live," she asked a tall, barefoot woman stirring a soup pot in a ramshackle shop on the straight road through town.

▨ ▨ ▨

When his bowlegged brown dog growled, Khun do-Chi's father stumbled from his thatch house to his dirt front yard. He didn't resemble his tall lanky third son; he was short in stature with a brushy gray beard, although the hair on his head receded the way Khun's had. When the father saw Rianna, his thick eyebrows tensed, but before he could approach her, his wife flew out the door, hair flying, overtaking her husband, her face red with her screaming. "You? You dare to come to my house? You think I wouldn't know my son's murderer anywhere?"

While her husband restrained the barking dog, and the roosters scurried, the hysterical woman lunged at Rianna and scratched the side of her face with a jagged fingernail, sending blood trickling down into the corner of Rianna's mouth, mixing with the saliva there, its sweet metallic aftertaste nauseating her. Rianna thrust her face forward, inviting disfiguring scars, craving visible marks of the terrible error she'd made.

Khun's father's voice trembled with helplessness. "Please go," he begged, and because she was causing Khun do-Chi's mother to slip into madness, Rianna left without apology or argument.

A hundred meters down the road, the youngest of Khun's brothers—the one called Skroi—caught up with Rianna and put a hand on her arm. "My mother doesn't understand," he said. "This wasn't your fault. This was an accident. Khun died in pursuit of an exciting life. And soon, I'll leave too." Skroi's words spilled out fast, as if he feared the universe taking notice of his self-involvement while his brother lay dead. "I'll go to America." He thrust out his palm. "Tell me what you see here."

"You have no future in America," she said without looking at his palm. What was in the palm came to the same thing with everyone everywhere: You want and want and want and then you are dead. She spat on the ground. "Your dreams are a fiction. Go home before your mother mourns another son." As soon as the words were out, she wanted them back. They'd come from her own desperate need. Again. Would crushing Skroi's dream expiate her guilt? Would it bring Khun back? As Skroi ran from her, she doubled over and vomited on the side of the road. "Run faster," she yelled after him. She scooped up a handful of water-buffalo dung and rubbed it into the scratch Khun's mother had made in her cheek. A water-buffalo dung infection left an ugly raised scar, a mark she needed to remind herself to keep her mouth shut and never again give advice.

After ten days of walking, eight of them in a feverish, hallucinatory state, her cheek inflamed and oozing pus, Rianna reached the steep footpath that led into the mountains and forced her aching body to climb up through the cardamom-scented forest. At nightfall she located a cave in the rocks, crawled into a dark inner passage and surveyed the rock surfaces with her hands for standing water before curling up on a dry narrow ledge. From the time she'd left Pin Dalie she'd barely slept, pausing only to nap for a fitful thirty or sixty minutes at a time, but in the morning, although she'd slept straight for ten hours, she awakened heavy with fatigue, cold, and shivering. When she emerged into daylight and saw her filthy clothes and scabbed feet, when she looked up and realized how distant the peak, it occurred to her she might not survive the climb, a circumstance she believed would serve her right.

Bruised by granite outcrops, feet so sore every step hurt, at mid-afternoon she reached a vantage point from which she spotted the several dozen rough huts of a hill tribe along a western incline. She made her way toward the clearing, at length picking up the crude road to the small tribal village. As she approached the wooden gate she saw the tribespeople ambling along the road to meet her, and from the heavy plugs in their ears, identified them as the Dyo Tribe. Rianna had seen this tribe in photographs on tourist brochures throughout Pin Dalie, the women in brightly colored woven skirts, ornate embroidered sashes to cover their breasts, silver ornaments in their hair, the naked children peeking from behind their mothers' skirts. When they reached her, she noticed that most of the adults, chewing betel nuts, were dreamy eyed and red mouthed.

"Aaiiii, buffalo dung," an old woman said, passing her fingers along Rianna's cheek. Then she turned her wrinkled face and spoke in rapid tribal dialect to the women behind her until they passed a small round mirror forward to Rianna who held it up to look at herself. Sleek, smooth, raised, and red, the fresh scar that crossed her cheek from the outer edge of her eye to the joint of her lips had yet to attain its full topographic dimension or develop the iron-rich earth tone it would acquire as it matured, but this face she'd intentionally altered matched the roughness she felt inside and seemed to her as if it were the face she'd been destined for all her life.

The tribespeople fed her and sheltered her for the night. In the morning, before she resumed her climb, they gave her a pair of battered leather hiking shoes that a tour guide had months ago tossed off his truck. They also invited her to choose a shawl from among many on hand the tribeswomen had woven as part of a weaving project funded by the royal family to add to the merchandise available for purchase by tourists driven up the mountain every day in rugged trucks.

"Do you know the woman called Zho," Rianna asked at the gate.

"Magazine lady," said a very pregnant woman with two dark-eyed toddlers clinging to her skirt.

"Up," an old man said, his hand pointing in the direction of the peak of the mountain.

It was a half day's walk to the next hill tribe and a full day's to the one after that. Rianna moved vertically, climbing for six days, sheltered in tribal villages for seven nights, the last two, above the timberline and tourist roads, poor and hardscrabble, reachable only by obscure narrow trails. When, as often happened, Rianna lost the trails, she clawed her way through bramble and dry forest scrub.

In the afternoon of her sixteenth day on the road, she reached the Koorins, the tribe that had settled at the highest mountain elevation of any of the hill dwellers. An agile people, stocky and small in stature, the Koorin told her it would take from ten hours to two days to ascend the peak depending on her mountaineering skills, for there would be no trail or soft ground until she reached the chain of small lakes in the summit caldera. Cheerful and generous, the Koorin sent her on her way with enough water for fifteen hours and would have given her food as well had she not declined the offer in favor of a lighter load.

Conditioned as a result of her weeks of walking, her body sinewy and visibly muscular, her hands and feet immune to blisters, Rianna nonetheless struggled on the rocky outcrops and moved with caution from boulder to boulder. At first she attempted to grab and hang onto the tough grasses that pushed their way out of cracks in the rocks here and there, but inevitably a clump pulled loose and she slid backward along the rocks, scraping her elbow on sharp loose talus, leaving a bright circle of blood on the left sleeve of her blouse. After that, she crawled up the steeper rocks on her hands and knees. The climbing was hard; the peak that appeared so near seemed no closer as the strenuous hours passed. Hot, spent, and still an unknown number of hours from the top, she lay down and closed her eyes. When she opened them, she looked toward a summit shrouded in clouds, and there in the mist, saw the figure of a slim woman with dark flowing hair. Distrusting the sight, she watched the clouds part and reappear, uncertain if what she saw was reality or the hallucination of an exhausted mind.

She'd never had a firm conviction that the woman the magazine called Zho truly existed. There were moments Rianna could believe she'd locate Zho and Zho would provide her with the story of the rest of her life, but during many more moments she felt she'd find nothing at the summit but a cold, hard wind. She climbed because she had no choice. Like Khun do-Chi, she'd been captured by the idea of an earned transition, a struggle—even one that risked death—as the price of a renovated life.

The climb to the high peak from the Koorin Tribe took Rianna seventeen hours. At the summit, where the wind whipped at her from four directions, she could make out a chain of three small lakes in the caldera to her right. Cold and tempted to scamper down to the first lake, she made herself pause to look at the view. From her vantage point she could see two countries—behind her, far below, lay the most fertile river valley of Ayama Na, a landscape marked by the wide Faro River and its myriad tributaries and by squares of farmland, distinct from each other by variations in the shades of green and furrows that changed direction. In front of her, in the distance, at the base of the gently sloping north face of the mountain, were the lights of Hiang Ree, the high-tech border city, home of the adjacent country's thriving movie industry and site of Khun do-Chi's elaborate dreams. To the rocks and the sky, she whispered in Khun's Marlon Brando voice, "You talk about vengeance. Is vengeance going to bring your son back to you? Or my boy to me?"

Shivering now, she descended to the first lake, where she stretched out in the tall grasses on its shore and slept, awakening at dawn to a sun-filled sky and with the sense

that she was being observed. She raised herself to a sitting
position and turned, and because she'd forgotten about
Zho, she expected to see a squirrel or a bird, but what she
saw was a couple of young hikers—one a young Cauca-
sian male, not too much older than Khun do-Chi, mid
twenties perhaps; the other a young woman, Ayama Nan,
wearing jeans and a T-shirt, tall, slim as a reed, her facial
bones high on her cheeks, her lips full, her dark olive skin
flawless, her black silken hair self-knotted at the nape of a
long graceful neck. She was barefoot, her toenails showing remnants of scarlet polish, and her shoes, Nikes with
socks tucked into them, were tied together and dangling
over a shoulder. The young man wore hiking boots and a
faded college sweatshirt over khaki pants with multiple
pockets. They stood at a respectful distance, arms around
each other's waists, watching her.

As Rianna studied the couple, she had a vision of the
young woman in a traditional Ayama Nan bridal cos-
tume of red and gold silk with gold braided trim, her
shining black hair loose and flowing to her waist, her
eyes rimmed with the blackest black. In the vision, the
young woman's body became transparent and Rianna
could see her liver, her stomach, her lungs, and her uter-
us, in which the heart of a tiny male fetus beat. In seven
months, the young man at her side, in white gown and
mask, would hold her hand as she lay on a hospital bed
and gave birth to his son.

"Do you have food?" Rianna asked. The young man
seemed to understand and answered in halting Ayama
Nan, thick with an American accent, that they had supplies at their campsite, further along the lake shore. The
young woman invited Rianna to come with them and
share their breakfast, and as Rianna rose, the young
woman said, "I'm Payat, and this is John."

Rianna ate ravenously. "Please," they said, pushing food in her direction, willing to give all they had. She was eating the supplies they had intended to last a few days, she knew that, but she was unable to stop herself. Energy bars, dried meat, nuts, rice balls. She must look crazy to them, she thought, elbow caked with blood, long jagged scar on her cheek, hair untamed, sitting there shoveling their food into her mouth. Finally, she wiped her lips with the back of her hand. "Thank you," she said.

Payat and John cleaned the site and sat opposite her on the bright blue tarp they'd unrolled for her, sat cross-legged, both of them shoeless now, John's hiking boots visible inside the door of their tent. "John and I met in Pin Dalie," Payat said. "My office sent me to take his English class so I could speak on the phone with American clients. We fell in love and now I am pregnant with John's child."

"I know," Rianna said, regretting her words, reaching to touch her scar, running her finger along it, making it throb.

Payat scooted forward and thrust her open right hand, palm up, toward Rianna.

"Don't do that," Rianna said, her voice sharp.

"Forgive me." Payat pulled her hand back and jumped to her feet. "In the city, it's the method. I'm not familiar with how you work."

John had risen when Payat did. "Please," he said, in his halting Ayama Nan. "We've waited ten days for you. Payat saw a sign in a cloud that you were on your way. We read about you in a magazine and climbed up here because Payat needs your help." He took Payat's hand as he spoke.

"Get away from me. I'm not who you think I am." She wanted to shout at them to run, but she was distracted by overlapping visions that came at her fast. Payat holding a baby boy in her arms. A big American house. Another infant—a girl this time. A bank in America. Farmlands in Ayama Na green with young rice.

"My family has arranged a marriage for me to a man from the next village. He's a widower, old, fifty-five, with 200 hectares. He promised my father fifty hectares for me, land my father needs to divide among my brothers."

"I want to marry Payat," John said, "and take her to America. But she fears harm will come to the baby—a deformity or blindness—as punishment for disobeying her parents. We love each other very much."

"Michael Corleone and Kay loved each other too. Even in the movies, love isn't enough."

"I don't understand," Payat said. She looked at Rianna, bewildered.

"Explain it to her," Rianna said to John. And just then another vision came to her, a vision of her husband, Haak, on the phone, calling her friends; also consulting the other clairvoyants on Prinsalasakaphorina Street, asking their help to locate his wife. He rang the doorbell at Mala's apartment—their old apartment—to tell her her mother had disappeared. Mala came to the door with their granddaughter, Irata, in her arms. Irata wore blue and yellow pajamas and had a spray of snow white blossoms in her straight black hair.

"Listen," John said, "Payat believes in your powers. I can't claim that for myself, but she's superstitious. If someone who didn't like your advice did this to you—" he pointed to the scar— "Don't be afraid. We won't hurt you no matter what you say. Please read Payat's palm and tell her the future you see for our child."

Rianna let her head fall back so the sun would shine on her face. Her body became still; her breathing slowed;

the dancing lights behind her eyelids settled into a uniform translucent white. Why should she look at another palm? Would it tell a different story than birth, old age, sickness, and death? And yet, didn't everyone have to navigate from one end of the lifeline to the other? Was it really irresponsible to help them steer the course with patience, effort, and attention to kindness?

"Show me your palm," Rianna said, opening her eyes. She placed her hand firmly around Payat's, clamped the thumb open, and because Payat expected her to, stared at the lines of her palm.

"You must do as I say," Rianna said finally. "Omit nothing."

Payat nodded.

"Leave with John. Go to America. Raise your children to respect their ancestors. Teach them to speak both English and Ayama Nan so they become a bridge between your two countries. As you and John prosper, send money to your parents and brothers. Do you understand?"

"Yes."

"Listen carefully. Before you embark on your new life, descend the mountain. Return to your home. Introduce John to your parents, describe your destination, say goodbye to your family, and promise you will help them."

"They won't talk to me," Payat said.

"Talk to them."

From the windy pass, Rianna watched John and Payat move down the southern slope, John leading the way, looking back after every few steps to check Payat's footing. Rianna tracked them until they vanished from her sight and then started her own descent. Once again, she had given the advice she needed herself.

She would retrace her steps to Pin Dalie, say goodbye, and then, with her scarred face and her calloused hands, she would inhabit her future, high in the mountains, north of the Faro.

Tea

The rain pounded on the living room window. Most days in the rainy season, it poured in the morning and then again between four and eight. Heavy cumulus clouds darkened the sky, and streams filled with litter ran down the gutters in front of the apartment buildings.

Pania hated the rain. The recent annual precipitation surges after the long drought that had upended her father's life struck her as an affront. If the climate had cooperated and the rice paddies and onion fields had prospered rather than drying up, her father and mother would be spending their old age on the farm instead of in the city, and she'd be growing up in the countryside without the temptations that were destroying her family life.

Pania was her mother's change-of-life baby, twenty years younger than the next oldest of her five siblings, four brothers and a sister, the only child still living in the country with her parents when the sand choked the chickens and shriveled the rice shoots. She could still remember shrieking with the pain of a scratched cornea as her mother ran with her to the edge of the rice paddies and yelled at her husband that she couldn't abide life on the farm for another second. Within a week, they had moved from Okapinala Province to Pin Dalie where Pania's older bothers and her sister already lived. Pania was four at the time.

Now she was seventeen, in her last year of high school, and seething as her father leaned back in the big red upholstered chair, the only comfortable chair in the third floor flat, staring at the TV screen, disregarding her pleas to continue their discussion. His silence infuriated her despite her understanding that no matter how intelligently or with what soaring passion either debated, neither would change the other's mind.

It was Monday evening, a half hour after the latest installment of the argument between Pania and her father that had disrupted the family's supper for the third straight night. Next Friday, at Pei Wei, an old-style noodle restaurant down the street, her father would host a dinner he had arranged so she could meet Nafal, only child of another Okapinala Province farmer robbed by Ayama Na's unpredictable climate of his country life, an acquaintance he hadn't seen in ten years but had bumped into a week ago on Mi-Lanippo Street where, in the ensuing catch-up, each discovered the other had a marriageable child.

"Don't do this to me," Pania begged. Her father cleared his throat and stared harder at the TV screen.

She had no intention of showing up at Pei Wei, a restaurant she could barely tolerate under the best of circumstances. Oily noodles, cheap incense, over-tenderized beef, worn-out red velvet seats, interminable conversations between her father and the proprietor—yet another dislocated rice farmer, this one with an influential relative who had set him up in the restaurant business—about subtropical humidity, tropical circulation, and recent weather patterns (as if meteorological conditions mattered to them any more), and this time, to add insult to injury, Nafal and his parents examining her as if she were a blouse in a shopping stall.

In the last three days, she'd told her father at least five times that she wouldn't appear, but he'd spent fifteen minutes with Nafal and had decided Nafal was the perfect husband for her. He was not going to call that dinner off.

"Please listen," she said. He coughed again and turned from her.

She grabbed her rain poncho and rushed out the door, calling back to him, even though she'd promised herself to refrain from harsh or disrespectful speech, "You're an old fool. You don't know what you're doing anymore."

Down the dim staircase two narrow flights and onto the watery street, she stood in a downpour amid the late dinner shoppers running in and out of Lin's Grocery with its fishy smells and Hsall's Seafood Market with its icy blue light, pulling on her poncho, fingers grappling with the tissue-thin plastic that stuck to itself, a final frustration that brought tears to her eyes. Tears of rage but also of shame because in her seventeen years, she'd never before insulted either one of her parents.

She pulled her cell phone from her pocket and called Kol, second oldest brother, third child in the family order. Could he meet her somewhere?

※ ※ ※

She waited for him outside 714825 Swadougkum-Pokaba Street, the address of the tiny café he'd suggested, reviewing in her mind her mean words to her father, anguish washing over her in unstoppable waves. She pressed her nose to the windowpane to see if Kol was already inside and through the narrow slats she made out yellow walls, tall ficus plants, and leathery heart hoya vines tangled into canopies overhead, so much greenery each of the tables inside the café seemed to occupy a private garden. There were no customers that she could see, and who'd want to stop in this place anyway, she thought, door a nondescript beige, plain windows hidden by those skinny slats, the name of the café, which was the same as its address—714825 Swadougkum-Pokaba Street—printed in all but unreadable script across the lower edge of the window pane. The cafés she and her friends chose had storefronts of wide corrugated metal that rolled up to allow rock music from the inside speakers to pour outside to the tables on the street. It looked to her as if 714825 Swadougkum-Pokaba Street could bore you to death.

The sky cleared at the exact instant Kol rounded the corner, creating the impression he'd banished the rain, just blown every big dark cloud away. His smile from the end of the street evoked in her the overlapping reactions she invariably had in that split second when she first glimpsed her brother, how funny-looking he was—his nose irregular, his ears elongated, his eyes too close together, his hair shaved to a stubble—but at the same time how kind, how magnetic, as if he really had stopped the rain and stopped it just for her. She'd seen mean canine strays sidle up and rub against his pant leg, that's how comforting the sight of him was. Filled with relief, she peeled the flimsy rain poncho from her sweaty arms and jumped into his. Head against his chest, tears rolled down her cheeks.

"Everything will be fine, Pania," he said.

"No it won't," she mumbled into his shirt, "He'll hate me forever, but if I give in, my life will be over." Maybe her brother could stop a storm or tame wild beasts, but he couldn't change their father's mind.

"Let's go inside before it rains again," Kol said, opening the door to the café.

"Why is he doing this to me? Why won't he listen?" Pania said as Kol extended a chair for her.

"We'll have tea before we tackle the problem."

"This Nafal—he's an *accounting student!*" she yelped, and would have continued to describe how their anachronistic and idiotic father had decided, after he'd heard Nafal laugh three times in their quarter-hour together, that he had a fine sense of humor and would make her laugh for the rest of her life, but Kol put a hand up to silence her.

"I know all about him," he said. "Take a moment to calm yourself."

In the family gossip chain, her mother's version of household events passed first to her sister, then from her sister to her brothers and their wives, and probably from there to half of Pin Dalie. No one, including Kol, had heard her side of the story "He won't listen to me. He doesn't care about me. He—"

"Please. Let's not speak of this yet."

She slumped in her chair, a deliberate pout on her face, tears rising again, irked by her brother's refusal to listen to her, an echo of the silence her father had subjected her to.

"If we're calm, we'll arrive at a solution more easily." His eyes remained on her, sober and generous. "Try to breathe slowly. Look around. Let the atmosphere here soothe you."

She'd didn't want to be soothed, but even if she did, this café had the opposite effect; it made her nervous. The masses of greenery, the unadorned walls, the absence of music, all felt claustrophobic and creepy to her. The roots of the tall ficus trees that screened the tables from each other had overgrown the rims of the pots, wound down and slithered along the wooden floor like water snakes. She didn't want to breathe slowly; she wanted to talk, to talk loud and fast while her brother listened to every word she said. "I'll run away before I show up at his dinner. He thinks…"

"Let's wait to be served."

"Will you please listen to me?" Exasperation rising, the tide of it coming in. "You and Vokar and Lem and Nee and Aa, all of you…"

"Pania, please don't talk until we've been served."

"But we haven't even ordered yet." She looked at her watch.

"The customers in this café don't order," Kol said.

"What are you talking about?"

"See the elderly couple over there? They own the café and they decide what to serve each customer who comes in."

"You're kidding, right?" Pania twisted her head and lifted a ficus branch. At a short end of the rectangular room an old woman with pure white hair stood at a sink rinsing suds from yellow mugs, while across the counter from her, seated on a three-legged mahogany stool, an elderly gentleman with a narrow gray braid that hung halfway down his knobby back read a book propped against an espresso machine.

"When they have a moment to spare, they'll observe us, and based on their observations and intuition they'll choose the appropriate beverages for us."

She stared at him, speechless.

"For example," Kol said, "if it's early morning and a patron stumbles in half asleep, they might serve an espresso with double shots of caffeine. For a cranky child, a mug of hot chocolate and a rice cake. For the agitated, a soothing green or jasmine tea. I imagine we'll be served tea, but perhaps a surprise. Regardless, they'll bring what we need."

"They're not looking at us, and we're the only ones here!"

"Try to have patience. Rest your hands on the table. It will help you wait."

"And I don't want tea." Tea! She wanted a Coke. Everyone, her mother, father, her older sister and her brothers, obviously even Kol whom she'd previously thought less controlling than the rest, considered it their right to direct her life, including her digestive tract. "I'm going to the counter to order, and I'm getting myself a Coke. What do you want?"

"I want to help you."

"Then help me get a Coke!" She stared at Kol, at the fine wrinkles around his eyes, at the stubble on his head already peppered with gray. He looked older than his thirty-nine years.

"That's not how it works here."

"You know what? I made a mistake. I should have called Vakor. He'd listen to me. And, if I wanted a Coke he'd get me one."

"But you didn't call Vakor. You called me."

At the ease with which he exposed her bluff, Pania felt herself deflate. Vakor, the eldest brother, the hothead of the family, not a subtle bone in his oft-inebriated body, would rant and rave as he always did until his sensible wife put a hand on his shoulder. Vakor would have offered extreme advice or confronted their father, escalating the problem— an unacceptable option because Pania didn't want a huge family fight, she wanted her father to change his mind. "Okay, you win," she said. "You want my hands on the table? Here—" She slapped her palms on the fine ecru lace, noticing for the first time the sleek rosewood it covered. "You satisfied now?" She poked the tips of her fingers through holes in the lace and studied what still showed of her fingernails, the cuticles neat, the nail beds a gleaming pale red. One of her sisters-in-law, Lem's generous wife, worked part time at Jiu's Nails on Weeskiescoopackiak Street and manicured the family at home for free.

"Good. Turn your hands over so they rest palms up," Kol said.

She did as he asked, surmising her hand position a signal he'd arranged in advance, a green light to the old folks to bring the tea.

"Can you sit up straighter?" he said.

She pulled herself out of her slump and forced her shoulders back.

"Close your eyes. Take a deep breath."

She bristled. This was too much. Her siblings, especially her sister, had warned her of the flaws in Kol's nature, defects Pania had heretofore refused to see.

In adherence to a vanishing country custom, a rite of passage en route to an ethical adult life, her father had taken each of her brothers in their sixteenth year to Wat Phra Spaq, a monastery on an austere ridge 500 meters up a granite mountain in a range north of the Faro, a compound at which they'd served for six weeks as guest novice monks. Phra Spaq was the same monastery her father had been taken to by his father for six weeks when he turned sixteen.

"You're not a monk and I'm not your disciple," Pania muttered, loud enough to make clear her disdain for the monastery tactic. Unlike Vakor, Lem, and Nee, who'd left Phra Spaq after the minimum six weeks and had, in short order, resumed their prior habits of profanity, arguing, imbibing, and gossip, Kol had opted to remain an additional six weeks, and from that day to this, as far as anyone knew, he never again ate meat, drank alcohol, swore, engaged in idle talk, or passed a beggar without giving him a few *ghree*. Whenever her sisters and brothers criticized Kol's *abuva luph*, Pania defended him and accused them of envying his virtue. Now she saw what they saw, how his holier-than-thou attitude got on your nerves, how it blinded him to other people's real and immediate needs.

"This is ridiculous. Motion them over here"

"They'll come when they think best. Just wait."

"Easy for you to say. No one's trying to wreck your happiness."

Kol put his finger to his lips to silence her, a gesture that made her angrier at him at that moment than at their father whose behavior at least had legitimacy, given his personal history. In his sixties when forced to move to Pin Dalie, he'd never adjusted to the city. Without an occupation, he spent a few hours daily selling lottery tickets on the street while his wife worked in a dress shop and his sons and his son-in-law contributed to his household income, leaving as a buffer for his bruised ego only his role as enforcer of the traditions. Kol, on the other hand, had been young enough when he'd left for Pin Dalie to fully grasp the uselessness of country traditions to urban life. What did he expect to accomplish with his stupid guru games?

Her back ached from the effort of sitting up straight and her right hand, having fallen asleep, felt detached from her body. She shook it at the side of the table until it stung with revived circulation and then replaced it face up as Kol had instructed. She'd outlast him, she thought. Periodically, she peered between the greenery at the proprietors of this absurd place, looking in vain for signs of their communication with her brother until, finally, her eyes closed by themselves.

The rain started again. She could hear it pound on the window pane, and when thunder shook the ficus leaves, she shuddered, the noise rumbling through her until the pelting rain invaded her thoughts: how long it took for water to wear away rock, how many eons nature required to carve out a canyon, how sometimes water seeped into small cracks and the shelf gave way in a huge crumbling slide that permanently altered the landscape. That's what she needed Kol for—cataclysmic erosion, her father's recalcitrance shearing and sliding away.

Pania opened her eyes when she heard Kol's chair scrape. He was getting to his feet, reaching under the table for his umbrella. "This is it? We're leaving?" she said.

"This café closes at 9:30." He transferred a 500 *ghree* note from his pocket to the table.

"What are you paying for? No one served us!"

"That happens sometimes. Perhaps they considered that nothing would suit us tonight, considering your state."

He was blaming her! Intolerable! Her sister was right about him. "Just wait. You'll see," Aa had said, and Pania did see. She saw her brother in all his ugliness, crooked nose, ridiculous ears, his charm stripped away. "Why are you leaving money? Do you have so much you can part with it for nothing?"

"We occupied a table even though we weren't served."

"Yeah and whose fault was that? I know ten other cafés we could have met at."

"No one's fault, just how it is," he said, rising and shaking her poncho out for her. But just as his arms spread apart to extend the plastic, the rain stopped, and he reversed the activity, folding the poncho patiently, squeezing the air out until it was the size and shape of a deck of cards, exactly the form of its original packaging. "We'll meet here tomorrow after you're out of school and I'm done at work. Things will go better."

Bags of garbage had appeared on the sidewalks in front of the shops for the predawn pickup, and the air smelled of pickled turnip and stale cooking grease as she and Kol walked to the corner of Swadoughum—Pokaba and Poteamandna streets where their routes diverged. When he reached out for a quick hug, she pulled away. "Tomorrow," he said.

"What makes you think I'll show up?"

※ ※ ※

At breakfast the next morning, at the round table her mother kept covered with a shiny red oilcloth, Pania sat across from her father, picking at a bowl of cornflakes and watching him eat his steaming crab and noodle soup without glancing up. To her mother's perfunctory questions, Pania gave curt one-syllable answers, angry at her too, for with her job in Pin Dalie's tourist sector exposing her to travelers from the entire world, she ought to have sympathized with her daughter's modern desires. But her mother's city clothes, fashionable biased-cut hair, and perfect French manicure—courtesy of Lem's wife—

barely covered her thatched-roof interior life. She had intruded in the argument between her daughter and her husband only once, the evening before, to ask Pania why she continued to harass her father when he'd made his decision clear.

"Whose side are you on?" Panya had demanded.

"Not yours. And in this house, we don't shout."

"In this house, we don't shout," Pania mocked. "In this house we just make people marry people they don't love."

"You will not talk to your mother that way," her father said, rising from the chair across the dinner table. And that's when he turned on the television, planted himself in the red upholstered chair, and declared he'd heard enough from her.

At school, Pania considered making good on her threat to stand Kol up that afternoon, reminding herself that even after eliminating Kol and the intemperate Vakor, she still had three siblings to turn to for help—Lem, Nee, or her sister, the bossy Aa. Any of the three would flatter themselves that she valued their counsel above the others, especially above their insufferable second eldest brother, yet she suspected that to keep her to themselves, they'd tell her what they thought she wanted to hear—ignore him, run away, you've got rights—easy answers that missed the point and failed to save her father from humiliation or prevent her estrangement from him. Pania knew (without knowing quite how she knew) that Kol, alone among her siblings, aimed to rise above the ardent, full time labor of prizing himself.

※ ※ ※

She arrived at the café that afternoon to find Kol in the chair he'd occupied the evening before, back straight, hands resting on his lap. Although yesterday she'd bristled at the quiet, today she hated that eight noisy businessmen had pushed potted plants aside and pulled tables together, disrupting the atmosphere. She wanted them to leave so she and her brother could have the café to themselves.

"They won't bother us," Kol said as he rose to pull out her chair.

She noticed that her brother's glasses needed cleaning, the lenses splotched with grime from the construction site. A thin patina of red dust covered his khaki shirt and heavy work pants.

Hot day, interrupted so far by a single half hour of downpour. Mostly the sun had blazed. "I'm thirsty. I'd like something to drink, if you don't mind," she said.

"It isn't up to me."

A lie, she thought, but she placed her hands on the table, palms up, sat up straight, took a deep breath, and worked at appearing serene enough to earn a pot of tea.

When the tea arrived, she felt herself leap inside. The plain white teapot and the two yellow porcelain cups in the middle of the table struck her as a personal triumph. They would drink their tea and Kol would tell her his plan for persuading their father of the inevitability of his youngest daughter's worldly desires. Grinning and excited, she reached for the handle of the teapot.

Her brother intercepted her hand in midair and held it in his. "The tea hasn't brewed yet, and you're too wound up to drink it."

"I don't believe this!" she said, pulling her hand away. Both teacups, chipped at their rims, showed irregular splotches of white through the glaze of yellow. What a fiasco this stupid place was. Rosewood. Lace. Defective cups. No way to order or get the drink you desired. She glared at Kol, furious.

After a long moment, he poured tea into his own cup. "I'll pour yours when you've calmed down."

"And meanwhile, what? You're going to sit there and drink your tea while I sit here parched?"

"Would you prefer I wait for you and remain thirsty myself?"

"You bet I would."

"All right," he said. He twisted the lid off and poured his tea back into the pot.

In spite of her anger, Pania reproached herself, knowing he'd given up family time to be with her, and at his job site, had labored as a brick mason for hours under the hot sun. She was selfish and horrible, also cowardly, for she could not bring herself to apologize or retract her words and tell him to drink his tea without waiting for her.

As self-recrimination, anger, and fear for her future, roiled inside her, her upturned fingers twitched. In the monumental effort to keep them still, to maintain ramrod posture, slow her breathing, and concentrate on calming herself, she forgot about the tea and her thirst. And only when she became aware of how quiet it was, did she realize that the businessmen had left, probably gone home to their dinners and their wives, and that evening had set in. Soon she and her brother would leave, another day wasted, yet he sat there as if time were limitless and her future without the slightest complication or peril.

According to family legend, Kol would have remained at Phra Spaq at the end of his twelve weeks had their father not declared that no son of his would live celibate with a shaved head, a saffron robe, and a begging bowl. Nee told her their father had summoned ex-monks to persuade Kol that the monastic life attracted misfits and fostered sniping, jealousy, and false pride. In Lem's version of Kol's history, there were no ex-monks.

He said Kol had pleaded for a week and then sought the intercession of the monastery abbot, who'd refused to come between a son and his father. Aa disputed both versions and claimed Kol had capitulated without a fight. Regardless, Kol had descended the mountain to work on the farm, marry the woman his father had chosen for him, and live the life of a laborer rather than that of a contemplative.

In other words, her father had stolen Kol's dreams, and it seemed Kol was willing to let their father rob her of her dreams as well.

Kol's chair scraped and when she opened her eyes, he was halfway to the cash register to pay for the tea no one drank. On return, he dug into his pocket and placed a 500 *ghree* tip on the table. The air came out of Pania's lungs with a hiss. Her brother earned barely enough to cover the expenses of a wife and three children, plus the stipend he insisted on giving her parents every month over their objections. How could he throw money away? She offered him the *ghree* in her purse, but he shook his head.

Out on the street she asked if he would answer a personal question.

"I will," he said.

"Why didn't you stay in the monastery?" She wondered why she had never asked him this before, why she'd relied on rumor and the selective memories of her less-than-admirable siblings to piece the story together. It came to her that until now, she'd never been truly curious about anyone's problems but her own.

"It wasn't the right life for me," he said.

"How do you know?"

"I know because the life I live now is the right one."

"Working at a construction site?"

"Yes. And my life with Sai and our daughter and sons."

"But suppose you'd been a monastic and loved that life. Maybe you'd tell me that was the right one."

"Probably, I would."

"See!" Pania said.

He smiled.

"What are you smiling at?"

"What do you think?"

"I think you're not telling the truth."

He accepted her statement without offense. "Let's meet here Thursday," he said.

"Thursday? The dinner is Friday. What about tomorrow?"

He reminded her that on Wednesday, after work, he coached Miala's soccer team.

"Come here yourself tomorrow," he said.

"Are you crazy? I'll go with my friends to a real café and get a Coca-Cola, and then I'll go to a movie made in Hollywood and watch beautiful people fall in love with each other and marry by choice."

"If that's what you want to do tomorrow, by all means then, you should."

⊠ ⊠ ⊠

If her father hadn't interfered, by now Kol could be the grand abbot of a renowned monastery or a wandering monk, meditating every day for hours in forest caves instead of stealing a brief moment of quiet for himself now and then on Swadougkum-Pokaba Street. Pania envisioned him seated on a square burgundy velvet pillow embroidered with gold elephants, the sash of a loose saffron robe on his knees, his lean body in total repose.

"Pania? Where are you?"

It was Lule calling her back from her brother's alternate life, the one he didn't get to live. Pania and Lule, along with three additional classmates—Fee, Vana, and Suliara—were at the Bom Café, one of the ice cream and coffee parlors they stopped at after school before going home to chores and algebra problems. In spite of the rain, busy young waiters in blue pants and white shirts rushed around to crowded tables and dipped their heads in and out of the freezer chest for one of the ice cream confections advertised on bright posters on the walls. Pania and her friends sat at a sidewalk table under a wide blue umbrella, shouting to each other above a blaring American-style rap CD and the steady pings of the raindrops hammering on the canvas over their heads. As Lule's question broke through Pania's reverie, she dragged her eyes from their hypnotic stare and realized the waiter was standing there, impatient for her order.

"A Coke," she said emphatically.

Even the fortunate among Pania's friends, the ones whose families had made it through relatively intact, suffered parents out of work, chronically ill siblings, homeless and sick relatives relocating into their own tiny dwellings. Lule, who had to baby-sit for the younger children, came to school, on average, every third day, and in February, a malaria flare nearly spirited Vana away. In comparison, Pania thought, her problem was trivial. Nafal's father had moved to the city in his thirties, had retrained as a cell phone assembler and subsequently earned enough money to send his only child to college. Her own father, in their three days of arguments before he stopped speaking to her, told her Nafal would likely be given an apartment as a wedding gift. He was educated and rich. What did she have to complain about?

With her index finger, Pania traced lines in the condensation on the Coke can, exposing the shiny aluminum and watching the droplets coalesce and trickle down the red and white letters, but she couldn't bring herself to pop the top open. She should have ordered tea, she thought, but suspected she wouldn't have been able to swallow a drop of that either. She didn't know what her state of mind entitled her to. Surprising herself, she rose abruptly. "I don't feel well," she said.

Suliara, who also lived in Pin Dalie Sector Twelve, asked if she needed assistance getting home. "I can manage," Pania said and handed Lule 1,000 *ghree* to pay for the unopened soda. Then she shoved her arms through the straps of her heavy backpack, pulled the poncho over both head and backpack, and ran hunchbacked in the downpour to 714825 Swadougkum-Pokaba Street, a couple of kilometers away. Breathing hard, she stood outside the café, hands on her knees, water dripping from the edge of her poncho in front of her face, waiting for her blood to stop rushing. She knew better than to enter 714825 Swadougkum-Pokaba Street in such an agitated state.

"Will you be waiting for your brother?" the old man said, lifting his eyes from his magazine when she walked in.

"I'm by myself today," she said, registering that he'd confirmed for her that he and Kol had talked. As she walked to the table she sat at with her brother, the old man continued reading, lifting a scrawny hand to the nape of his neck to straighten his braid.

At the sound of musical tones, she looked through the ficus branches to the adjacent table and saw a young boy, nine or ten, seated with his grandmother, practicing scales on a small black and silver harmonica, his free hand cupped professionally around the instrument to make its sweet sound resonant.

The old woman approached Pania's table with a heavy left foot that made a small thud as it dropped into place, an infirmity not uncommon in Ayama Na where a typical punishment in the aluminum mines had been a blow to the foot. Pania studied her arthritic hands, toothless mouth sucked into a straight line, and the old argyle sweater with the missing two middle buttons she wore in spite of the heat, and thought with a pang of grief that this old couple could as easily be mother and son as husband and wife, the sole survivors of a once large and happy family. After resting a small tray on the edge of the table, the shaky old hands transferred a can of Coke and a tall glass of ice to the lace.

The Coke must be a mistake, Pania thought, a drink intended for the young musician at the next table. All that caffeine and sugar couldn't have been destined for someone in her frame of mind. At Café Bom, she'd figured that much out for herself.

"Are you sure this is for me?"

The old woman nodded.

Although Pania didn't believe anyone here read anyone's mind, she expected these fake seers to convey their metaphors in good faith, and the Coke seemed an egregious symbolic breach. Unless—the thought upset her—unless they'd meant the Coke as an insult, a statement that without Kol at her side, she was, in their eyes, shallow and dismissible, not worthy of their best thoughts or effort.

She straightened her back, placed her hands on the table palms up, inhaled slowly, and settled herself. She would prove herself superior to that aluminum can.

What did it matter if Kol couldn't or wouldn't help her with their father? In three months, she'd graduate from high school, get a job, move out, live as an adult in charge of herself. Away from her father's house, she'd avoid the insistent, turbulent emotions of family life and accomplish what even Kol hadn't managed to accomplish at her age—she would choose her own destiny.

At the thought, her heart became so still it barely seemed to beat, a sensation foreign to her and deeply consoling. Although she couldn't maintain the state, she kept her eyes closed until she heard the clink of ice. When she opened her eyes, the old man was removing the tall glass and the Coca-Cola can.

※ ※ ※

At dinner, Pania's mother commented on how quiet she seemed, odd because she'd hardly spoken a word to either parent since her father stopped talking to her, but her mother had gotten it right. Her rage had spent and exhausted itself. Instead, she pitied her father and, not only her father, but herself as well. According to her father's understanding of the world, a world disappearing on him, his motives on her behalf hadn't been cruel, they'd been beyond reproach, and one day she'd be debilitated by age and her children would find her irrelevant too. This was the inescapable, sad, hurtful truth of life, but unlike her father, she'd be aware of the inexorable march of time and grant her children the right to their own dreams, their own wishes, their own fully lived lives, no matter how much it hurt or how much patience it required. Too sad to swallow, she dragged the chopsticks back and forth through her mother's fiery stir-fry of prawns and morning glory greens.

"Silla expects you tomorrow after school," her mother said. "I told her to cut your nails short and use colorless polish, so don't make a fuss. And your hair is too long. If you don't get a cut before Friday night, you'll pull it back from your face with a clip. And, Pania, no perfume."

It was Wednesday night, and for the first time since Monday when he stopped talking to her, Pania looked straight at her father, searching his face for clues that he understood the futility of her mother's instructions. She found him looking straight at her too.

The night before, Pania had heard him on the phone with his chum at Pei Wei, finalizing the details of Friday night's menu, discussing the pros and cons of the booth at the window versus the oval table near the marble lion-head fountain. She knew he wouldn't let her resume their discussion, wouldn't listen if she tried to talk him out of the dinner, but she thought perhaps he would revisit the topic himself, for what would happen the day after her absence humiliated him at that matchmaking dinner? Would he declare her dead to him? Would he expel her from the house before she finished high school? Would he risk such a confrontation? Or abide never seeing her again?

His eyes continued to hold hers, even when her mother initiated another round of annoying chatter, this time about the outfit she, herself, might choose to wear on the fateful night. As her mother prattled on, Pania had a sense that she and her father were engaged in a silent conversation, the sort that occurs in films when two brave warriors who face a battle that will end with one of them dead wordlessly acknowledge each other's courage. Whatever happens, Pania thought, she would have this moment of reciprocal respect and adversarial connection between herself and her father for the rest of her life, a link so strong it left even her mother out.

And then her mother asked her father a question. "What do you think, Ri? Should I wear the pink or the green?"

"The green," he said, turning at once to his wife and smiling at her with a warmth Pania had forgotten him capable of. "Definitely the green, your best color. And wear the golden snake bracelet and the white silk scarf, the one with the serpent design where the fringes start."

Frightened, feeling lightheaded and at the same time heavy with mourning, Pania closed her eyes, rested her hands face up on the table on either side of her plate. She would lose her family, lose her father's protection and love. She forced her back straight, pretended she was at 714825 Swadougkum-Pokaba Street, and tried to calm herself. With envy, she thought of Kol's discipline and wished she possessed a fraction of his composure. Patient, impervious to others' judgments and slow to rush to judgment himself, above trivial conversation and divisive opinion, Kol was sheltered by wisdom and inner contentment from adversity and the altering landscape. But she wasn't like Kol, she was like nearly everyone else. She wanted too many things, not only shinier hair, rounder eyes, and a mother-of-pearl barrette, but other people's permanent good opinion of her. Yet, she gossiped, she craved exclusivity, she suffered impatience and dissatisfaction. She was like her sister, Aa, someone who deluded herself, a person unworthy of respect.

"Pania? Are you all right?"

To her mother, a woman characterized by hands that never rested and eyes that inspected in every direction, her stillness must have seemed a symptom of illness. On another night, Pania might have responded, *How could I be all right?*, but her bruised thoughts restrained her. Besides, her mother answered the question herself.

"You're tired Pania. Try not to think so much." She tapped the table. "Finish your dinner and go to bed early tonight. We don't want dark circles to spoil your eyes."

▨ ▨ ▨

Pania slept restlessly. Only a single day remained for Kol to listen to her, take her side, and sway her father, and if she didn't manage to sit up straight or appear unperturbed, the next day would pass as futilely as the previous three.

To compose herself before Kol's arrival, Pania skipped her last class (Beginning Economics, taught by Mr. Sam Leetoto, who had one real and one artificial leg) and arrived at the café before her brother.

Pania assumed the requisite 714825 Swadougkum-Pokaba Street posture and hand position. It hadn't rained yet that day and the air seemed less hot and humid, a sign that the winds had reversed and the rainy season might have been swept away, although it was only mid-March and until the last of April, the monsoons could return. Mr. Leetoto had devoted considerable energy to the warming of the earth, stressing that social and economic upheavals had occurred as a result. You don't say, Pania had thought.

She felt Kol's kiss on the top of her hair and simultaneously heard the soft thud of the old woman's approach. When the white teapot and two yellow porcelain cups were placed on the table, Pania recognized the chips in the yellow glaze. These were exactly the same cups they'd been given on Tuesday when Pania had refused to let Kol drink his tea.

She knew better than to reach for the teapot, nor did she allow herself to experience the fatal pride or excitement Kol had noticed the last time around. She would not only wait calmly for the tea to brew, but to make amends for her previous selfish behavior, she would tell Kol to drink his tea while she composed herself for another moment or two.

"I'll pour for you," he said.

"No, please, you go ahead. Pour for yourself and begin." She closed her eyes. "I need a moment."

"All right," Kol said. "You tell me when you're ready."

That she'd undone her error proved a source of unexpected satisfaction, but the feeling didn't last, for it excited her and made her proud, and that was unsettling. As she admonished herself to settle down, she heard tea flowing into her brother's cup and experienced another disturbing shift of feelings, an intense disappointment at Kol's failure to consider her actions worthy of comment or credit. Her spirits plunged further at the disheartening realization that what she'd really wanted was not to make amends but to earn her brother's praise.

But why hadn't he at least thanked her for her kindness on his behalf? She grew agitated, imagining that he hadn't thought about her, that their prior encounters had failed to move him or register her plight. At the same time, she detested herself for her inability to exhibit generosity for its own sake. She was exactly like her sister, in it for herself. It would serve her right, she thought, if the old folks took away her tea cup and brought her a Coke and a glass of ice.

She heard rustling and tearing, must be Kol lifting a paper tube of sugar from the bowl on the table and ripping off the end. Then the grating and swishing of a spoon running itself along the bottom of a cup, then her brother's leisurely sips and swallows as he sat there unconcerned, drinking his tea, without a thought of time running out.

No matter the outcome of her dilemma, it was all the same to him because, in or out of the monastery, married to this one or that, drinking tea or not, he was content. If he intended her to learn that lesson from him, all was lost, because she could never be like him. Never. She couldn't settle for a marriage or a life she didn't choose.

An accounting student! Someone she hadn't selected of her own free will. Someone who laughed three times in fifteen minutes in the company of her father. How did that make Nafal a person with a sense of humor? It made him a fool or a nervous type. Or at the very least, a kid who considered this matchmaking caper a great big joke and had probably agreed to appear at Pei Wei to come by a story for the amusement of his friends. Having grown up in the city, he couldn't want to marry her any more than she wanted to marry him. He probably expected her to be so unattractive and so stupid she couldn't utter an articulate sentence.

At least her father had seen Nafal and could testify that he didn't drool all over himself. Nafal would need his alleged sense of humor to get through Pei Wei's front door not knowing if the person inside—his intended bride—was fat and ugly and dumb as a leaf. She'd like to see the expression on Nafal's face when he realized she was not only pretty but also one of the smartest students in her high school class.

And fast on the heels of that startling thought, she envisioned the two of them—she and Nafal—sitting side by side on those faded red velvet chairs by the marble lion fountain sharing a laugh at their situation. He'd wink at her and she'd wink back, acknowledging the mortifying absurdities of growing up in the city with these irrelevant parents. She and this Nafal, whoever he was, both knew the dilemma of having one foot in the new world and one in the old, split by the push and the pull, by the struggle to choose between oneself and one's ancestors. And wasn't it just possible that since they shared the same predicament, they could find the solution together?

All at once, she felt high, as excited as she'd felt a few months ago in school when her literature teacher asked her to read her essay on Kio Lu's *Mountains of Marble* to the class, declaring it the best paper turned in, even more excited than that, her feet fidgety, her eyes dancing under their lids. And if Nafal didn't possess the requisite sense of humor or courage to show up, well his absence would solve her problem too.

She'd lost her equanimity again: too low when things went wrong, too high when things went well. Kol would deem it as big a mistake to be excited about Nafal as an ally as it had been to be angry or sad or chaotic inside. Long way to go, she thought, to maintain a mood in a steady state or even to know if she would ever choose to return to this strange café. She tried to keep her eyes closed, and while the remains of the tea grew cold, she made a stab at pulling her mind back to ground level, but every time she cracked her eyelids a bit, she saw Kol smiling at her and her excitement surged again.

Before long, Kol paid for the tea and left his custom-ary 500 *ghree* tip. As they exited the café, walking into the blue-gray dusk of the descending evening together, Pania was thinking about what color to wear to Pei Wei so she wouldn't clash with the red velvet chairs. As they hugged at the corner of Swadougkum-Pokaba and Pateamandna streets and went their separate ways, the skies opened up, and big drops of rain fell out.

E leanor Bluestein has worked as a science teacher, editor of science textbooks, and designer of multimedia educational materials for Internet delivery. For a decade, she co-edited *Crawl Out Your Window*, a San Diego based literary journal featuring the work of local writers and artists. She lives with her husband in La Jolla, California, where she writes fiction and volunteers as a court appointed special advocate for foster children. *Tea & Other Ayama Na Tales* is her first book.